PRAISE FOR
SITA BRAHMACHARI

'This is a story of an escape, and the discovery that the world is not as propaganda tells it. The book, despite the hardship it chronicles, is lavishly written and full of love of the natural world, and of stories – and families and friends'

Sunday Times, on *Where The River Runs Gold*

'This is a book with real warmth, carefully drawn characters and sensitive relationships. There are strong themes of trust, love and the meaning of family . . . A gripping read'

Books For Keeps, on *Where The River Runs Gold*

'This is so much a book for our troubled times, pinpointing the idiocy of our Earth-trashing ways, while celebrating the healing power of Nature. All that embraced within a pulsating adventure story, with compelling and inspirational characters, reaching out to both young

uns Gold

Also by Sita Brahmachari

Artichoke Hearts
Brace Mouth, False Teeth
Car Wash Wish
Corey's Rock
Jasmine Skies
Kite Spirit
Red Leaves
Tender Earth
Worry Angels
Zebra Crossing Soul Song
Where the River Runs Gold

SITA BRAHMACHARI

Orion

ORION CHILDREN'S BOOKS

First published in Great Britain in 2020 by Hodder and Stoughton

1 3 5 7 9 10 8 6 4 2

A CIP catalogue record for this book
is available from the British Library.

ISBN 978 1 51010 543 0

Typeset in Adobe Garamond Pro by Hewer Text UK Ltd, Edinburgh
Printed and bound in Great Britain by Clays Ltd, Elcograf S.p.A.

The paper and board used in this book
are made from wood from responsible sources.

Orion Children's Books
An imprint of
Hachette Children's Group
Part of Hodder and Stoughton
Carmelite House
50 Victoria Embankment
London EC4Y 0DZ

An Hachette UK Company
www.hachette.co.uk

www.hachettechildrens.co.uk

For my mum and dad – nurse Freda Brahmachari and the late Dr Brahmachari – and all the millions of people from around the world who have given their lives to working in the National Health Service and social care. Your and your ancestors' lives matter deeply.

'Perhaps it's true that things can change in a day. That a few dozen hours can affect the outcome of whole lifetimes. And that when they do, those few dozen hours, like the salvaged remains of a burned house – the charred clock, the singed photograph, the scorched furniture – must be resurrected from the ruins and examined. Preserved. Accounted for. Little events, ordinary things, smashed and reconstituted. Imbued with new meaning. Suddenly they become the bleached bones of a story.'
Arundhati Roy, *The God of Small Things*

Newspaper Baby

'I'm not sleeping in no dead person's bed. Can't I take mine with me?'

As soon as the words were out of her mouth, Imtiaz clocked Delyse's deeply furrowed scowl. This was exactly the sort of 'double negative attitude' that Delyse was on a mission to coach Imtiaz out of. The closer the day came for Imtiaz's adoption, the more Delyse got on her case and the angrier Imtiaz blew. She would never understand why Delyse couldn't stop being a social worker to everyone else in the children's home and just look after her. *What else will Delyse have to do when she retires?*

'There's still time to change your mind,' Imtiaz pleaded. 'You said no one's forcing you to leave the country any more, so stay, and you and Merve can foster me! You're always saying how I should accept an apology – well, the government have said sorry about how they treated you, haven't they?'

'Immy.' Delyse shook her head, exasperated. 'Remember you promised not to keep on with this. We've made our decision.'

Delyse placed a comforting arm around Imtiaz's shoulder. 'Don't worry about the bed. I'm sure you'll be getting a new one. Just wait and see your beautiful new ship of a room.' Delyse winked at Imtiaz. 'And don't look at me like that. All will be revealed. You'll see! That top deck's beyond your wildest dreams, I promise.'

'Doubt it,' Imtiaz mumbled, pulling away from Delyse.

'I'm telling you, Immy, this is meant to be. I can't tell you how happy it makes me that I've been able to settle this adoption. When I think about how it's all fallen into place, it does feel like a little miracle. Me meeting Merve and discovering his family wanted to adopt. *And* them sharing the same surname as you! Like it was God's will!'

'Don't go bringing God into it! You said you called me that because you had a school friend with that surname. Just so happy it's all been so convenient. At least you get to wash your hands of me now, before you go sailing off into your Caribbean sunset!'

Delyse took hold of Imtiaz's flailing hands before she could whip herself up into more of a state. 'That's enough, Immy!'

Imtiaz caught the fire in Delyse's eyes and knew not to push any further.

It was no use anyway. Last year, when Delyse was arrested,

had changed everything. Detained for, as far as Imtiaz could understand, *nothing*, except for Delyse's parents not travelling with documents for her as a baby on the ship called *Windrush* like, half a century ago. It still didn't make any sense. But at least they had released Delyse quickly and given her the money that was called 'reparation' because it was supposed to repair the damage done for arresting her. When she'd heard about this, Imtiaz had got her hopes up and she'd sprung at Delyse and hugged her. 'So you don't have to go, then?' Great sobs had heaved out of Delyse as they'd held each other. It was the first time Imtiaz had ever seen Delyse cry like that, so Imtiaz had cried too and wished she could look after Delyse for the rest of her life, like Delyse had looked after her.

'No money could ever repair how I feel. This country doesn't feel like home any more,' Delyse had whispered when she'd finally calmed down.

Imtiaz knew in her heart there was no point arguing with Delyse. She supposed there was one advantage in Delyse hooking up with Merve. She'd learnt more about the Joseph family than anyone being adopted would normally know. Not that all the getting-to-know-you meetings had got any less awkward over time. Mostly Usha had just sat quietly while her mum and dad, Tanvi and Lem, banged on about how much Usha had always wanted a sister. Just a shame Usha herself couldn't even be bothered to look her straight in the eye, let alone attempt a smile.

'Every time you meet it'll get a bit easier between you,' Delyse constantly reassured Imtiaz. But it didn't. Maybe they would have had more of a chance to talk if they'd had somewhere chill to go, instead of having to compete with all the comings and goings on the ground floor of the house, the bit they called 'The Hearth'.

'What even is a hearth anyway?' asked Imtiaz.

Delyse's face softened. 'A kind of fireplace to gather around, and find a bit of warmth at. As you know, it's refugee people mostly. Good name for it, don't you think?'

Imtiaz shrugged. 'I didn't see no fire in there!'

'I didn't see *any* fire!' Delyse corrected.

'That's because there isn't one!' Imtiaz grinned and despite Delyse's nitpicking at the repeated double negative, her face broke into sunshine.

'Why couldn't I be in a family where I'm the only one who needs help?' Imtiaz complained.

'That's not like any kind of family I've ever heard of! They're a busy, caring crew, the Josephs, always helping people. I think you'll soon settle.'

'As long as I'm not just another of their charity cases! Maybe that's why Usha's so weird. She probably just wants her house to herself – and now she's got me to deal with.'

'She's shy and sad about her gran dying, that's all. Give Usha a chance. She's had a lot to deal with too.'

'All I'm saying is they'd better clear out all her granny's stuff.'

Delyse placed a finger over her own mouth – her signal for Imtiaz to choose her words more carefully.

'Anyhow. Weren't you supposed to be at their ashes sailing-ceremony thing?'

Delyse shook her head. 'I was invited but I said my goodbyes at the funeral and I've still got so much to organise before we go. I'm handing over to the new manager later. *You're* all sorted though!' Delyse scanned the bare, posterless walls of Imtiaz's room, settling on the suitcase and crate of belongings stacked and waiting to be picked up.

'I haven't got that much!' Imtiaz shrugged. Everything she owned could more or less be fitted into a case and a crate. Not exactly impressive for eleven years of growing up here.

'I'd better get on.' Delyse stood stiffly and reached up to the shelf above the bed.

Taking down a card, she waved it at Imtiaz, her face growing stern. 'Immy! You told me you'd sent this!'

Imtiaz shrugged. 'I was waiting for Usha to invite me to the funeral or at least this ashes-spreading ceremony. In any case, I couldn't work out what to say. Never even met Usha's gran. Anyway, isn't it too late to send now?'

Delyse thrust the card into Imtiaz's hand. 'Just write something nice.'

'Like what?'

'Tell her you're sorry for her loss and that you're looking forward to seeing her soon.'

Imtiaz puffed her cheeks and released a pent-up gush of air.

'You want to try out that lido, then write the card. We can post it on the way back and they'll get it after the ceremony.'

With a surly scowl, Imtiaz took the envelope from Delyse and pulled out the revolting card. One of the reasons why she hadn't been able to send it was just how gross it was, with its shiny lily on the cover and the no-sense message inside. 'It already says "sorry for your loss". What else do you want me to say?'

The staff-only phone in the office rang. Delyse wagged her finger at Imtiaz on the way out of the room. 'I mean it, Immy! No condolence card, no swim!' she cautioned, hurrying out along the corridor to the office.

I need that swim, thought Imtiaz. One thing she *was* looking forward to was seeing the lido at the end of Usha's road, where Tanvi, Usha's mum, said she could swim all year round if she was brave enough! Sighing at the card, she thought, *Not in a million years would I ever choose this for anyone I care about. But who* would *I care about enough to send one of these to?* She came to the conclusion that the only person she would ever be truly sorry about dying or going away was Delyse.

Sorry for your loss.

Eugh. What's that message even supposed to mean if you don't know the person you're writing to, or the person who's died? Imtiaz's pen hovered over the card. *It feels fake!*

She pictured the impossible-to-read face of Usha. At least in looks they could just about pass as siblings: same-ish height, similar rich brown skin tone, dark eyes and shiny black hair – Usha's a tangle of curls and Imtiaz's cut short at the nape to fit inside her swim cap. But in every other way . . . *Us two, sisters? No!*

Every time she thought up something, it sounded wrong. *How can it be so hard to write a few words?*

Swim, I need to swim. Just write anything to get Delyse off your back, Imtiaz told herself, still hesitating over what she should say.

I'm not sorry for Usha that her grandma died, I'm sorry for me! Sorry that Usha will be miserable. From what Delyse told her, Usha and her gran had been pretty much best friends. In a way she felt more sorry for Usha. Maybe Delyse was right and she would soon 'come out of her shell'! But even so, *I'm not pretending to be someone I'm not. I didn't get the name 'say-it-how-it-is Imtiaz' from nowhere,* she thought as she wrote:

Dear Usha,
I'm sorry about your gran dying.
See you soon,
Imtiaz

Licking the envelope left a bitter taste in her mouth. Grabbing her swimming kit from the crate, she peered through her doorway where she could still hear Delyse talking.

What am I supposed to do now, with everything packed away? Imtiaz wondered, idling over to her crate and taking out her 'life book', containing the cutting about her first days in the world. Though she'd memorised every word, reading it always brought tears.

'NEWSPAPER BABY'
SOCIAL WORKER FINDS NEWBORN IN LONDON FIELDS

Local resident and experienced social worker Delyse Lovelace was walking her new rescue dog in London Fields on Thursday evening when her dog, named Tug, drew her attention to a bin on the far side of the park. After several attempts to recall Tug, Ms Lovelace was forced to cross the park to pull her dog away from the debris.

'I thought it was a bit of chicken and chips he was scavenging around for,' Ms Lovelace explained. 'But when I got close, I realised he was gently nudging open a newspaper and to my horror a newborn baby rolled out on to the grass. I was in shock but I swaddled her in my coat and took her straight to the hospital.'

There is a police search for the mother. No note or identification has been found. The child is presently without a name.

'In all likelihood this was a hidden pregnancy,' Ms Lovelace said. 'I assume the mother could be very young, frightened and in need of medical assistance.'

Laying the clipping aside, Imtiaz took out the rolled-up newspaper and, out of habit, sniffed it, despite the fact that the paper her baby-self had been wrapped in had never smelt of anything but damp and a slight whiff of mould. A familiar heat of anger rose in her. *As if I was a piece of rubbish.* The paper had grown soft and smooth to the touch, like a worn blanket, from so many handlings. *What's the point of keeping this?* She had the urge to rip it up into tiny pieces. *I never want to see this again. Why did Delyse save me and look out for me for so long, just to abandon me? If she's going to make a fresh start, why shouldn't I?*

Imtiaz tore through to the office, where Delyse was *still* on the phone. Ignoring her whispered questions, Imtiaz held her article and newspaper blanket over the shredder that turned everything to spaghetti.

'Immy! Stop! What are you doing?' Delyse grabbed Imtiaz's shoulders, pulling her away from the shredder with such force that Imtiaz lost her balance and toppled on to the floor. 'Sorry! Immy, are you hurt? I didn't mean . . . What were you thinking? You can't destroy your past like that!' Delyse soothed, kneeling next to her.

Tears rolled unchecked down Imtiaz's cheeks. Taking the card out of her pocket, she flung it at Delyse. 'Here! It's a crap past! So why shouldn't I? What about *my* loss? Who's writing *me* a card to say sorry?'

9

While Delyse held Imtiaz in her arms, the pent-up feelings she had not known how to express opened like a dam, rushing out of her. 'You said that someone in the government shredded your parents' landing papers and now nothing can be repaired and it's too upsetting, so you've decided to make a new start. Well if you can go off with Merve and pretend you're just setting out on some sort of adventure, then why can't I shred everything sad and start again too? Why should anyone else read my story? It's literally rubbish.'

Imtiaz held the newspaper in her hands as the words shot out of her in wild sobs. She clenched her fists as if she was about to crumple it. 'What's the point of remembering?'

Slowly, softly, Delyse unravelled the scrumpled paper blanket and placed it over Imtiaz's shoulders.

'Because this contains one of the most precious little souls I've ever met.' Delyse swaddled Imtiaz in the flimsy paper as if it still contained the newborn baby she had found and named. Delyse's chest heaved up and down, struggling to control her emotion too as Imtiaz's tears darkened the paper. She kissed Imtiaz on the forehead so tenderly that it felt as if she was being touched by a feather.

'Immy, my little warrior miracle, you hold on to that fight in you.'

'Please take me with you?'

Delyse's heavy sigh spoke for her.

'Then take this, so you won't be able to forget me,' Imtiaz said, thrusting her newspaper blanket at Delyse. 'Don't you get it? I'll never be Immy to anyone except you!'

Blue Mirror

The blue of the pool and the sky admired each other in a still, clear mirror. As ever, when Imtiaz was near water she felt her shoulders ease away from her ears and her spine lengthen, as if her body knew better than she where it belonged. Not that she had any time for Delyse's horoscopes, but she had to agree that Pisces the fish was definitely the right zodiac sign for her. *How can Usha live so close to this place and not like swimming?* she wondered. *Maybe I could get her into it.*

'Hurry up, Delyse,' Imtiaz called into the changing room, surveying the vast expanse of water stretching out in front of her. She pulled her goggles over her head and secured the taut elastic behind her ears. 'Can't believe we're the only ones here!' she said as Delyse emerged in her flip-flops with a bright turquoise towel wrapped around her middle. *She does look quite old*, Imtiaz thought as she watched Delyse cautiously pad her way to the water's edge.

Flicking off a flip-flop, she tentatively dipped her toe in and gasped.

'I need heat!' Delyse shivered overdramatically.

Well, you'll get it soon, Imtiaz was tempted to snap back.

'It's not that cold. You've just got to jump in!' Imtiaz yelled as she made a star of her body and flopped on the water, splashing a mini-waterfall over Delyse's dimply legs and arms.

'Aargh! That's ice, not water!' Delyse shivered as she wrung out the end of her towel. 'Thanks! What's the point of all those diving lessons I got you, if you're just going to belly-flop?' Delyse's infectious laughter echoed joy around the pool.

I will so miss Delyse's laugh, Imtiaz thought as she watched her unravel the towel stowed under her arm, wrap it around her shoulders and head towards the viewing platform.

Looking up, Imtiaz caught the expression on the lifeguard's face as she sat on her ladder watching her one responsibility like a hawk, making her risk assessment. *I'll show her!*

Imtiaz smiled to herself as she hauled herself out again and prepared her best dive. Balancing her feet on the edge of the pool, knees bent and braced, concertinaing her power for a second like a flattened spring, body poised, sleek and arrow-sharp, she made her leap. Arching down, propelling herself under, then rising, her arms grew into butterfly wings sweeping through the water.

In slow, even strokes Imtiaz pushed wave after wave of doubt away as she ploughed on, surfacing and dipping down, letting her new reality ripple over her.

My new family
Usha
My new family
Tanvi
My new family
Lem
Usha
Sister
Usha
Sister
Usha
Ushhhhhhhha

Breathing Usha's name to the end of her breath, she snatched a deep gulp before fully reaching the surface. Her lungs gagged as the chlorinated water gushed in where air should have been. She coughed and spluttered violently. The lifeguard was halfway down the steps when Imtiaz waved to reassure her that she was fine. Over on a bench Delyse's head lolled on to her chest while she dozed. Ignoring the lifeguard's suspicious stare, Imtiaz pushed off the side and floated on her back, feeling her knotted sinews untangle. Wanting rid of the screen between her and the water, she pulled off her goggles and threw them poolside, blinking several times at the stinging sensation as chlorine seeped in.

Rubbing her eyes to clear the blur, her attention was caught by a woman wearing a white sari walking barefoot to the water's edge, her long, grey plait swaying heavily. As the woman approached, the pale green trim of her white cotton sari dragged through the water. She was now in touching distance of Imtiaz, who reached under the gentle waves to lift the cloth out. But as she did, it seemed to slip through her fingers, fold after fold unravelling into the choppy waves like fast-moving clouds. Imtiaz dived down to catch the ends, but it dissolved at her touch. When she surfaced, bleary-eyed, the woman had gone. Scanning all around the pool, she found only the now bored-looking lifeguard and Delyse stirring from her sleep.

Heart pounding against her sternum, Imtiaz flexed her feet and kicked hard off the side. *Get a grip, Imtiaz Joseph. The problem with swimming,* she thought, *is it loosens up your imagination so much you feel like you're dreaming.*

She let herself drift. Releasing her arms behind her head, Imtiaz lengthened her spine against the blue diamond tiles that line-divided the bottom of the pool. She felt like an ancient creature of the deep: huge, powerful and peaceful, navigating her way along shimmering channels. The sleep-lulling whale song she had listened to every night when she was little sounded through her, so that she felt like a vast underwater being, moving through its own sparkling habitat.

And I think Usha's weird! Imtiaz smiled to herself, greedily gulping air as she surfaced to reality, to find Delyse standing above her.

'I'm freezing,' Delyse grumbled. 'I'll meet you in the café for a hot chocolate when you're done, and then we can get Usha's card posted.'

'Did you see that woman in the white sari?' Imtiaz asked, grabbing hold of Delyse's foot.

'No! But then, I had a little snooze,' Delyse admitted, heading for the changing rooms. 'Don't be long!'

Swim, just swim, Imtiaz told herself. After a while she stopped counting the lengths, stopped worrying about someone else breaking the pattern that she was making in the water, the pattern that made her feel like she could do anything, be anyone, and really have a new family that would love her as if she was their own. Every so often she would turn her head to the side and scan the pool for signs of the woman in the sari.

Imtiaz and Delyse walked down the the wide, tree-lined road towards Usha's house; it was all so different from the noisy double lines of traffic outside Acorns Children's Home. Taking the envelope from her pocket, Imtiaz climbed the steps to the house that would soon be hers. The sharp-pronged metal railings to the left and right and the imposing pillars seemed suddenly jail-like. The impressive black door that had always been wide open for the people at The Hearth, shouted, 'Do not enter.'

To her left, in the side bay window, delicate paws peeled back white lace curtains and a cat's curious face stared at her with one brown and one green eye.

'I didn't know they had a cat?' Imtiaz smiled.

'Nor did I. Just pop that in the letterbox!' Delyse urged. 'We don't want to disturb anyone today.'

I wish I'd written something better now. Imtiaz winced as she heard the card drop into a metal cage and joined Delyse, who stood on the pavement, neck straining upwards, her hands open as if ready to catch something.

'Just look at those roses!' Delyse gasped as a flurry of white petals drifted down.

Imtiaz opened her palm and caught them. 'Like confetti!' She laughed and threw them over Delyse. 'When you and Merve get married you'd better make me your bridesmaid. I'll be yours and Usha can be Merve's. But just so you know, I'm not wearing a dress! I've looked it up. You can get wed on a beach in St Lucia.'

'We're way past retirement age, Immy! I think we're both a bit long in the tooth for that. Our plan is to just sail away into the sunset together.'

'You're sailing there? I thought you said you booked a flight?'

Delyse chuckled. 'Immy! You've got to learn not to take everything so literally!'

Imtiaz sighed and linked her arm tightly through Delyse's like she would never let her go.

Uncharted Waters

'Right! Time to get dressed, Ush! There's so much to do before the ceremony. I thought I'd go and collect some rose petals. You want to help?' Usha's mum tutted as she caught sight of Spirit arching her back and stretching on Kali Ma's bed.

Yawning noisily, Usha smiled as the cat yawned too.

'That stray still making herself at home? You shouldn't let her on the beds,' Tanvi complained.

Too late for that! Spirit seemed to have already claimed Kali Ma's bed as her own. Maybe by the time Imtiaz took her old bed and she moved over to Kali Ma's, the cat would trust her enough to let her near.

'Spirit!' Usha called and the cat paused and turned slowly, head tilted, eyes questioning. 'I think the name suits you,' Usha whispered to the delicate white cat now padding across the deck, steadily surveying her from the safe distance of the anchor.

Usha had named her Spirit because the cat had half scared her to death when, on the day of her Kali Ma's funeral, her trembling hands had unfolded the bedcovers and discovered nothing more ghostly than a hissing cat that had peered at her with its one green eye, one brown eye, looking just as surprised as she was. Now it felt strangely comforting not to be alone, even if Spirit was only a stray that had come to keep her company for a while.

Ignoring her mum's complaints, Usha crept across the uneven floorboards, past the giant anchor that Spirit had claimed as her lookout post. Usha loved to follow the cat's path down the sunken steps into the heart of the room to her own anchor den with its comfy cushions. There Spirit either curled up or braced herself to leap on to the anchor's feet, deftly climbing to the zenith point on the curve of its rusted spine that floated halfway between floor and ceiling. From there Spirit's eyes now followed her as she drew closer to Kali Ma's boat-bed, which she'd insisted she didn't mind moving into so that Imtiaz could take hers. But now the time had come to swap, she wondered how she would ever sleep in it.

There had never been sides to their room when Kali Ma had been alive. It had always been just one big open space. All in all, Usha thought that the new layout worked quite well. Pushing both beds away from the walls further out towards the anchor and using the triangular 'sails' as screens had achieved what she'd wanted and created privacy for both of them. When closed, their bed sails made one room into two.

The anchor was their room divider and formed a corridor to the Globe Window leading out on to the roof terrace. Usha pushed her bedside sail screen closed. From behind, it did really feel like this was her side of the room. *I wonder if we'll ever open these to talk?* Usha pondered, pushing the bamboo pole that held the triangular sail taut. It swung open easily, sending Spirit leaping off the anchor and scarpering across the floorboards, out through the half-opened giant eyelid of the ship's porthole. The window-come-glass-door that her Pops Michael had found in the reclamation of an ocean liner's wreckage – 'the Globe Window', he'd called it, and the name had stuck. 'Our very own porthole on to the world.' Spirit had knocked it on her way out, causing it to tilt fully open. Now a dazzling stream of light snaked across the bleached floorboards, illuminating what Pops Michael's sailing obsession had turned into – the top deck of their family ship.

'That cat nearly sent me flying!' Tanvi called from the terrace.

Usha walked over to the anchor and sat on the top step that led down to her cushion-scattered den.

'Breezy out here! Give me a hand, Ush. Plenty of petals to collect!' Tanvi called.

'I'm getting dressed, Mum!' Usha called back, but didn't move. Her hair lifted off the nape of her neck, flowing behind her. Glancing over to Imtiaz's boat-bed, she felt a pang of resentment. Even though the new room plan had been her idea, the top deck now looked suddenly shrunken and cluttered. Impossible to believe that this harbour of peace and quiet, that had always belonged to her and her Kali Ma, would have to be shared with a stranger with eyes as piercing and unflinching as Spirit's.

Usha closed her own eyes against the mounting tension at her temples that seemed to flare up whenever she thought of Imtiaz moving in. 'This sister idea was such a mistake. Can I say I've changed my mind?' Usha muttered. *You have to stop talking to Kali Ma*, she reminded herself. Realising she had broken her own new rule, she flattened her hand over her mouth. But no matter how many times she told herself not to, she seemed incapable of breaking the habit.

'What if I say I can't do it? That it's too soon after you've died to even think about Imtiaz moving in?' Usha imagined her Kali Ma reaching for her hand, reassuring her. 'You agree, you think I should tell Mum and Dad, then?'

Usha took a deep breath. It was all too much. Pressing her spine against the anchor's metal curve, her mind drifted to the silty sea beds of her Kali Ma's stories, which she in turn said had once been told to her by Pops Michael. *Tiny iridescent fish darted through inky depths among flowers of bright coral . . .* Kali Ma and Pops Michael's voices fused in her ear. Tears rolled down her cheeks. 'Why did you have to die now, Kali Ma?'

Scanning the walls, Usha took in afresh what she had hardly noticed just weeks before: the vintage black and white pictures of her Kali Ma's fashion shoots, the thick misted glass of the ancient navigation clock, the shiny dark wood of the rafters that her Pops Michael had lovingly collected from old ships. Even their beds were carved in the shape of boats, with sails attached now too. 'To think that Pops Michael made all this for you, Kali Ma.' Usha smiled through her tears as she raised her hand into a dust-stream of light, picturing the spirit of her Kali Ma floating towards a waiting Pops Michael. 'How long does it take to pass from the land of the living, Kali Ma? Where are you now?'

'That cat snuck back in?' asked Tanvi, appearing at the Globe Window carrying a basket of rose petals.

Usha shook her head.

'I thought you'd be dressed by now,' Tanvi sighed and eased herself down beside Usha on the anchor steps.

Usha winced into the sunlight. 'My head hurts.'

Tanvi sighed. 'We'll all feel more settled after today, Ush.'

This is my last chance, Usha thought. 'Mum! You know how you were telling me I should say what's on my mind?' Tanvi nodded, drawing closer. 'I should have said before, but now Imtiaz is actually coming, I don't think it's a good idea.' Usha hesitated, attempting to soften the blow. 'I mean, it doesn't seem like a good time for her to move in.'

Tanvi smiled gently, wrapping an arm around Usha's shoulders. 'Let's get through today and then we'll talk about everything. Adopting Imtiaz is a big deal for all of us. It's

22

natural to have some last-minute nerves.' Tanvi peered over to Kali Ma's bed, opening her hand to reveal a pressed rose petal. She raised it to her own nose and offered it to Usha. 'Remind you of anything?'

'The perfume I used to make for Kali Ma!'

Tanvi smiled and rubbed the petal over Usha's wrists. The sweet memory-scent brought tears.

Resting her head against her mum's shoulder, Usha allowed Tanvi to smooth over her tangle of curls as she used to when Usha was little. The light from the Globe Window shifted, rippling a river of light across the floorboards.

'Nothing's in straight lines any more, Mum,' Usha sobbed, letting the grief rip through her, feeling her mum's heart beat against hers, torn breath by breath until finally her chest began to ease.

'You know what, Usha, I think you've been up here on your own with your Kali Ma for too long, and it's our fault for always being so busy in The Hearth. I've got an idea that Imtiaz coming might help to take you out of yourself, make it easier to get on with people your own age, so when you start secondary school after the summer—'

Usha's shoulders tensed as she shrugged her mum off. 'I don't want to think about school now.'

Tanvi tapped Usha's knee and picked up the rose petal basket. 'You're right! Come on, let's give Kali Ma the final send-off she ordered. You can't do that in your PJs. Ma would not approve of that! "Come on, Myush . . ."'

'Get your glad rags on!' Tanvi and Usha chorused together, bringing smiles.

Tanvi nodded towards Kali Ma's enormous floor-to-ceiling dark wood wardrobe casting a shadow over the bed that was now to be Usha's.

'But Mum, if Imtiaz is coming she can't keep wandering over to my side and anyway, I'm not having her going through Kali Ma's things.'

'OK, we'll work it all out.' Tanvi kissed Usha's wild hair. 'And give that mop a brush!' she said, heading downstairs as if something had been agreed.

'I wish you'd told me what you wanted me to wear, Kali Ma.' Usha pulled back the sail screen and climbed over her bed, her bare feet padding across the soft rug to the wall that Kali Ma's bed had once rested against, the space now taken up by Kali Ma's pride and joy of a wardrobe with its fruit-engraved panelling. Laying her hands flat against the heavy oak doors, Usha took a deep breath and pulled both sides open together, scanning from her own clothes on one side to Kali Ma's collections on the other. *There is no way Imtiaz is putting her things in here.*

'Don't worry, Kali Ma, I won't let anyone replace you,' she whispered.

Kneeling, Usha scanned the rows of satin shoes in every colour, and, hanging above them, she admired row after row of Kali Ma's sample fashion collection. *Start with the shoes! Always start with the shoes, Myush.* Usha smiled at the memory of Kali Ma speaking her nickname as she reached into the bottom of the wardrobe.

Pulling out a single shoe, she dropped it again at the sound of mewling. Spirit emerged, dislodging the matching one. 'OK, here's the pair! Clever cat!' Usha placed the slipper-like shoes on her feet; slightly loose at the back, they fitted a bit like her summer espadrilles. From the drawers in her side of the wardrobe she grabbed her underwear, a white T-shirt and a pair of jeans while Spirit climbed further in, meandering along the rows of kimonos and silken coats. 'Come on then, Kali Ma. It's your day, you choose.' Closing her eyes, Usha let her hand drift through the soft silk and cotton materials, the lengths of sari cloth, the bright-coloured print samples, jackets and dresses. As Spirit's tail brushed her hand she opened her eyes. 'Trust me a bit more now?' Usha asked, and in answer Spirit pawed at the hem of a gaudy orange kimono-coat.

Usha stared at Spirit's mismatching eyes and the cat returned her stare unflinchingly. 'If you were going to come back as anything, Kali Ma, you would definitely be a cat – with your style and serious attitude!' Usha sighed at the wildness of her own thoughts. 'It's your fault I've got all this reincarnation stuff in my head.' Spirit pawed at her as if to say, 'Get on with it.'

'OK!' Usha threw on the coat and checked herself out in the long wardrobe mirror. 'Well, *you* love clashing colours, so . . .' Usha reached up to her bare neck.

Bending down, she eased out the lacquered chest where

25

she had tucked Kali Ma's precious things. Removing the lid and sliding her hand in, she attempted to retrieve the necklace without having to unpack the whole box again. It must have slipped to the bottom. Everything would have to come out. Carefully, Usha laid the conch shell, satchel and a box of slides on the floor. 'Feels weird to go through your things without you, Kali Ma.'

The lacquered box was empty now, but there was no necklace. *I definitely put it in here.* Usha frowned, confused. Unless her mum had taken it? Usha picked up the satchel that had belonged to Pops Michael and shook it. Something rattled inside. Peering into it, Usha sighed with relief as she caught sight of the jade skull necklace that her Kali Ma had gifted her the day before she died.

Placing it over her head, she checked herself in the inset mirror of the wardrobe door, inspecting the soft smokiness of the jade beads. *It's just a necklace*, she reassured herself as, forehead furrowed, she tried not to stare at the hollow cheeks, bumpy skulls and deep eye cavities that had always seemed a bit grim but now with Kali Ma gone, felt full-on gruesome. The necklace lay like a dragging weight against her chest. 'How did you wear this every day, Kali Ma? I'll put it on today because I know how much you love it. After that, it's going back in the box.' Usha glanced down to where Spirit was busy sniffing around the satchel.

'Let's see?' Picking it up, she unbuckled the worn leather straps and opened it fully. Empty! But, flattening her palm, she felt around inside a document compartment and was amazed to find a thin, brown book. She had always assumed the satchel was empty. Carefully she pulled it out. 'You didn't show me this, Kali Ma?'

Spirit rubbed her head over the book's cover as Usha attempted to decipher what was written there in unevenly formed childlike letters. Her spine fizzed with anticipation to discover something of her Kali Ma's that she'd never seen. Handling it as if it might fall apart on touch, Usha read:

Esimorp Book
by Kali Gopal
Aged 11

How strange and comforting it felt to be holding something that had belonged to her Kali Ma at her own age. 'Your handwriting was terrible, Kali Ma! Is that why you didn't want me to see this? What's "Esimorp"?' But now Usha's attention was caught by a yellowing label, in old-fashioned typewriter print, stuck below her Kali Ma's writing, with the words:

In consultation with Dr N.K. Mistry

'What is this, Kali Ma?' Behind Usha, Spirit sniffed the air and circled restlessly around the upside down conch shell, setting it rocking next to her on the floor. Usha carefully leant the book on her knees and turned the pages. Every bit of space was covered by her Kali Ma's drawings. Reading it felt like collapsing time between them. It also felt wrong, like she should be asking for permission to look. Usha bit her lip. *Kali Ma is dead. You've got to stop talking to her and accept it.* In any case, now she'd taken this peek into her Kali Ma's childhood she couldn't stop herself from reading on.

Young Kali Ma had chalked and charcoaled many pictures. Usha flicked back and forth through its oddly repetitive imagery of a woman in a floaty dress with a long plait trailing down her back. In her hands she carried something that looked like a shell and at other times a round, pink smudge like a bowl or perhaps a ball of wool?

'Who's this Dr Mistry? Why were you seeing a doctor? Is this like Mum's art therapy class with people at The Hearth?' Usha smiled as her eyes scanned the images. They seemed so childish. No way could anyone be able to predict from looking at these rough sketches that Kali Ma would one day be destined for art school. Usha couldn't quite work out what was strange about the sketches, except that they looked like they'd been done in a frenzy, as if she was desperate to show someone her dreams – or nightmares? As Usha touched the pages, the chalky drawings smudged a little, releasing dust, but something else too, that came creeping over her like a smell – an unsettling pent-up energy rose from the pages. Peering closer at the repeated image of the woman, Usha realised that the ankle-length gown with fishtail folds was not a dress at all but a sari.

Spirit's sharp miaow pierced her concentration.

Usha dropped the book, her heart pounding hard, feeling like an intruder on her Kali Ma's childhood but unable to pull herself away as she began to notice that here and there, a few words and names were repeated. 'Michael. Is this Pops Michael? You knew him then, didn't you?' Usha leafed through the pages to where they turned into thin-lined tracing paper at the back, searching for an explanation. If this was some kind of therapy book, here is where the doctor's notes should go, but the only thing she found were a few made-up words dotted around: Terces, Ykcul, Esimorp, Niagrab.

'Or maybe you were supposed to write something yourself? All those sari-covered notebooks you gave me telling me to write down my thoughts. Why didn't *you*, Kali Ma?'

Does Mum or Merve know anything about this? Usha wondered, placing the book back in the satchel and closing the worn brass buckles. 'I'll look after it for you, Kali Ma. I promise.'

Stowing the satchel back in the box, Usha turned around to find Spirit purring loudly, stretched flat out on the floor, her head nestled in the smooth ear of the conch. Usha gently eased the shell away from the cat, remembering how sensitive Kali Ma had been when she'd handled it. Lifting it up, she smoothed her fingers over the pale pink inner, noticing for the first time how it spiralled into the invisible centre of the shell like the delicate folds of a giant ear.

'Why did you keep this locked away?' Usha was about to place it back in the box when Spirit began a persistent protest.

'Come on, Spirit, we'll put it in the shell garden if you like it so much. It can't do any harm.'

Spirit stuck close by her ankles as Usha stepped through the Globe Window and walked out into the roof garden, padding over the decking, through the long, swaying grasses, to the family's summer camp. She placed it among the other shells in the raised bed next to the driftwood bench where she and Kali Ma had whiled away so many hours together.

Usha sat down and looked to her side. 'So strange not to have you next to me. If you were here right now, I'd ask you why you hid the most beautiful shell away.' Only the breeze in the whistling grasses drifted back in reply. Spirit lay on the sun-drenched decking, resting her head inside the smooth conch ear. 'OK, you stay here then, listening to the sea,' Usha whispered. 'Lucky you! I have to go.'

The cat raised her head and nuzzled Usha's hand for the first time, as if she understood.

From the hallway staircase distorted voices rose through her open doorway, amplifying a hollow echo as if their whole house had become an empty shell.

Usha crept down to the turn of the stair, pausing at the sound of her mum's voice contorted with anger. Was she crying? Crouching low and out of sight, she peered through the banisters at her parents as they stood in the hall. From here they looked so far away . . . like miniature figures in her old doll's house. The pulse at her temples pounded.

Tanvi held a letter in her hand and was reading over it, pausing every few minutes to vent her outrage. 'What do they mean by needing *proof* of permission for the downstairs to be for community use? They can't give us so little time to find a legal document no one's seen since my grandma's era. How can they spring this on us now? Those developers have been sniffing around here, and that councillor up the road with all his complaints – I bet they're in on this together.'

'Let's not allow this to spoil today. We'll deal with this later.' Lem attempted to calm Tanvi down but she threw off his hands.

'When, later? When they're forcing us to move out of The Hearth? Looks like we've got weeks! When they brought this up last time I asked Ma and she hadn't got a clue either.'

Usha struggled to understand why her mum was getting herself in such a state. She had never known her so upset, not even at Kali Ma's funeral. Straining closer, she heard her dad's response.

'This isn't exactly out of the blue, Tanv. We've had letters before, asking us for proof of business use. We'd better start looking as soon as we get back. Kali Ma wasn't especially organised – maybe it's somewhere among her papers.'

'And if not?' Tanvi asked.

'Then we'll have to talk to the council.'

Tanvi leant her head on Lem's chest and pointed through to the communal room. 'What about all the people who depend on The Hearth? If we can't run it from here, we'll have to move. We couldn't afford separate premises.'

Winded by this revelation, Usha lay back on the step, where she could still glimpse them through the banister slat, and listened to her mum's rising panic and her dad's attempt to calm her.

But Tanvi refused to be consoled. As a new wave of rage surged up, she pulled away from Lem and brandished the offending envelope in the air. 'The cheek of it! Sending us this leaflet about "Investing in Communities", offering funding to help us relocate The Hearth to a more "appropriate location"! What have they got against us? First all those complaints about keeping "the fabric of the house up to street standard", now this? I swear there are people around here trying to hound us out, with all their whinging about our clients queuing for help. How can a few people lining up outside our door be causing an obstruction? There'd be room for half of Hackney on this one street!'

Usha leant forward to see her dad wrap his arms around her mum's shoulders and hug her close. 'A home isn't just bricks and mortar, Tanv, is it? If it came to it, if we had to, we could build another Hearth and home somewhere else.'

Tanvi laughed, a bitter laugh that Usha hadn't heard from her mum before. 'And Nilam, where would she work? And all the friends we've made who just pop in?' Tanvi peered up the stairs. Usha flattened herself against the steps out of sight. 'And what about Pops Michael's top deck? It'd break

Usha's heart to have to leave that. Mine too. And Imtiaz? We've promised her a stable home . . .'

'Come on, Tanv, don't let Usha hear you like this, you'll frighten her.' Enfolded in her dad's arms, her mum whispered something that made her dad straighten up. 'I agree. She's got enough to deal with. We'll keep this to ourselves. No need to worry her about any of this.'

Usha took in the stark reality of what she'd heard. Her hand was still clasped firmly over her mouth. Panic rose in her as her insides scorched and she had to remind herself to breathe. *How can they tell me to open up to them, when they're keeping the secret of having to leave the house I was born in?*

Leaning on the banister, Usha stood up as quietly as she could, setting off at a trot down the steps as if she'd only just left the top deck. Hearing her coming, her parents sprung apart and pasted tense smiles on their faces.

'Look at you! Bright and beautiful, just as Kali Ma wanted!' Her mum's bloodshot eyes settled approvingly on her outfit.

'Your voice sounds weird,' Usha tested.

'Sorry! Just feeling a bit emotional about today. Better out than in!' Tanvi reassured Usha, straightening up. 'Now I've had my cry, time to celebrate. That's what Ma would have wanted. You got the music, Lem?'

He nodded, picking up Kali Ma's vintage record player box by the handle. 'You've got the ashes, Tanv?'

Tanvi shot Lem a look that said, 'How could I forget my own Ma's ashes?' But she checked in her rose-petal-filled basket anyway, took out an envelope and handed it to Usha. 'Before I forget, this came for you this morning. I think I saw Imtiaz and Delyse drop it in.'

'Thanks, Mum!'

'Looks like a card. That's kind of her. Don't you want to open it?' her dad asked as she placed it in her pocket.

'I'll read it later.' Even having to think about Imtiaz today, when they were supposed to be saying goodbye to Kali Ma, seemed like an intrusion.

Feeling as if her brain was being squeezed in a clamp, Usha could not rid herself of the suspicion that since her Kali Ma had died, something in the ship house had shifted. Its anchor was raised and now they were all setting sail into uncharted waters.

The Farewell

The trees lining the Embankment gently swayed in the afternoon sunshine. Craning her neck up at the London Eye, Usha's chest tightened as her mind flashed back to the the outing she and Kali Ma had taken just after her Pops's ashes-scattering ceremony. Just the two of them sitting high above the river in a glinting pod on a bright winter's day three years ago.

'I'll have a last boat trip too, like Michael.' Kali Ma stood up and pointed past the Houses of Parliament. 'Right there, Usha, floating in the tides of history, is where my ashes are going!'

'Don't be silly, Kali Ma. You're so young . . . you'll live for ever!'

Kali Ma shook her head. 'Promise you'll tell Tanvi and Lem this is what I want when my time comes? No stress, no speeches . . . just make a wish for me and spread my ashes on the water, that's all I ask. And maybe you can hang out my bunting and play a few of the old tunes. Make sure you wear one of my best threads – and I'll have dancing, of course!' Kali Ma laughed at herself. 'I don't want much!'

As they approached the boat, Usha turned to the Eye and whispered, 'See, Kali Ma, I haven't forgotten my promise.'

Farewell

Usha caught sight of the plaque on the side of the boat they'd rented as Tanvi and Lem made small talk with the guests slowly gathering. As soon as they were on board, Usha shied away from the chatter, picking out a few people she recognised. She smiled at Nilam from The Hearth, who had sometimes kept Kali Ma company while Usha was at school. Apart from Nilam, she wished that today could have been only family.

'How you doin', me darlin'?' She felt a hand on her shoulder as Uncle Merve came to stand by her side. 'Anything I can help with?'

Usha hugged him tight, feeling his heart beating through his blazer jacket, just as she had felt her Kali Ma's only weeks ago.

Feeling her sobs, Merve rocked her soothingly. 'I know, my love, I know . . . but we're all in the same boat!' Uncle Merve detached himself from her and did his one at a time

36

eyebrow-raising trick . . . and despite herself, she laughed through her tears. 'Come on, let your old great-uncle help!'

Usha dried her eyes and pulled Kali Ma's bunting out of her mum's basket. Merve whistled in admiration as triangle after triangle of Kali Ma's designs unfolded. As she and Merve hung the bunting around the guide-ropes, she felt bolstered by Kali Ma's colours.

Merve examined an orange triangle and pointed to the pattern on Usha's silken kimono-coat. 'Snap!' He laughed. 'My brother Michael was a lucky man. He may have left us too young, but what a blast those two had. Such an adventurous pair, and he met his match in Kali. See all that she's left behind.' Merve wasn't looking at the bunting but straight into Usha's eyes as his own switched from shine to cloud. 'Fitting tribute, you wearing her clothes.' Merve pointed to the necklace and mock-shuddered. 'Those skulls always freaked me out a bit though!' he admitted as they wandered around the boat, hunting for places to string the bunting from.

'Thanks for that, you two! Looks so pretty.' Tanvi kissed Uncle Merve's cheek as she busied herself greeting guests. 'No Delyse today?'

He shook his head. 'Working. I'll have to find another dancing partner!'

'Ah. Well, you two love birds will soon be away!' Usha watched her mum meander between people, greeting and smiling, greeting and smiling. *I suppose that's what's called 'putting on a brave face'.*

Now all the bunting was hung, Usha tied the ends in a slip-knot and for the first time realised that the one thing that she and Imtiaz would soon have in common was missing people they loved and that those two people, Uncle Merve and Delyse, loved each other too.

Merve winked at her and wandered off to greet an older woman carrying a guitar case on her back. 'So glad you came, Peggy!' Merve turned to Usha and grinned. 'I thought your Kali Ma deserved a bit of live music for her send-off!'

'Well, I'm just about alive!' Peggy joked.

'Here, let me help you.' Merve took the guitar from Peggy and walked her over to a red velvet chair where a music stand had already been set up. Next to it was a table where Kali Ma's record player was open beside a stack of vinyl, ready and waiting to be played.

Usha shoved her hand deep in her right-hand pocket, scowling as she transferred the card from Imtiaz to the other side. A single rose petal floated free. For a moment she was transfixed as she watched it bobbing on a stream of air over the railings and falling into the murky water, growing heavy and disappearing. Suddenly she knew what she must do. 'You want *me* to scatter your ashes, Kali Ma?'

There was a brief pause while all the guests gathered.

Peggy nodded and began to strum a few chords.

'Better get my handkerchief out!' Merve whispered and the chatter gradually stilled as Peggy began singing in a voice Usha thought she recognised. It sounded rich and warm and a bit crackly, like an old radio recording.

'Many rivers to cross . . .' Usha knew the words of Kali Ma's favourite song by heart but was afraid to sing along in case it set her off crying again. Merve placed an arm around her shoulder and they sat in silence listening to the music, feeling the freshening river air play over their skin.

'Thanks for inviting Peggy,' Usha said under the ripple of applause at the end of the song.

Merve waved his hand away as if to say, 'It's nothing.' 'Shame Kali couldn't be here really, to see this. You've done her proud.' The sun's reflection blinked off the pod at the top of the London Eye.

'Oh! And I nearly forgot!' Merve reached into his pocket and handed Usha a tiny brightly painted statue.

'Michael brought it back for me as a present from India after their honeymoon. The goddess Kali! She's for you.'

Usha felt herself tearing up again at the thought of having to say goodbye to Uncle Merve too, even if they would see each other for holidays. *Why does everyone I love have to go away?* she thought and kissed Merve on the cheek to thank him.

'Now, enough tears!' Merve dabbed her cheek, then his own. 'Your Kali Ma wanted a send-off party, so a send-off party she must have!'

Tanvi waved Usha and Merve over.

'Shall we' – Uncle Merve ceremoniously stood up and linked arms with Usha – 'go and make a wish for your Kali Ma?'

Her parents waited together on the staircase above a small floating platform. Tanvi held the ashes boat in both hands. It was a simple rowboat shape, made more beautiful by Tanvi attaching two plain triangles of bunting for sails. As far as Usha could tell, the miniature boat was made of cardboard that had been dipped into some kind of protective wax that was supposed to keep it afloat for a while. Tanvi had already stowed the ashes in the hull and replaced the top, where a small candle in the shape of a lotus flower waited to be lit. Lem stood ready with his lighter, just as they had rehearsed. Usha felt in her pocket for the petals she'd taken out of the basket.

'Can I talk to you, Mum, for a moment?' she asked.

Tanvi smiled gently, nodded and walked Usha out of earshot of everyone.

'There's no pressure, Ush. If you don't want to scatter the petals you can stay here with Uncle Merve.'

'It's not that,' Usha whispered. 'I want to set the ashes free myself.' She glanced up at the Eye. 'I promised Kali Ma I'd sort all this out, so I think I should do it on my own.'

The worry lines on her mum's face softened into a broad smile. 'You organised today, so whatever you want to do is fine.' Tanvi took Usha's hand and walked back to inform Lem of the change of plan.

'Proud of you, Ush!' her dad whispered as he lit the candle, placed it in the bow of the ashes boat and passed it to Usha.

Head held high, Usha walked slowly down the steps to the raft platform. Her body swayed as it bobbed up and down, troubled by the river's constant lapping. Feeling light-headed now, she cupped the ashes boat in both hands and kneeled down so that all that separated her from the water were the safety railings and the cat-flap-sized gate she was to open to set her Kali Ma's ashes sailing free. Her mind flashed bright with an image of Spirit tapping at the Globe Window. Down here, so close to the river, she could feel every tilt of the water. Closing her eyes, she breathed in and out, slowing her heartbeat to the rhythm of the waves.

Opening the tiny gate, she placed the ashes boat on the water and let go. At the sight of all that was left of her Kali Ma bobbing alone, Usha had the urge to pluck the boat out again, but it had already sailed out of reach. Through tear-washed eyes, she watched the candle flicker casting a glowing light over the water as the bunting sails set fire and burned brightly.

'As long as the flame stays lit, you're still here with me, Kali Ma,' she whispered.

Behind her, Tanvi called out a reminder, 'Don't forget the petals, Ush.'

Moving as if in a dream, she reached into her pocket.

Feeling the velvet softness of the rose petals, she began to scatter them on the water, where they trailed behind the ashes boat. Within moments, the waxen paper began to grow so heavy that the last of the flaming sails met the water, soon to be snuffed out.

Make a wish before the light goes out, make a wish before the light goes out, make a wish before—

'I wish . . . I wish . . . I wish . . . that you'd come back.'

It's too late. Her heart sank at the same time as the little boat dipped beneath the surface of the grey river. Usha felt a sudden deadening pang of guilt. *Why didn't I wish for Kali Ma to be at peace, or reunited with Pops Michael?* she berated herself, and, unfurling her fingers, she found the miniature figure of Kali indented into her skin.

Usha stared at the murky river. The light was extinguished. It was over and all she felt was a dull ache of emptiness in the pit of her stomach. Her legs collapsed under her and she sat cross-legged on the floating platform, watching the rippling water.

In the exact place where the boat had sunk, the afternoon sun formed a glistening light pool. The surface dipped and the rose petals were caught in a swirling vortex into which the sun shot millions of shards of light; emerald green, purple, red and bright yellow sparks formed a rainbow pathway across the Thames.

Hypnotised by the river's beauty as if Kali Ma had created it herself, Usha leant forward to touch the colours on the water. Holding her breath, she squinted into the sun and gasped to find a slender wreath of smoke – *or steam?* – shooting up from the river, just where the boat had sunk. *Only a trick of light and shadow*, she reasoned as she peered closer. But the force of the water built and now spurted violently upwards, splashing her, propelling her trembling body backwards as Kali Ma rose from the Thames on the shiny grey mass of a *whale's* back. Frozen to the spot, Usha willed her legs to move but she could do nothing but stare in horror at the sight of her Kali Ma, just as she was in life, surging towards her. Cowering away, Usha bashed against the railings as the platform listed violently sideways then steadied itself, returning, shaken, to the water with a loud thud as the great whale dived down and the rainbow river smudged back into mucky brown. Her heart racing, struggling to catch her breath, Usha turned to find her Kali Ma sitting beside her.

'You're dead!' Usha gasped.

'What sort of greeting do you call that?' Kali Ma threw her head back and laughed. Usha opened her mouth to speak several times but her tongue was numb. 'I'm as surprised to find myself back in the land of the living as you are, believe me, Myush. Whales are not a mode of transport I'm familiar with! Boat, plane, hovercraft, submarine, yes. Rickshaw, even. I've swum with dolphins, but never a whale.' Kali Ma stood up, shifting from foot to foot as if testing her ability to stand, brushing herself down, her clothes already miraculously dry. 'But what a novelty to have my energy back,' she said, turning to where Tanvi, Lem and Merve stood at the top of the steps calling for Usha to join them, waving at her now as if they had felt and seen nothing to disturb them.

'But why were you being carried on the back of a whale?' Usha asked, still shaking her head in disbelief.

'Well, you know how your Pops Michael loved his whale watching. Maybe he came to pick me up and I've been diverted! Who knows the mysteries of life and death. We're sitting on the border of unknowing here.' Kali Ma grinned and clapped her hands at the sight of her bunting blowing in the breeze. 'You remembered, my angel.'

Usha nodded. 'Have I dreamed you up? Have I willed you here?' she whispered.

Kali Ma shrugged. 'Don't ask me! All I know is I'm here by your side and you're talking to me. And I have to admit, I always fancied turning up to my own funeral! So come on, Myush, let's make the most of it while it lasts.'

Usha scanned around the deck to see if anyone else showed any sign of alarm at the appearance of the whale, or if they'd felt it butting at the boat, but all the guests chatted away peacefully. Usha sensed her Kali Ma's presence as a warm glow as they walked back up the steps together.

'Kali would have been so proud of you,' Merve said, leaning in to confide in Usha. 'I think that's why they don't usually have sails in ashes boats – see how tall those flames grew . . . fitting for such a firecracker, I say!' He smiled, wrapping his arms around Usha's shoulders, and as he did,

Kali Ma collapsed like a flickering flame and emerged on Usha's other side.

'Dear old Merve. There's no *would have been so proud* about it! I am, am, am proud!' Kali Ma chipped in. 'All a bit sombre, isn't it? What happened to the music?' Kali Ma took in the gathering and her face lit up as she spotted Peggy sitting with her guitar across her knee. She hurried over to her. 'Bless you, Peg!' she said.

Usha watched closely for signs that anyone else could see her Kali Ma. It didn't seem like it, but as Peggy picked up her guitar her mood seemed to shift. 'I feel the spirit take me!' Peggy said. 'Time for a bit of Janis, I think!'

Before Usha knew what was happening, Kali Ma was in front of her, swaying her hips, encouraging her to dance along.

'Kali Ma, stop. I'll look weird,' she muttered.

'Don't be so self-conscious. Who cares what anyone else thinks! Go on, Myush, let that gorgeous hair down!'

Following the flicker and glow of Kali Ma's movements, Usha found herself twirling around too.

Merve smiled and came to stand nearby. 'If I'd have known that little statue would bring out your confidence like that, I'd have handed you the Kali force ages ago!'

'Grab him, Myush! Come on, Merve! Let's dance!' Kali Ma laughed.

Heat surged through Usha as she reached her hand out. Merve took hold of it and joined them in their wild dancing, heads thrown back, arms flung to the sky.

'Steady!' Merve warned. 'You must have inherited that wild streak from your grandma! She always loved a dance!'

If only Merve could see her Kali Ma linking arms with him. Usha glanced over to her mum and dad, who watched in amazement as around them, one by one, people began to dance too as if drawn to an invisible flame.

After the dancing, Kali Ma moved among the guests saying goodbye to each of them. Usha was sure now that none of them could see her Kali Ma as she did, but had the feeling that each in their own way felt her energy glowing brightly and more often than not, her presence turned tears into smiles.

'Such a sudden way to go, the old ticker stopping in my sleep! Don't get me wrong, I'm happy I went out with a bang and not a whimper.' Kali Ma snapped her fingers. 'But I have to say, it's good to have a little time to say goodbye.'

Drawing near to Tanvi, Kali Ma gently placed her arms over her daughter's shoulders and tried to rock her like a baby. Usha watched as her mum swayed and the tears flowed down her cheeks. Finally Kali Ma beckoned for Usha to walk with her, back down to the floating platform.

'Thank you for this beautiful send-off.' Kali Ma reached towards Usha's tear-stained cheek and her skin tingled. 'Don't get me wrong, Myush, it's been a pleasant interlude. Finding my dancing feet, having a chance to say a fond farewell, but if it's in your power to hitch me a return ride on that whale, I'm keen to sail away now. It's my time.'

'But how?'

'I don't know. How does it usually work? Click those red shoes of yours together, call on your Kali statue, pray on my skull beads. Seems like anything's possible! Hurry up though, we're heading back to shore.'

Usha closed her eyes and attempted to wish the wish she should have wished. That Kali Ma could be at peace. She tried three times, after each wish opening her eyes to check, but Kali Ma was still standing beside her.

'I did wish for you to come back, but that can't be why you're here. What if there's another reason?' Usha whispered.

'What reason could there be to raise the dead and keep me from sailing to my Michael?' Kali Ma's shoulders tensed.

'Maybe we need you. There's something happening with our house,' Usha blurted out. 'Mum and Dad have to find some legal papers, they're really worried about it.'

Kali Ma turned to face Usha, her forehead deep-scored with frown lines. The energy seemed to be leaking out of her and she looked suddenly exhausted. 'What business do I have with worldy goods now? I'm done with houses and wanting things. Please, Myush, wish harder before it's too late.'

But they were already approaching the shore. 'Come on, Ush!' Lem called as he untied the last piece of bunting. 'Let's get home.'

'I imagine the dead go free!' Kali Ma chuckled as she swept on to the bus past Usha, Tanvi and Lem swiping their Oyster cards.

Maybe I should be afraid, Usha thought as she followed Kali Ma to the back seat.

As they pulled up at a bus stop, Kali Ma pressed her nose against the glass and inspected the shop window displays. 'Has the kaftan made a comeback? *Not* flares again!'

I thought you weren't into high street fashion or worldly things, Kali Ma? Usha wanted to ask, but her mum and dad sat in the seats opposite. Her stressy pulse pounded her temples. *How am I going to handle a ghost as well as Imtiaz coming, and maybe even having to move house?*

Her dad smiled as he checked his iPhone. 'Apart from the small sail fire I think that all went off quite smoothly.'

This cannot be happening. Usha wrapped her arms around herself. Kali Ma nodded towards her. 'If it's any consolation, it has been heard of for whales to lose their way and swim up the Thames so perhaps my mode of transport is not as fantastical as it seems. My question is, how do I get back?'

Usha had so wanted to see her Kali Ma again but now that she was here by her side and didn't even seem that keen to stay, everything was wrong. Placing her hand in her pocket, she felt for the envelope from Imtiaz. As she lifted it out, a petal that had clung to its surface floated lose and on to Kali Ma's lap.

'At least I'll get to see my roses in full bloom again.' Kali Ma pointed to the card. 'Open it, then! It might be about me!'

Usha shrugged Kali Ma away. In all her grief she had created a version of her Kali Ma, remembering only the bits she loved the most, and managed to completely forget her bossy side, the way she always took charge. Tearing open the envelope, Usha pulled out the card and inspected the cover image.

'Yuck! Lilies! Not my favourite.' Kali Ma scrunched her nose in distaste, as she bent in closer, and together they read the few words written inside.

Dear Usha,
I'm sorry about your gran dying,
See you soon,
Imtiaz

'Direct and to the point! Atrocious handwriting, though. Mind you, you should have seen mine when I was her age!'

Usha checked on her mum and dad, who were chatting quietly, worry lines etched on both their faces. Usha craned towards Kali Ma, timing what she said with the announcement for the next bus stop. 'I know how bad your writing was. I found your Esimorp Book.'

'My what?' Kali Ma pulled away from Usha and faced her, demanding an answer.

Usha's skin prickled and she felt an angry heat flush her own cheeks. 'What's the matter? Why are you so upset?' Then the realisation hit her as her heart raced out of control. 'Do I feel what you feel, Kali Ma?' Usha whispered.

Kali Ma shrugged. 'How would I know?' But Usha felt the annoyance sparking through her own body just as she'd felt joy when she'd danced on the *Farewell*.

'Sorry, Usha, what did you say?' Lem sat forward on his seat and tapped her knee.

Usha stared at her dad, struggling to find a convincing reply. 'I . . . I . . . just said I'm tired!' Usha lied, feeling Kali Ma turn away from her. She tried to remember what was written on the cover of the book she'd found in Pops's satchel. The name – Dr Mistry, plus Kali Ma's name and age and the title. Feeling suddenly dizzy with the strangeness of it all, she nudged closer to Kali Ma's turbulent heat and breathed on the window, writing the word she had seen on the cover.

Esimorp

'I used to do that backward writing when I was your age!' Tanvi smiled. 'Kali Ma taught it to me.' Her mum blew on the window by her side and wrote 'Promise' on the glass.

How could I have not seen that? Kali Ma nodded, making Usha feel slow.

'Remember what I said, Ush. Anything troubling you, don't keep it to yourself. No secrets between us . . . Esimorp?'

'I heard you this morning, talking about the house.'

Lem leant forward. 'Sorry, Ush, we didn't want to worry you. We've got to find some legal papers to show the council, and we need them for a tribunal at the end of the month.'

'I said I heard!' Usha mumbled, her attention torn between

50

Kali Ma and her parents. As Kali Ma stared intently through the window, Usha got the feeling that she might be hiding something. Her mind flooded with questions she needed urgent answers to. *If Kali Ma knows something that can help save The Hearth and the house, and if I'm the only one who can see her, then it's up to me to find out.* When they were on their own she would get out the Esimorp . . . Promise Book, she corrected herself, and see if Kali Ma could shed some light on it.

'Wipe that word away,' Kali Ma ordered, pointing to the window. Usha blew on it and the glass clouded over. 'If only it was that easy to forget old promises. Seems like this is unfinished business.' Kali Ma sighed.

So she does know something. Usha closed her eyes and tried to visualise the other scattered words in the book in her mind's eye.

Esimorp

Promise

Ykcul

Lucky

Sterces

Secrets

Niagrab

Bargain

When she opened her eyes again, she found Kali Ma snoring softly. *Why are you here, Kali Ma? What promise did you make? Why can't your spirit rest?*

The Promise Book

Kali Ma's silent treatment ended as soon as she saw the top deck again. She was full of praise for the new room layout. Her only criticism was that no one had thought to use one of her Kali Prints for the sail screen material. Usha didn't have the heart to admit that she had chosen the plain cream muslin because sometimes all Kali Ma's colours were a bit too over the top for her.

Kali Ma was out on the roof garden admiring the roses when she first met Spirit and let out a scream.

'What's the matter? It's only a cat, Kali Ma!' Usha explained. 'She's just a stray.' Usha bent down reaching for Spirit . . . but the cat moved away, intent on keeping track of Kali Ma.

'I don't like its odd eyes!' Kali Ma complained, shooing it away.

Usha laughed. 'I think they're pretty.'

Usha spent the weekend on the top deck with the ghost of her Kali Ma, blasting out music on her old record player, dancing around together, even camping out under the stars in the roof garden. Surreal as it was, Usha didn't want their time together to end but she could not ignore the tension that rose through the house beneath them as her mum and dad searched for the legal documents. It felt wrong that she and Kali Ma were so happy in their own little cocooned world when her mum and dad were pulling their hair out with stress.

So, even though Kali Ma kept repeating how she was done with worldly things (while insisting Usha model all her old outfits), Usha finally plucked up the courage to take the lacquered box out of the wardrobe. At the sight of it Kali Ma's smile faded instantly and the lines around her mouth hardened.

'What do you want to go through all that old stuff for? The past is the past, put it away!' she snapped, her voice growing so sharp that Usha felt afraid of her.

'But you're here, Kali Ma! And all these problems Mum and Dad are having about the house must have something to do with what happened in the past.'

'Party's over, I see.' Kali Ma sighed and the warm glow Usha had felt since her Kali Ma's arrival turned suddenly chilly.

'Let me go now, Myush, please.' Kali Ma flinched as Spirit stalked towards her.

But what you said on the bus . . . Usha persisted. 'Since I found your Promise Book in Pops Michael's satchel I can't stop thinking about it.' Usha took the lid off the box and lifted it out.

'Get this cat away from me!' Kali Ma snapped. 'You have no business, Usha, rummaging through my things.' She winced. Kali Ma only ever called her Usha when she was really angry. The force of her Kali Ma's reaction rattled her. Now she turned her back on Usha, just as she had at the mention of the book on the bus. Usha was sure now that the Promise Book held the clue to why Kali Ma's spirit could not rest.

'What does "Lucky" mean, Kali Ma? You kept drawing this same picture and writing backwards words . . . *Lucky, Secrets, Promise, Bargain.*' Still Kali Ma refused to turn around. 'Who was this Dr Mistry? Please tell me, Kali Ma. I don't want to upset you but it might help us work out why you're here.'

Usha carried it over to her bed and began leafing through the pages. Kali Ma cursed as Spirit sped past intent on following Usha.

'You have no right to stir all this up again.'

Usha had the strangest feeling that Kali Ma was talking to the cat.

'Stir what up?'

Kali Ma shook her head and walked out into the garden to sit among her beloved roses. It was as if just the sight of the Promise Book made her unhappy. No matter how guilty Usha felt for not letting it rest, time was running out to ask about it. Tomorrow when Imtiaz moved in, how would she even talk to her Kali Ma without looking like she was out of her mind?

Carrying the book outside into the garden, Usha found Kali Ma sitting on the driftwood bench that had always been their favourite place for talking. The whispering grasses seemed to calm Kali Ma, who sighed in resignation and nodded for Usha to sit down beside her as they watched Spirit shove her head inside the conch ear, prodding it with her paw.

'If the conch ear's opened it's too late anyway . . . Spirit knows,' Kali Ma sighed.

Usha scowled, picking up the Promise Book. 'How can a cat know? Who is this woman you kept drawing? Was it a dream? Or something you were haunted by – like you're here with me – but scary?' Usha turned to the front cover and pointed to the Dr Mistry label. Smiling gently at Kali Ma she asked, 'Was drawing all this your way of telling the doctor about your nightmares?'

Kali Ma shook her head and stared at Spirit, her mouth formed into a tight, sealed line as she stood up abruptly, leant on the rose balcony and looked out over the city. 'This street has changed a lot since Michael and me were your age. Well' – she tilted her head from side to side – 'it has and it hasn't. Tell me about this trouble with The Hearth.'

Usha came to join her so that they stood shoulder to shoulder. Spirit climbed elegantly along the rose-tangled balcony, picking her path between thorns, balancing back and forth as Usha relayed what she knew about the documents that needed to be found to keep The Hearth open.

'So you don't know where they are either?' Usha studied her Kali Ma's face. She shook her head.

I believe her, Usha thought. 'So why did you ask about The Hearth?'

Kali Ma grimaced, glancing at an open page of the Promise Book in Usha's hands. 'You've no business raking over the past like this. If you have to know, I was haunted all through my childhood by that silent ghost I was trying to draw. Her name was Lucky.'

Spirit settled beside Kali Ma, staring at her. 'How did you know her name? If she couldn't speak?'

'It was sewn into her sari.'

Usha nodded, looking again at the childish drawings. Kali Ma pointed accusingly at Spirit. 'She had eyes just like that cat's.'

Usha pulled away from Spirit, who followed Kali Ma's every move.

'She can see you, can't she?' Usha asked softly.

Kali Ma nodded. 'Oh yes, she sees me all right, whether I decided to put all this haunted house stuff behind me long ago, or not.'

'But Kali Ma, I found the Promise Book and then you came back. So, if you're here something's not settled . . .'

Kali Ma blocked her ears and returned to the driftwood bench. 'If you don't mind, Usha, I think I need a bit of time to myself. I didn't ask to be alive again.'

Feeling as if she was about to explode, Usha left Kali Ma alone in the garden.

Sitting on her bed, Usha leafed through page after page of chalk drawings, looking for clues and noticing that the only colour used in the book were a dot of mossy green and brown on the woman's eyes and a touch of pink for whatever she held in her hands. Spirit settled at the end of the bed and blinked at her. 'Same eyes as yours!' Usha whispered, and for the first time the cat let Usha stroke her head and began to purr.

Reaching into her bedside table drawer, Usha took out a green sari-covered notebook, one of Kali Ma's presents from a trip to India that she'd never once been tempted to write in until now.

Once she started, Usha was amazed to find that her pent-up words poured so easily on to the page.

Maybe I need a Dr Mistry too. Someone to talk to about what's going on here, somewhere to go to try and work out what's happening here. Because even though she felt guilty for writing out her thoughts about being haunted by Kali Ma and the prospect of Imtiaz coming, the tension in her head eased as her words hit the page.

I wish I'd never mentioned I wanted a sister.

If I was going to have a sister I can't think of anyone who would be worse.

Usha flicked forward a few pages and wrote *Imtiaz Invasion.* That felt about right, and she began to list the ways it would never work between them. There were so many . . .

Usha was so engrossed that she did not see Kali Ma until she was sitting on the bed beside her.

'Sorry, Myush. I didn't mean to snap.' Usha closed the book and Kali Ma smiled. 'Glad you're putting it to some use . . . Can I read?'

Biting her lip, Usha tucked the book under her arm. 'It's kind of private,' she whispered.

'Is that so?' Kali Ma nodded meaningfully and lay on the bed beside her as Usha placed the book back in her bedside drawer. 'You see, Myush, everyone has some things they want to keep to themselves.'

'But, Kali Ma, what if the things you know can help us?'

Spirit crept closer towards them, peering at Kali Ma as if waiting for her answer.

'I need to sleep now. I've never been so tired in all my . . . death!'

Usha cringed.

'Don't look at me like that, Myush. I haven't got the energy to speak now.'

Within minutes Usha heard the familiar sound of Kali Ma's snore, but now there was nothing comforting about it.

Welcome to the Ship House

Imtiaz read the handmade banners of the protestors approaching from the opposite end of the street. Delyse slowed and signalled for Imtiaz to stick close as the group came to a standstill outside number four.

Residents' Rights First

REFUGEES NOT WELCOME HERE

RELOCATION, RELOCATION, RELOCATION

'Might have known *he* would be here!' Delyse muttered, eyeing a tall man in a white linen suit handing out leaflets to passers-by.

'Looks like he thinks a lot of himself. Who is it anyway?' Imtiaz asked.

'A councillor! He lives on this street, just two doors down.

Tanvi says he's always complaining and stirring things up about The Hearth. Doesn't like having it on his street! He's the one I heard nothing back from when I complained about my case.'

Imtiaz had the urge to knock the banners out of the protestors' hands. 'Call yourselves neighbours?' she said, loud enough to be heard.

'Just walk past as if we're not going in and I'll call Lem and Tanvi to tell them what's going on.'

'No way! This is going to be my house. I'm not hiding from anyone!'

Delyse squeezed Imtiaz's hand tight. 'You're right, Immy. Running away is no way to deal with things.'

'Like you are, you mean!' Imtiaz jibed.

Delyse winced, marched up to the councillor and waited for him to give her a leaflet.

Hesitating, he reluctantly handed one over. 'Don't I know you?' he asked.

'I shouldn't think so, but *I* know you, Councillor Buttock!'

'No way!' Imtiaz giggled.

'Councillor Puttock,' he corrected, scowling. 'Yes indeed, but today I'm here as a resident. We're a local interest group simply demonstrating to have The Hearth relocated to a less residential area, more in keeping with the needs of the . . .' Councillor Puttock searched for an appropriate word. '. . . the clientele.'

Delyse nodded a few times, but her gaze grew more steely

as she listened. 'Clientele! It's not a hairdressing salon! You mean refugee people, displaced people? But . . . Councillor Puttock –' Delyse made the 'p' pop like bursting a bubble – 'where is this more "in keeping" place? Where would you have 'clients', as you call them, go for help? Is it, by any chance, anywhere except your street?'

A muscle in Councillor Puttock's cheek began to twitch as his skin flushed a ruddy purple. 'There's a legal case to be made.'

'Oh, cut the crap! I know why you're protesting and you know too. Bad, old-fashioned racism.'

'How dare you accuse me of that!'

'I dare, because it's the ugly truth of why you're standing here. I never thought I'd see a time when it would raise its ugly head again, this shamelessly.'

It was all Imtiaz could do to stop herself from cheering Delyse on.

'You don't get my vote for this kind of . . .' She looked up at the banners. '. . . vileness! I hope your conscience is as clean as your suit. You should be ashamed of yourselves.' Delyse paused to listen to the music blasting out from the roof garden. 'This place brings heart to your street.' She pointed to the councillor's chest. 'And it seems like you need it. Why don't you put your energy and resources into helping people instead of making your neighbours' lives a misery?'

'It's precisely disruptive influences like you we want to avoid attracting to the street,' the councillor said pompously.

Imtiaz had been doing her best to keep out of it, but this swipe at Delyse was too much. Lunging forward, she batted the bottom of the councillor's hand, sending the leaflets flying. Jumping off the pavement, pretending to lose her balance, Imtiaz trod them into the dirty puddle, sending water splattering up Councillor Puttock's crisply ironed trousers. Then she got right up in his face, wagging her finger. 'Don't you dare disrespect Delyse like that! *She's* no fake. *She* actually *does* help people!'

The councillor's eyes widened. 'Stand back, everyone. Get this on record, and that noise pollution from their balcony!'

'It's called music!' Imtiaz chimed in.

'And make a note of that name – Delice!' The councillor's voice rose in panic as he summoned the banner-carriers like cavalry.

A woman laid hers down, lifted up her iPhone high and started taking photos.

The councillor tutted at the sodden leaflets, waving his hands from Delyse to Imtiaz as if *they* were the rubbish on the pavement. 'This little fiasco certainly won't help your cause! People like you don't belong in a street like this.'

'Well people like you don't belong in this century,' Imtiaz shouted.

'Let's just get inside,' Delyse whispered, taking Imtiaz's arm. But it was too late, the flame was lit.

'Why don't you just go do one? Better get your suit

cleaned up. You don't want to lower the tone of the neighbourhood!'

'That's enough now, Immy, leave it.' But it was Delyse's trembling, not her call for calm that got through to Imtiaz. Ever since Delyse had returned from being in detention, whenever she got upset her hands shook uncontrollably so that she had to clasp them together to still them. Imtiaz linked arms with her instead and felt Delyse lean on her.

'Back off, will you!' Imtiaz shouted and the protestors and the councillor stepped away into the road.

The music from above cut out and rose petals tumbled from the roof garden. Imtiaz looked up to see Lem appear over the balcony's edge.

'What's going on?' Lem yelled, waving as he spotted Delyse and Imtiaz. 'One minute!' he shouted, disappearing again.

Imtiaz scanned the length of the balcony, feeling suddenly nervous. *Usha could at least wave a welcome to me.*

'Don't worry! This place won't be open for much longer,' a woman shouted from a distance.

'Ignore!' Delyse muttered, turning her back on the protestors. 'These lot can all – what did you say? Go do one!'

Imtiaz laughed and sprung a huge hug on Delyse.

Finally, Merve opened the door. 'Come in, come in! Sorry, we were blasting out a few old tunes while we lit the BBQ. What's up?' he asked, taking Delyse's hand and steering her in.

Lem stood in the hallway, shaking his head. 'Sorry you had to bump into them. And we wanted to give you a full-on Joseph family committee welcome! We've hung the bunting out for you and everything!' Lem nodded to where the staircase was decorated with bright triangular colours.

'I like this material,' Imtiaz said, stopping to inspect a batique-printed triangle.

'These are Kali's designs. They go all the way up! She was quite prolific.'

Imtiaz nodded, letting the triangle drop. *I'm only on the stairs and her dead granny's things are all over the place.*

'Come on up,' Tanvi called from above.

'Your things arrived this morning, they're already here waiting for you to unpack,' Lem explained.

Imtiaz nodded and tapped her fingers on the smooth wooden banister, straining her neck to follow its spirals up through the tall house. As she placed her foot on step after step, it felt like she was climbing a tower – so different from the low-ceilinged regulation rooms and corridors she was used to.

Lem paused on a landing to peer through a long, arch-shaped window that extended all the way from ceiling to floor. 'Good riddance to them! I wish they'd get off our backs,' Lem muttered as he watched the protestors disperse. Imtiaz glanced sideways at Lem, at his close-shaven hair, his crumpled shirt – sleeves rolled up – and his kind expression, never far away from breaking into laughter. *This is actually happening!* Despite her nerves, for the first time Imtiaz allowed herself to believe that this was not a dream. Her chest flooded with emotion. *This is going to be my family . . . my home.*

'That's our room!' Lem said, pointing to the right of the window, into the chaos of a large, bedsit-type living room.

'We've been sorting through a few old files so it's a bit of a tip at the moment, but anything you need, if we're not in The Hearth, that's where you'll find us. You can watch the TV in there too when we're a bit more sorted!' Lem pushed the door closed.

'I'm not exactly tidy, either.' Imtiaz smiled.

'Understatement of the year!' Delyse called down from where she and Merve waited at the top of the stairs.

Beyond the landing the staircase grew narrower. Reaching a sharp turn, they were forced to walk in single file. Lem led the way. Imtiaz's fingers caught on the bunting twisted around the stair posts. *Maybe it's just because I know Usha's grandma died up here that this bit of the house is starting to give me the creeps.* She shivered as she disentangled her fingers from a black and white design she now realised were skulls.

'Hurry up, Immy! You have no idea how hard it's been for me to keep this a surprise!' Delyse's eyes shone bright as she and Merve steadied their breathing and waited for her and Lem.

Joining them at the top, Lem pushed open a small door. 'That's your bathroom.' Delyse rolled her eyes. 'En suite!'

Looking down through the spiral staircase to the ground floor, Imtiaz's stomach somersaulted.

'Ready?' Lem grinned. 'Eyes closed, then! It's a top deck tradition.' Imtiaz grimaced. 'Go on. Humour me.' Lem smiled.

Imtiaz closed her eyes and allowed herself to be led by Delyse. From inside came a tense rustling and a sound of whispering; Tanvi's voice and Usha's were some way off.

'Can I open my eyes yet? I feel like a real idiot standing here like this,' Imtiaz asked, transferring her weight impatiently from foot to foot.

'Now you'll see why I wanted to keep this as a surprise. Go on then!' Delyse nudged her.

I don't care about the room, just let Usha be happy to see me, Imtiaz thought as she slowly opened her eyes to find . . . no Usha, only Tanvi standing in front of her, smiling warmly.

'Welcome to your birth, Imtiaz.'

Imtiaz scowled at the weird greeting. Registering her bewilderment, Tanvi clarified. 'Your and Usha's *berth.* Your room!' she explained, scrunching her nose. 'We call this a berth, because my dad designed it to feel like you could be on a ship.'

What am I supposed to say to that? Imtiaz wondered.

'Thanks!' she managed. Looking beyond Tanvi, she gasped, struggling to take it all in.

'See! And you accused me of talking it up,' Delyse giggled. 'It's not often you'll see Immy lost for words.'

If anything, the 'top deck' was even more amazing than Imtiaz had imagined, definitely more like a ship than a bedroom. In the centre of the room was what looked like an enormous sculpture of . . . *no* . . . *it is a real anchor.* Imtiaz could hardly believe what she was seeing. How had they managed to sink that into the floor? *So this is what Delyse was going on about.* Imtiaz nodded as she took in the sails that made the beds into boats. Beyond them her eyes were drawn through a huge round window to the dance of tall bamboo grasses swaying on the terrace . . . As she took in the walls covered in bright textiles and photos, she realised that the swish and sway of the grasses made it sound like they were at sea. Imtiaz's stomach rumbled as the smell of BBQ – *halloumi* – drifted to her from the roof garden. *Usha's probably out there getting things ready for me,* she reassured herself, checking out what she figured, by the colourful quilt, must be Usha's bed. On the wall beside it stood a giant wardrobe, the biggest Imtiaz had ever seen, and the oldest-looking. *How ancient is it?* Glancing to the other side of the room, she was relieved to find that her suitcase and crate were stacked up beside her bed. *At least I don't have to sleep under the shadow of that wardrobe*, she thought.

Imtiaz jumped as she heard something shift in the centre of the room and was shocked to see a hand appear and rest on the anchor. Usha eased herself up out of what Imtiaz now saw was a collection of bright mirrored floor cushions, fitted snug, at the bottom of the anchor steps. *Has Usha been hiding or worse . . . spying on me?* Usha turned to Imtiaz and nodded in her direction. Her lips seemed to be constantly moving. *She might be saying 'Hi'?* But then again Imtiaz thought that could be wishful thinking because in one hand she was holding a green cloth-covered notebook. She stared at Imtiaz for a moment and wrote something down. *Is she writing about me?* Whatever she was doing, it was hard to think of a way she could have made Imtiaz feel more uncomfortable. *You're as bad as those protestors! How can anyone look so miserable when you have all this?* Imtiaz wanted to run over to her and shake Usha out of her silence. Imtiaz stared back, matching Usha's unsmiling gaze. *You want to play it like this, Usha, see who wins!* Imtiaz swallowed hard. *Why can't you just be pleased to see me? How come I always have to fight for everything I get?* she thought, holding back hot tears of rejection.

'Usha, why don't you come and show Imtiaz around?' Tanvi fixed her eyes on Usha, willing her to get involved.

Still Usha didn't move. She followed the path of something invisible to Imtiaz across the room and seemed to be recording what she saw in her notebook. *Maybe she writes instead of talking?* Imtiaz wondered.

'Usha's a bit shy, but she'll come out of her shell,' Tanvi whispered apologetically. 'So! Here you are, your boat-bed!' Pointing to Usha's matching one, Tanvi pulled the sail screen back and forth to demonstrate how it could create privacy when closed.

'We made these for you out of some old sari material. Lem knocked up the bamboo frames and I stitched the sails. These were Usha's idea, so you can both have a bit of your own space or open them to chat.'

'Sure she didn't want to build a wall?' The words were out of Imtiaz's mouth before she could curb them.

Tanvi shook her head and, lowering her voice, said, 'I think Usha's still coming to terms with her Kali Ma's death. But you'll soon get to know each other, don't worry.'

I doubt it, Imtiaz thought, checking out her bedside table, lamp, drawers and bookshelves. 'Sorry for snapping,' she whispered, lifting her suitcase on to her bed and unzipping it.

'Arrange everything as you want!' Tanvi smiled. 'Usha will show you around properly later, won't you, darling?' Tanvi said, more as an order than a question.

Usha nodded distractedly and continued mumbling to herself and writing in her notebook.

And Delyse was worried about me *being rude! If I did that, she'd go off on one. Maybe Usha's just a spoilt brat.*

Imtiaz gazed out through the enormous window to the garden where Merve and Delyse were standing talking. *And you're going to leave me here with her?* Imtiaz sighed heavily.

'The BBQ's not far off being ready. Why don't you settle in and we'll let you know when it's done?'

Imtiaz nodded and watched on as Tanvi had words with

Usha. She noted the tension in Tanvi's shoulders as they stood head to head, whispering and clearly heard her last words as they pulled apart. 'Come on, Ush, you were the life and soul of the party the other day. Just make Imtiaz feel at home.'

So she isn't always shy? Imtiaz felt like punching through the sail screen and screaming at Usha, *You should be showing me around, not your mum!*

'So, I'll leave you two girls to it!' Tanvi spoke pointedly to Usha. 'Perhaps you can help Imtiaz unpack her things.' And with that, she headed out into the garden.

Imtiaz waited for Usha to finish off whatever she was writing. Then, glancing Imtiaz's way, she sighed and walked up the steps from the anchor towards her bed, swinging open her sail. Imtiaz saw now how they worked. When pushed wide open they became a kind of headboard. *If I open my sail screen right now we can talk.* As if Usha had read her thoughts, she swung her sail back. *Like closing a door on me.* Imtiaz sighed. *Shut me out before you've even said hello, then.* But through the thin material of the sail, Imtiaz could still track to where Usha placed the book in her bedside drawer. *The first chance I get, I'm seeing what she's been writing. What does Delyse say? "Forewarned is forearmed." I might as well know the truth.* Edging closer on her pillow, Imtiaz watched Usha walk over to the wardrobe, open the huge door, take something out, return to her bed and lie down.

Just when I thought it couldn't get weirder. Imtiaz froze as great shadows wafted across the room like wings. Staring closer, Imtiaz realised that the wing shadows were attached to Usha's hands as she wafted a fan in wide arcs as if cooling someone beside her. *A fan! Who uses a fan like that?*

Imtiaz saw in black and white how it was going to be. *She can try and spook me as much as she wants, but I never dreamed I would ever live anywhere like this and I'm not going to let her drive me out – she doesn't know who she's dealing with!*

She could cope with out-and-out combat, but she would have to work out how to deal with Usha's sullen, brooding silence and her weird whisperings. *Well, let her try to psych me out! No use tiptoeing around someone like her.* If Tanvi and Lem wouldn't tell Usha straight, then *she* would.

Imtiaz reached for the suitcase on the end of her bed and started unpacking. *Just face her up*, she coached herself. Pushing open the sail screen, she picked up a pile of clothes that needed hanging. *This is a joke, me actually hanging up clothes, but it's one way to test how much Usha hates me being here.* She set off across the room, but hadn't even reached the anchor when Usha punched her sail screen open.

'You can't put your things in my Kali Ma's wardrobe,' she shouted, jumping up and heading over to the wardrobe as if she was chasing after someone.

In seconds, Usha was flinging open the doors, gathering armfuls of bright-coloured clothes and flinging them on her own bed. Imtiaz backed off. *Is she sane? This makes no sense. Saying she won't share the wardrobe but makings space for me anyway?*

'Forget it! You think this is easy for me? I know your game and it's not going to work.' Imtiaz spat the words out.

At the sound of raised voices, Tanvi came running in. Imtiaz retreated, carrying her clothes back to her side of the room. She closed her sail screen but listened to every word. *At last, she's finally getting a telling off!*

'What on earth's got into you, Usha? Why are you making such a scene? I know you wanted separate wardrobes, but there's no need to fly into a temper. It just makes sense to share for now.' Tanvi closed the wardrobe door. 'Food will be ready soon. Perhaps leave unpacking till later,' she called over to Imtiaz.

As soon as they were alone again, the air bristled with tension. It felt like a stand-off as Imtiaz watched the constant movement of Usha's lips, whispering to herself again, silhouetted behind her sail screen.

Play it like that then, see if I care. Not being able to see your face makes it even easier for me to say what I have to.

'Did you get my card about your gran?'

Imtiaz's question was greeted with a yawning pause.

'Yes, thanks.' Imtiaz heard Usha's voice above the music from the garden but only just.

'Let's cut the crap. I don't want your thanks and I know you don't want me here. What's with the fan?'

'It was my Kali Ma's . . .' Usha said her silhouetted shape turning away from Imtiaz as she started up her fanning again.

Clever! Imtiaz thought. *How much does she not want me here that she's gone to the trouble of working out how to make those freak shadows loom at me.*

Imtiaz turned on to her back, staring at the ceiling as she spoke. 'I get it. Here you were, living in your own little palace and now I've turned up, invading your space. But I'm telling you straight up. I'm not going to let you spoil this for me. I've never had anywhere like this, somewhere to dream . . . You might be used to it but I'm not, and when Delyse and Merve have gone off to St Lucia I've got no choice. I'm not going back to Acorns if Delyse isn't there. I'll make this work, whether *you* like it or—'

A high-pitched cry came from the direction of Usha's bed. Imtiaz shot up. Shoving open her sail screen, she crossed the room. 'I'm sorry, I didn't mean . . .'

Now she'll probably say I've been vile to her and she'll have what she wants. Idiot, playing right into her hands. Imtiaz berated herself but paused as the crying grew louder and wilder. She opened Usha's sail screen to find her pulling open the wardrobe door and backing away from a snarling white cat.

'What's that doing in there?' Imtiaz gasped. Ignoring her, Usha cautiously reached in, but the cat swiped the air and retreated further inside.

'What's its name?'

'Spirit,' Usha whispered. 'She's a stray, I think. Not that friendly!'

'Neither would I be if you locked me in a wardrobe.'

'I didn't lock her in!' Usha protested.

'Here, let me try.' Imtiaz chewed her lip, drawing closer to Usha, feeling more wary of her than she did the cat. '*Ps ps ps*, Spirit . . . it's OK,' she soothed as gradually the cat grew calmer and allowed Imtiaz to stroke her back.

'We made friends the other day, when I dropped your card in. Just call me the cat whisperer,' Imtiaz joked, but Usha's haunted expression didn't shift. The cat began to purr and let Imtiaz pick her up. 'Seems like the friendliest thing here to me. Love her different coloured eyes, like marbles.' As she said this Imtiaz looked Usha straight in the eye. 'I know this is all part of your plan to freak me out and, just so you know, it's not going to work!'

'I'm sorry, Imtiaz. I know what it looks like, but what's happening here, it's complicated.' Usha fidgeted, looking to her left and blinking furiously.

Does she have a nervous twitch? Imtiaz wondered, easing back slightly, softening her tone. *How am I ever going to get through to you?*

Imtiaz sighed. 'OK! But I don't see how it's that hard to say hello. Even if you aren't feeling it, you could make a bit of an effort.'

'It isn't how it looks, Imtiaz. I promise you.'

'Whatever!' Imtiaz lifted Spirit to her chest and stroked her cheek against the cat's soft fur.

'She's been really nervous. Maybe she doesn't like me that much.' Usha shrugged.

Imtiaz kissed Spirit on the forehead, set her down and followed the cat towards the Globe Window. Turning at the last minute, unable to hold her rage in any longer, she flung back. 'Can't think why!'

Ghost Sister

Imtiaz followed Spirit out on to the top deck garden and found that it was even more beautiful and spacious than she'd imagined from the glimpses she'd snatched. It was so like a ship's deck that, looking over the balcony, she could easily believe she'd find the sea. *Maybe if I'd grown up in a place as awesome as this I wouldn't want to share it either,* Imtiaz admitted to herself as she walked along narrow decking into a den of grasses covered overhead by a large canvas sun-screen. Under the blind, Lem and Tanvi were turning skewers on the BBQ while Delyse and Merve sat on a low bench made of driftwood, next to a shell garden.

'So, what do you think? Beyond your wildest dreams or not?' Delyse asked, smiling at Imtiaz.

She nodded, biting the inside of her lip.

'Let me show you around. Want to steer the ship?' Delyse lowered her voice. 'Need a chat?'

Who will ever know me like Delyse? Imtiaz thought as she

took Delyse's arm. They walked together through the grasses, past a rusty ship's pulley, then balanced over a bridge that led to a wall. There, lengths of rope hung from brass hoops fixed either side of an ancient wooden ship's wheel that turned slowly.

'They call this "the Helm"! Go on then. Steer!' Delyse smiled as Imtiaz reached up to hold the wooden spokes, her hands fitting into the well-worn grooves. She turned the wheel slowly.

'Feels like the whole house is going to move!' Imtiaz said, setting it off spinning again as she grabbed hold of a rope by its side. Leaning back and pushing her feet against the wall, she tested her strength then collapsed on to the decking where Delyse was already sitting, hands folded in her lap, waiting for Imtiaz to speak.

'This place is great, but Usha hates me and she's trying to weird me out,' Imtiaz finally blurted out.

'Grub's up!' Lem announced from inside the swaying grasses.

'We'll talk later,' Delyse sighed, 'I promise.'

'You'll be gone later!' Imtiaz mumbled as she followed Delyse back over the rope bridge.

Usha was already sitting at the driftwood bench, tucking into a halloumi skewer.

'This turns into a tent. If the weather stays like this you two can camp up here all summer!' Merve pointed to where the thick canvas material that made a sun canopy was rolled and tied at the sides. He pulled a rope and one side unfolded. 'Clever, huh! All my brother's, Usha's Pops's work. Michael got the brains, I got the looks!' Delyse bashed Merve on the arm playfully.

'Do you camp out here a lot then?' Imtiaz asked Usha, as it was clear she wasn't going to start up a conversation, even to impress the adults.

It seemed to take her ages to answer anything, like there was a time lag between her brain and her mouth. It made the atmosphere hang heavy.

'With my Kali Ma quite a lot. I mean, I used to.'

Imtiaz waited for more, but it seemed that was all Usha had. *Awkward.*

Tanvi stepped into the silence. 'I'll set it up and you can have your meals and sleep out here if you want. Your skewer's on its way . . .'

'Thanks!'

Imtiaz watched Spirit balance her way around the rose balcony, through the den of bamboo grasses and finally pad over to Imtiaz's ankles, where she circled then leapt up into the shell garden. There she began to nose at the largest shell. Imtiaz picked it up and placed it to her ear. 'That's weird, I can't hear the sea . . .'

Usha sprang forward, upsetting her plate and cup, and grabbed hold of the shell as if she was ready to fight Imtiaz for it. Stunned, she released her grip and Usha snatched the shell away so hard she almost fell backwards. 'Sorry! It was my Kali Ma's . . . it's delicate. She didn't like people touching it. Just leave it there.'

'Usha!' Tanvi snapped and her eyes flashed with an unspoken reprimand. 'Come and get Imtiaz her food.'

Imtiaz raised her eyebrows and nodded to Delyse as if to say, 'See what she's like?' *How am I ever going to get on with someone who's so protective of her turf, who won't even let me touch her precious shell?*

'Give it another go. Be the bigger person?' Delyse whispered as Spirit jumped on Imtiaz's knee, nestling down and licking her hand with her rough tongue. The cat seemed to sense how close she was to crying.

'Thanks! Looks delicious!' she managed to say when Usha handed her the plate and attempted to lift Spirit off her lap, but the cat clung to Imtiaz.

'Leave her, I can manage like this.' Imtiaz held the plate above Spirit's head to demonstrate.

I'm eating. It's up to you to break the silence, Imtiaz decided. She finished her skewer and corn first course, then Lem brought over desert and she was almost done licking the chocolate from around her mouth from the baked bananas when Usha finally spoke.

'I found Spirit under the sheets in my Kali Ma's bed after she died and she frightened me. She had no collar, so I named her Spirit, because at first I was convinced it must be the spirit of my Kali Ma come back.'

Weird and weirder! Is she comparing me to a stray? Of all the things I was expecting . . . An apology for losing it about a shell would have been a start. Now Imtiaz was sure that everything Usha said and did was designed to make her feel as uncomfortable as possible, but bringing up the ghostly granny did seem like a new low. The sweet food, music and the warm welcome of Tanvi and Lem could not mask the bitter chill that Usha wafted around her.

'Sure you didn't call her Spirit to weird me out?'

Usha shook her head, staring at the shell garden.

Imtiaz sat on her bed with Spirit on her lap, grateful for the privacy of the sail screen and that she and Delyse were finally being left in peace to talk.

'Clever how they've organised your separate spaces.' Delyse gestured to the bedside table, drawers, bookshelves and the rope weave mat identical to the one on Usha's side of the room.

Imtiaz nodded as Delyse helped her unpack her clothes, laying the things that needed hanging up to one side. Even though she'd thought Usha pathetic for freaking out about the wardrobe, she'd already decided that it wasn't going to work, her having to cross over to Usha's side to get her clothes. She told Delyse as much.

'I'll speak to Tanvi and Lem. I'm sure that can be resolved quite easily,' Delyse reassured her, sitting beside Imtiaz on the bed. 'Have you had a chance to chat a bit more, you and Usha?'

Imtiaz stroked Spirit's head and sighed. 'Only for her to tell me a ghost story about how she thought the cat was her dead gran . . . That's why she called it Spirit. Like that makes sense!' Imtiaz shrugged off her frustration. 'If you ask me, Usha feels more like the ghost around here.'

Delyse's eyes widened in alarm halting Imtiaz in her rant-track. *What if Delyse gets so worried that she decides it's not going to work after all and then I'll be back at Acorns without Delyse and lose out on having all this?* One thing Delyse had drummed into her was how actions have consequences, but words do too. *Rein it in, Imtiaz, rein yourself in.*

Imtiaz sighed. 'Like you said, she's the shyest person I've ever met, and she seems like she's always kind of somewhere else, writing in her book or daydreaming. So considering that, we're doing OK, I suppose.'

Delyse placed her hands on Imtiaz's shoulders. 'Give her time. Maybe that story was just her way of telling you how much she's missing her gran? Try asking her about her writing. Now, do you want this going-away present or not?' Delyse smiled and reached for a large oblong-shaped object covered by a turquoise towel.

'Like the wrapping!' Imtiaz smiled. Opening its folds, she found an enormous framed poster of a whale swimming through a shimmering ocean. Her smile grew as she took in the tranquil sea. 'Thanks, I love it.'

'Remember when you couldn't get to sleep without me playing you whale song? If you ever have trouble sleeping

81

now you can imagine this one singing to you. Maybe one day you and Usha can come to stay with us and we can go whale watching together.' Delyse's voice cracked as she stood up and hung the framed poster on the waiting hook.

Imtiaz's chest felt tight enough to split open. 'Please, Delyse, change your mind and stay a bit longer to help me get on with Usha,' she pleaded.

Grasping the ends of the turquoise towel, Imtiaz drew her legs close under her chin. She pushed her head into the towel that still smelt of chlorine. Instantly, it transported her and she imagined herself swimming along the blue diamond floor of the lido, held by the water, as she attempted to still the sobs that rose up in her. But they kept coming; no matter how many times she tried to picture herself moving smoothly through the water, her chest convulsed. Imtiaz clung to Delyse and wouldn't let her go, only vaguely hearing the reassuring words Delyse kept offering.

'You'll find your way, Immy.'

'But what if I don't?' she sobbed.

Delyse gave Imtiaz time to collect herself before she spoke. 'Remember when we watched that episode of *Blue Planet* about a whale's eyes being on the side of its head?'

Imtiaz blew her nose on the tissue Delyse had offered her and nodded as she stared at the whale.

'I've been racking my brains trying to recall what they said. It was something like . . . each eye sees a different world, and somehow that . . . imaginary third eye! I think that was the gist. Well, try to be like that. How about thinking of yourself as one eye and Usha as the other, and try to make sense of things together. Meet at the third eye!' Delyse chuckled at the 'what-are-you-on-about' look on Imtiaz's face. 'Just remember to be patient, and that there is nothing Lem and Tanvi won't do for you.'

As Imtiaz snuggled close in Delyse's arms, Merve and Usha wandered in together and Merve sat on the end of Usha's bed, chatting.

'She's still clinging onto that shell, making sure I don't touch it again!' Imtiaz whispered to Delyse as she watched Usha through the thin muslin cloth edging closer to hear their conversation.

'No big goodbyes. Either we'll come and see you, or you'll visit before long. But we all have to try and settle first.' Merve's words echoed Delyse's and Imtiaz wondered if they'd rehearsed how the goodbyes would go.

Tanvi and Lem closed the latch on the Globe Window.

'Sorry, Delyse, we have to go,' Merve whispered.

As Delyse squeezed Imtiaz's hand tight, she pulled away and snuggled up with Spirit, refusing to lift her head, shielding herself from the torrent of emotion that threatened to drown her.

Imtiaz listened to the adults' voices retreating down the long hallway stairs. Laying her head close to the cat's, Imtiaz whispered in Spirit's ear, 'At least you're not leaving me.'

Once they were alone, Imtiaz peered through the sail

screen, beyond the metal arms of the anchor and waited. *Maybe if I let her make the first move*, Imtiaz reasoned, struggling to calm her churning stomach.

Say something. Are you all right . . . anything to make me believe you actually care if I'm here or not. Imtiaz willed Usha to talk, but she didn't even glance her way. Instead, she coolly placed the conch shell close to her sail screen so it magnified. Imtiaz supposed to big up her 'hands-off-my-things' point. She then opened her drawer and took out her book. As Usha began to write she whispered to herself, occasionally pausing to turn in Imtiaz's direction, but not once did she attempt to speak.

She hates me! My supposed-to-be sister hates me and the way she's being, I'm starting to hate her, too.

Dr Mistry

Usha lay cuddled up to her Kali Ma, listening to her breathing change as she drifted into sleep. Usha ached with tiredness herself but felt the need to read over all she'd written, if nothing else, to try and figure out how to untangle the mess she'd made of her first day with Imtiaz.

She heard Imtiaz yawn and switch off her bedside light. Breathing a sigh of relief to be alone with her thoughts, Usha caught sight of Spirit stirring. She couldn't get over the way the stray had attached herself so easily to Imtiaz when it had taken so long for her to gain its trust. *Maybe Spirit could be a kind of bridge between us?* Usha pondered, shivering and pulling her duvet higher. Milky moonlight illuminated the places around the top deck where the nightmare moments of the day were seared into her memory. It had been like walking a tightrope between Kali Ma's constant interruptions and Imtiaz's accusatory looks.

Embarrassed by the venting she'd done about Imtiaz,

Usha flicked to the middle of her notebook and started reading over the words that had poured out of her so easily a few minutes ago.

Imtiaz Invasion
Day 1
It was stupid of me but I figured just before Imtiaz came was my last chance to talk to Kali Ma about the Promise Book again. I pushed it too far and right at the moment when Imtiaz walked through the door Kali Ma had a full-scale meltdown. I thought my head was going to explode. Mum gave me a look like she wanted to shake me. She needn't have bothered because Imtiaz's cold stare makes me feel about as big as a pea (she's not the sort of person that I'll ever really get on with anyway - she'd think I was weird even if I didn't have Kali Ma on my case).

It all just got to me. As if it's not bad enough having to share this place with Imtiaz and have Mum and Dad on at me about welcoming my new sister, without Kali Ma having a go at me about rooting around in her old things and how I should concentrate on making friends with Imtiaz.

When she was alive I hardly ever argued with Kali Ma, but when she shouted at me so sharp in my ear, telling me to throw all her clothes away and give Imtiaz some space to hang her stuff, railing on about how she didn't ask to be brought back from the dead, I actually wished her gone because of the way she's been bossing me around and making me look like there's something wrong with me. What must Imtiaz have thought when Kali Ma made me grab that conch out of her hand? If only Imtiaz could have seen how wild Kali Ma was, ordering me to take it back inside and screaming at me that I had no business to have even touched it. I wanted to shout back at her, 'You're dead, Kali Ma,' but I couldn't say anything because a few times I'm sure Imtiaz has already caught me talking to her. I've seen the look on her face like, 'How come I get dumped with a sister as weird as Usha?'

Closing the notebook, Usha turned to her Kali Ma as she lay beside her, snoring away. 'Why are you even here?' she whispered.

'I'm here because I have every right to be here!' Imtiaz snapped, batting open her sail screen, making Usha jump.

Kali Ma sat up too, bleary-eyed. 'What's going on, Myush? It's the middle of the night, settle down.'

'Shh!'

Usha's hands trembled as she eased her sail open and climbed out of bed to find Imtiaz slowly walking towards her. Even through this dim light, Usha gleaned by the set of Imtiaz's shoulders that she was squaring up for an argument.

Spirit circled as the two girls faced each other.

'No one tells me to shhhh!' Imtiaz's jaw clenched. 'I'm

telling you straight out. I'm not going anywhere. No matter how much you try to freak me out.'

'You don't understand, Imtiaz.' Usha felt like crawling into her anchor den and hiding. She was already so tired of having to argue her case with Kali Ma, and now she had to start again with Imtiaz. 'You really don't understand!' she whispered.

'Then make me!'

Feeling light-headed, Usha clung on to the anchor. Behind her, Kali Ma was sitting up now, eyes wide, hair dishevelled. She backed away from Spirit, who approached her and leapt on to the end of the bed and begun hissing and swiping at Kali Ma, teeth bared, hackles up.

Usha turned and shooed her away.

'What's the matter with you? You can't even be kind to the cat!' Imtiaz accused, shaking her head.

'I wasn't shhhhing you or being mean to Spirit. But if I tell you what I'm dealing with here, you won't believe me.'

'Try me!'

Usha looked over at Kali Ma but she lay her head back down on her pillow, refusing to meet her eye. Sighing deeply, Usha began. 'OK. The ghost of my Kali Ma is right there, sleeping in my bed, and Spirit can see her too and Kali Ma's wary of her. I know this sounds weird but the way she just appeared like that when Kali Ma died . . . Spirit might be a ghost too.' Usha tangled and untangled a strand of hair. 'And my Kali Ma's been ranting on at me all day long so I couldn't welcome you properly.'

'Or at all!' Imtiaz stared at Usha for a while, her eyebrows meeting in a sharp 'v' as she struggled to take in what Usha had said. For a moment, Usha thought she might believe her, or at least be trying to give her the benefit of the doubt, but then Imtiaz's face contorted with contempt.

'You think this is funny? At least Spirit actually made me feel welcome and now you're trying to frighten me off making friends with the cat! You are way out of order. I think you need help.'

'I don't want us to be enemies,' Usha whispered.

Imtiaz shrugged. 'OK then, stop making up ghosts and give me the conch as a peace offering!'

Usha hesitated, then, taking a deep breath, nodded. 'OK.' *If this is what it takes to show her I'm not her enemy . . .*

As Usha approached, Kali Ma stood and attempted to block her way from the bed and held it to her own ear. Returning over to the anchor steps, Usha handed it to Imtiaz. 'My Kali Ma never even wanted me to touch this. She used to keep it out of sight in the wardrobe.'

'Weird!' Imtiaz exclaimed, holding the conch to her ear, then switching sides. 'I can't hear the sea.'

Imtiaz shook it and curled her finger around the shiny spiral folds and discovered something soft inside, wedged too deep to pull out.

'Can I borrow your hair grip a minute?' Imtiaz asked. 'There's something blocking the sound.'

Usha glanced over to Kali Ma, who had turned her back on them both, but now Usha was as curious as Imtiaz to see what was inside. Pulling the hair grip apart so that it became one long wire, she passed it to Imtiaz, who stuck her tongue out in concentration as she dug around in the shell. For a moment she got purchase on something in the bottom, then lost hold of it.

Sighing in frustration, Imtiaz handed Usha the long grip. 'Here, you try. It feels like make-up-remover pads or something stuck inside.' After a few attempts, Usha eventually managed to ease out . . . a square of white material like a handkerchief. Stunned, she examined an embroidered corner of a little pomegranate fruit and, stitched below it, the name 'Lucky'.

'Did you stuff this inside?' Imtiaz asked.

Usha shook her head. 'I've never even listened to it.' Her heart was pounding impossibly fast. 'Lucky's the woman Kali Ma was trying to draw in her Promise Book. Ykcul, Ykcul,' Usha whispered under her breath.

'What are you on about? Sure you didn't sew that yourself?' Imtiaz asked, doubtfully.

Usha shook her head. *How can I make you believe me?* Then the thought came to her. There is a way. She sprang up, ran over to her bedside drawer and took out the Promise Book. Ignoring Kali Ma's stern expression, she returned to

Imtiaz and was about to open the first page when Kali stood up abruptly and headed for the roof garden beckoning them both to follow.

'Kali Ma says she needs some air,' Usha explained. 'She wants us to follow her,' Usha explained. 'She says you should bring the conch and the handkerchief and I need to carry the Promise Book.'

'Whatever, Usha.' Imtiaz sighed. As she opened the latch on the Globe Window, Usha's head ached with the effort of switching from Kali Ma's demands to wondering what Imtiaz must think of her behaviour. She turned and gestured Imtiaz over as she followed Kali Ma through the hushed whispers of the long grasses, past the rose balcony and across the rope bridge to the Helm.

'Just so you know, you don't scare me and I don't believe in ghosts.' Imtiaz grabbed hold of a knotted rope and twisted it nervously, levering herself to sit cross-legged underneath the ship's wheel that turned slowly above them.

'Spin your story, then!' Imtiaz mocked as Spirit tripped lightly over the bridge.

'See that?' said Usha, pointing. 'Strange how it didn't even sway. Same with Kali Ma when she walks over it.'

'*Shut up!*' Imtiaz shook her head. 'Spirit hardly weighs anything! That's why! Go on then, if you have to tell me another of your ghost stories.'

'Not mine.' Usha shook her head. 'Look, Imtiaz, I don't

know what's going on here any more than you do, but it looks like we might be about to see.' Usha took her orders from Kali Ma, leafing through the pages to find the pictures of the woman with a white sari. 'Look at her eyes – one green, one brown, just like Spirit's,' Usha said, pointing to the woman's face and the pink thing she held in her hand that Usha had thought was a bowl or a ball of wool. She picked up the handkerchief square with the embroidered fruit in the corner. 'That's a pomegranate, isn't it, Kali Ma?'

Kali Ma nodded. 'Myush . . . I think you're right . . . No one's going to get any peace around here' – she eyed Spirit – 'until I tell you what I know. A conch symbolises truth and it seems like the way to that has been blocked.'

'Hello!' Imtiaz waved at Usha in frustration. 'Remember me? I'm actually here!'

As Usha listened intently to what her Kali Ma said and repeated it, Imtiaz leant in closer to the Promise Book and read the words underneath the drawing.

'Ykcul. Lucky . . . Backwards writing?' Imtiaz's eyes flashed with anger. 'You made this, didn't you? Lovingly prepared for my arrival. It's pathetic, Usha! Going to all this trouble to scare me.'

Heart racing, Usha ignored the accusation, holding the handkerchief and waving it at her Kali Ma. Spirit curled up on Imtiaz's lap and she cuddled her close. Usha felt sorry for Imtiaz; even though she sounded tough, she looked like she needed Spirit to comfort her.

'Start at the beginning.' Kali Ma sighed deeply.

Usha turned to the front page of the Promise Book and pointed to Kali Ma's name and Dr Mistry's.

Imtiaz ran her fingers over the cover, sneering, 'Got to hand it to you, Usha, trying the old tea-stain trick? I did Egyptian parchment-making at school too, you know!'

Usha didn't blame Imtiaz for not believing her, but the act of sharing her discovery of the Promise Book seemed to release the pressure behind her eyes a little. *If only I could be free from this tug of war. I have to get Imtiaz to believe me.* Her desperation spurred her on.

'It looks old because it is. It belonged to my Kali Ma when she was our age in the 1960s.'

Exasperated, Imtiaz laid her head against the rope wall, following the shadows cast by the ship's wheel as it turned. 'Go on then!'

'I found the Promise Book and the conch in Kali Ma's box of precious things. Before you came I asked her about it.'

'Is that before she was dead or after?' Imtiaz asked, doubtfully.

'After, but Kali Ma says if you're going to keep interrupting we'll be here all night. She says I have to report exactly what she says, then maybe you'll believe me, OK?'

'Whatever!' Imtiaz raised her eyes to the stars and stroked Spirit's head. 'She sounds feisty.'

'She is,' Usha admitted and scrambled to catch up. 'I am Kali Ma, Usha's grandmother . . . And I think I know why my spirit won't rest . . . When I was your age, I was visited by a ghost called Lucky.'

'Runs in the family, then,' Imtiaz mumbled.

Usha ignored her and carried on. 'She would come to me all the time, not just at night. She followed me around wherever I went, a quiet spirit but an insistent one. In the end I told Michael about her.'

'Who's Michael?' Imtiaz asked.

Usha gestured around the roof garden. 'You know! My pops, Kali Ma's husband, Merve's brother, the one who made all this. They knew each other from when they were at school.'

'Sweet!' Imtiaz picked up the book and ran her fingers over the name 'Dr Mistry' and nodded like she'd finally understood something and smiled. Usha's heart leaped. *She's starting to believe me.* And she thought that it was the first time she'd seen true kindness in Imtiaz's eyes.

'I get it now. You're making me piece you together. But I'm no whale, I can't put my eye to yours and see what you're seeing,' Imtiaz said.

Usha pulled back. *There's no way she can know how Kali Ma arrived.* 'Why did you say that?' The vision of Kali Ma surging up through the water on the back of the whale flashed through her mind.

'Don't lose your rag. Just something Delyse said about seeing things from your point of view. Anyway, what I'm saying is you don't have to make all this up about ghosts. Just talk to me. You miss her. I know how that feels. I'm already missing Delyse.' Imtiaz stroked Spirit's head.

Tears of frustration filled Usha's eyes. *How am I ever going to get her to believe me?*

Imtiaz sighed. 'OK! OK! Don't cry. If this is how it has to be, go on.'

Usha wiped her eyes, took a deep breath and continued speaking Kali Ma's words.

'Dr Mistry was in fact my father's – Dr Parv Gopal's ingenious invention when he realised that I found it easier to speak to a made-up doctor about my nightmares. Mostly Dr Mistry just talked to me about the difference between dreaming and being awake.'

'Is that what you're doing now? Imagining I'm your Dr Mistry?' Imtiaz asked, but Usha ignored her as she listened to Kali Ma's voice. Usha felt sick as the strength of Kali Ma's feelings began to surge through her as if they were her own. 'I told my mama that I'd seen the ghost of an Indian woman but she started shaking and ran into the surgery. After, I stood outside the surgery door and I heard my mama complaining to Baba that his Dr Mistry method was making me worse.'

'The Hearth was a surgery?' Imtiaz asked.

Usha nodded, feeling as if she was disappearing and that Imtiaz was talking direct to Kali Ma now.

'It was a surgery in those days. It was my parents who converted it. Anyway, I kept having these nightmares about this woman called Lucky. So Mama took over and one day she said she would be Dr Mistry instead of Baba. I picked up the conch shell she kept on her desk and, in its ear, I heard a woman whispering to me, "If you believe me it sets my voice free," or something like that. There were other words too that I whispered to Mama but she went pale and took the conch away.'

'What other words?' Imtiaz asked.

'Can't remember. It was so long ago. Anyway I kept it all secret after that, started writing in invisible ink. I pretended Lucky had gone away, because everyone was happier that way.'

'Let me see the book again?' Imtiaz asked, leafing through the pages and letting her fingers discover the backwards words. 'Secret, Promise, Lucky, Bargain.'

'But I kept seeing her in my dreams and after that, I used invisible ink to write all the words I'd heard in the conch that day. Gradually I grew up and the ghost faded and I never saw the conch again till my mama died.'

'What was your Kali Ma's mum's name?' asked Imtiaz.

'Sara . . . her name was Sara. Mama was such a gentle soul and was hardly ever angry with me, so after she died the Promise Book and the conch felt like a tainted memory of her. Anyway, I didn't know what to do with her things, it's like that when someone dies . . . Usha knows! There are some things you can't bring yourself to throw out, but you don't really want them either. So I shoved the Promise Book in Michael's old satchel and the conch in a box. I had no idea Mama had blocked the listening canal with a handkerchief like the one I saw Lucky carrying. To be honest, some part of my mama was always a bit of a mystery to me.'

'Like?' Imtiaz prompted.

'Like when we went on our big adventure to India to see Papa's family and all my cousins she seemed so distant, as if she didn't want to be there. Not me! I couldn't get enough of India, taking everything in. I remember asking Papa why we knew so little about Mama's family and he didn't know either, but told me we must simply respect her wishes. I remember he said, "There are times when you just want to look forward. For some people it's too painful to dredge up the past."'

'I get that. But where was her family?' Imtiaz asked.

'She said she didn't have one.'

Imtiaz nodded. 'Some people don't know who their family are. I don't.'

Usha wanted to pause for longer to let her explain, but, held in the grip and pace of Kali Ma's storytelling, she had no choice but to continue.

'So I told Michael that I lived with a ghost, and as we got to know each other, riding around on our tandem, falling in love, Michael helped me exorcise my ghost and I always loved him for that!' Usha's voice broke with emotion.

'You OK, Usha?' Imtiaz asked.

She couldn't help it – as Kali Ma spoke about Pops Michael, the emotions welled in her and the tears poured from Usha's eyes. Without thinking, she wiped them on the handkerchief. 'I feel what she feels.' Usha sobbed, slowly lifting the conch to her ear, her arm a coiled spring, ready to pull it away. But her breathing settled as she listened. 'I can't actually hear anything except the sea,' Usha said, relief flooding through her. 'Here!' Usha reached over to Imtiaz. 'Kali Ma thinks you should try.'

'I think what I *should* do is go and get Lem and Tanvi.' Imtiaz shifted uncomfortably, leaving Usha holding the conch mid-air, but Spirit stuck her claws into Imtiaz's pyjamas, fixing her to the spot.

Reluctantly Imtiaz took the conch.

Maybe she does believe me, her hands are shaking, Usha thought as Spirit jumped off Imtiaz's knee and faced her like an audience. Usha, Kali Ma and the cat studied Imtiaz in hushed anticipation as she listened, closing her eyes in concentration, then slowly opening them again and shaking her head . . . 'No voices, like you say. Only the sea.' She sighed, lowering it from her ear and levering herself up on the knotted rope.

'What kind of knot is this?' Imtiaz asked as she stood and inspected it closer.

'A reef knot,' Usha answered, her voice still gravelled with emotion.

'Sure it's not called a grief knot?' Imtiaz asked.

Wrung out, Usha let her head rest against the wall. It had taken all her own strength as well as her Kali Ma's to speak these memories.

'I don't care what you think. I'm not imagining this,' Usha insisted as Imtiaz offered her a hand up.

'We should get some sleep. Delyse said you were good at making up stories but I never imagined my first day would be anything like this!'

Usha smiled faintly and accepted Imtiaz's hand as a tentative peace offering. But as Kali Ma returned to their bed and Usha secured the latch on the Globe Window, the grasses bent and bowed, whispering wildly, and nothing felt at peace.

Dream Pieces

Spirit padded restlessly around Imtiaz's space, eventually settling on the chair beside her bedside table. Now, as Imtiaz pored over the pictures in the Promise Book, it struck her how much the woman in the drawing – 'Lucky's' – eyes, did resemble Spirit's.

Get a hold of yourself, Imtiaz. Tomorrow I'm going to tell Tanvi and Lem that I think Usha's made up the ghost of Kali Ma because she needs help. Either that, or she's just making this up because she wants me gone.

But as she looked at drawing after drawing, the woman she'd seen at the lido filled her mind. So maybe Delyse had said something to Merve about her and Usha had overheard it and used it as detail to creep her out? Imtiaz looked through the gauze screen to where Usha was still writing in her notebook. *Maybe she's just a really good actor.*

Spirit blinked at Imtiaz, opening her jaw in an enormous yawn, and closed her eyes.

Pulling Delyse's turquoise towel round her, Imtiaz pressed her nose against the sail screen. The way Usha's lips were moving, it looked to Imtiaz like she *was* in a constant argument with herself. Unless Usha really did think her Kali Ma's ghost was by her side?

Be patient, Delyse's voice whispered in Imtiaz's ear as reflections of swaying grass shadows played over her poster, so much so that the whale looked almost as if it was swimming through the waves towards her. The misty moonlight that now bathed the top deck had the eerie effect of making Usha's bed seem further away. It was like they'd been launched out on to an ocean from opposite sides of the world in two tiny boats, with only a faint hope that one day they might meet.

Imtiaz picked up the conch and placed it over her ear. *I'm not going to let her grief, or whatever it is that's going on with her, get inside my head,* she reassured herself as the distant sound of the sea lulled her into sleep.

Spirit stalked across the floorboards and climbed on the anchor, and the cat grew before her eyes. The sail screen opened and a woman in a white sari beckoned Imtiaz out of bed. The woman turned, smiled gently and patted her hands against her heart. Imtiaz followed her over to the Globe Window and she gestured for Imtiaz to release the locks and bolts. I'm dreaming this, I'm dreaming this, *she told herself, following the woman out into the roof garden, where she stood looking down on the streets below.*

Turning round and pulling the train of her sari from over her shoulder, she offered Imtiaz the end. Slowly pirouetting, she unravelled the top layer of her material, where a small square had been cut out. She unfolded more cloth to reveal another space. Mesmerised, Imtiaz watched the woman's feet drum the ground as she turned faster and faster, until she stood in a sari blouse and petticoat skirt, the fine white length of cloth caught on the breeze like a cresting wave.

Now, reaching into her blouse, the woman held a handkerchief square up to Imtiaz . . . in the corner was an embroidered pomegranate and a name. The woman clutched it to her chest.

'What are you saying? Is this yours? Are you Lucky?' Imtiaz asked.

The woman smiled and sat on the driftwood bench, then, turning to her side, she picked up the conch and placed it on her knee, nodding towards the length of sari and waiting.

Bending down, Imtiaz placed the piece of cloth in the first gap . . . it was too small. Now in the second . . . the shape was different, but in the third, it fitted exactly.

'The handkerchief we found in the conch. Is it cut from this sari?' Imtiaz asked. The woman nodded.

'You are Lucky.' The woman tilted her head from one side to the other as if Imtiaz was both right and wrong.

'Sitting here in my dream with you feels like being with Delyse,' Imtiaz whispered, feeling a calming sea breeze wash over her. 'I don't want you to go. Please don't go.' Lucky held out *her hand and counted off three fingers, pointing to the two other gaps in the sari. 'Why can't you speak?' Imtiaz asked.*

Lucky placed the conch to Imtiaz's ear. Her mind flooded with the powerful surge of the sea and, beyond, deep in the wave's roar, she heard a distant whisper. 'Promise to piece me together or my story's lost for ever.'

Lucky raised the conch to her mouth and produced a sound, deep and mysterious, that swelled in power, like a ship's horn calling across oceans.

AAAAAAAAAAAAAAUUUUUUUUUUUUUUUU
UUUUUUUUUUUMMMM.

Drenched in sweat, Imtiaz woke to find the shell sticking into her arm. *I've let her get to me.* Heart thrumming, she turned to find the silhouette of someone standing watching her within touching distance on the other side of the screen. 'Usha! You've gone too far now!' she gasped.

But across the room Usha pushed open her sail, while next to Imtiaz stood a woman in a white sari. Imtiaz's breath caught as she batted the screen aside, but the woman from her dream melted through it. Imtiaz staggered backwards. *You're still dreaming, this is in your head,* she told herself. *There is no Lucky . . .*

'What's the matter? Can you see my Kali Ma, now?' Usha asked.

Imtiaz retreated, shaking her head, her mouth gaping open. She desperately wanted to shout out, but no sound came. Backing away from the woman's pleading outstretched arms towards the anchor, Imtiaz collapsed to her knees, eyes fixed on the woman, who slowly approached. Struggling to breathe, Imtiaz caught her legs up under her, every sinew coiled.

'Is this your Kali Ma's ghost?' she whispered.

'I can't see anyone. My Kali Ma's over there, on my bed.'

Usha took Imtiaz's trembling arm and they sat together for the first time on the anchor steps.

'This whole thing is doing my head in,' Imtiaz said. 'I don't believe in ghosts and all that stuff you were going on about, but I had a dream.' Imtiaz clung to Usha. 'Am I still dreaming?'

'Tell me what you see, Imtiaz.'

'She's here! Right there by the Globe Window, smiling at us . . . the woman in the sari – the one in your book. And I think I've seen her before at the lido.'

Usha frowned and wrapped her arm around Imtiaz's shoulders to comfort her. 'Where's Spirit? Did you let her out?'

They both cast around but there was no sign of her.

'I think Spirit turned into Lucky!' Imtiaz whispered.

Usha's eyes grew wide in wonder. 'The woman Kali Ma drew – the name on the handkerchief piece?' she asked.

'Only, it's not a handkerchief. It's part of her sari!' Imtiaz corrected.

'I can't see her, Imtiaz. What's she like? Is she talking to you? Describe her to me.'

Imtiaz shook her head. 'She's small, gentle-looking and her hair is parted down the middle. She keeps holding her hands to her mouth. And' – Imtiaz struggled to catch her breath – 'her eyes . . . are the exact same colours as Spirit's.'

Usha returned to her bedside table, taking out the cloth square and grabbing a throw from her bed. She placed it over Imtiaz and handed her the sari piece as she sat back down. 'Here, you're shivering. Are you afraid of her?'

'No! I mean, I'm terrified that I'm seeing a ghost now too . . . but it doesn't seem like she'd hurt us. She looks kind . . . I think she wants something from me.' Imtiaz opened her clenched palm and inspected the sari square that she'd discovered blocking the conch's air canal, and her fingers traced over Lucky's embroidered name. Feeling stupidly self-conscious, Imtiaz held it up to the ghost. 'Is this one of your missing pieces?' The woman held her hands together in prayer and nodded. Imtiaz breathed deep; since her dream she'd felt as if she'd been swimming underwater, *but I've surfaced now. I'm awake and reality feels as wild as my imagination.*

Usha placed a tentative hand on Imtiaz's arm and whispered, 'I know how this feels.'

Dazed and struggling to speak with all that was happening on her first night in her new home, Imtiaz asked Usha, 'You can't see her, but how about your Kali Ma?'

Usha turned round to her bed. 'Not any more, she says, but what you've described is just like it was for her when she was our age . . . She's sure the woman in the white sari is Lucky, but she thinks only some children can see her.' Usha hesitated. 'Children who need looking after.'

'Why can't *you* see her, then?' Imtiaz bristled, turning the pages of the Promise Book. As her fingers touched the drawings some of the chalk dust came off in her hands, smudging the features of the woman. 'You should fix this or it'll rub away. Hairspray works. I used it in art once,' Imtiaz suggested, but Usha seemed distracted.

'OK, calm down, calm down, I know where it is, Kali Ma!' Usha said, heading off to the bathroom and returning with a golden can of spray. 'Imtiaz! Didn't Kali Ma say she wrote in invisible ink?'

Imtiaz nodded.

Usha waved the can in the air. 'She's remembering now – when she used the pen the instructions said hairspray would work to reveal the secret words. Some kind of chemical reaction.' They both held their breath as Usha shook the bottle and carefully lacquered over each page. The lines firmed and darkened, and the figure of Lucky came into focus along with the repeated, familiar words:

Esimorp
Niagrab
Ykcul
Sterces

Imtiaz started coughing at the fumes as new words appeared.

Promise
to
piece
me
together
or
my
story's
lost
for ever

'That's what Lucky said to me in my dream,' Imtiaz gasped.

'Kali Ma remembers now exactly what the conch voice said . . . "Your belief in me sets my voice free".' As Kali Ma spoke through Usha, Imtiaz began to uncover the very same words in the Promise Book.

Your
belief
in
me
sets
my
voice
free

'What does your Kali Ma have to say about this secret promise, bargain, or whatever it is?' asked Imtiaz.

'She says she's just so sorry that she failed Lucky and that now this is all visited on another generation. She's told us everything she knows. Kali Ma thinks whatever Lucky needed from her, she's still searching for it.'

Imtiaz opened the end of the blanket for Usha to wrap it round her shoulders too.

'That means it's down to us two now to find out what she wants,' Imtiaz said, shaking her head in disbelief.

Anchor

The girls woke in the anchor den, necks aching, backs crunched, limbs entwined. They stretched and attempted to untangle themselves from each other.

'This is the longest night of my life.' Imtiaz yawned, staring up at the fading patterns of moonlight that played between the rafters.

'Your ghost still here?' Usha asked.

'She's not my ghost.' Imtiaz searched the room for Lucky, to find her sitting patiently on the end of her bed. 'But . . . yes, she is! What time is it?' Imtiaz asked suddenly, searching for a clock and, through Usha's open sail screen, spotted one on the wall beside the wardrobe.

'That's a chronometer,' Usha explained. 'It's a navigation clock to find your way at sea.'

'Mmm, useful.' Imtiaz sighed. 'Delyse and Merve should be setting off for the the airport some time around now. Delyse said they had to leave at an "unholy hour".'

Now Delyse's coaching about the whale's third eye sprang into Imtiaz's mind. *Try to work out how Usha sees this,* Imtiaz reminded herself.

'Where's your Kali Ma now? What does it feel like, having her around?' Imtiaz asked.

'She's sitting on the side of the bed, listening to us.' Usha glanced in her Kali Ma's direction. 'At first, she felt like heat and flames and fire.'

Imtiaz smiled. 'I think we got the wrong ghosts. Mine's like you and yours is like me!'

'Like me? How? You don't even know me.' Usha's jaw tensed.

'Sorry. You're right. I don't know Lucky, either . . . I meant, you're both quiet . . . Well, she's silent, but she's reaching out to me now.' Imtiaz closed her eyes. 'This is a kind of game Delyse used to get me to play to help me to see someone else's point of view . . . Lucky feels like clouds, a soft blanket, like floating on calm, blue water in the sunshine and' – Imtiaz sniffed the air – 'there's a sweet smell of—'

'OK . . . I don't mind being like those things.' A faint smile hovered around Usha's lips. She held up her hand. 'Don't tell me. Let me ask Kali Ma if she remembers a scent.' Usha waited and her smile grew. 'She says where do you think her obsession with roses came from – Lucky's rose oil, of course!'

Imtiaz nodded. 'Sounds like our ghosts are a bit extreme! Fire and water.'

110

Usha nodded, picking up the conch and pressing it against her ear, unsure if they were talking about the ghosts or each other. 'Maybe you can hear something now?' she said, offering the shell to Imtiaz.

Cautiously, as if she still half suspected that Usha was playing an elaborate trick on her, Imtiaz placed it to her ear and felt Lucky draw near.

Sea swirled in her inner ear. Grey cresting waves calmed her breath. She was about to give up, when through the rhythmic surging surf came the wisp of a whisper. The closer she listened, the louder it grew. It held her like a magnet. Imtiaz glanced beside her, to where Lucky cradled her own arms as if rocking a baby.

'I can hear Lucky's voice. She's humming . . . It sounds like a lullaby!' Imtiaz gasped and as she began to hum, felt Lucky's voice soothe her. 'Wait! Usha . . . there's more! She's speaking through the conch.'

'What's she saying?' Usha whispered urgently.

Your belief in me sets my voice free
Promise to piece me together
Or my story's lost for ever
To find peace in this house
Sew my patchwork
Of forgotten promises
Pomegranate pieces
Bargains broken
Secrets unspoken
Free my story
To free this house
Save my memory
Set my spirit free

Watching the silent Lucky, who though moving her mouth, released not a sound, Imtiaz understood. No matter how strange this was, what Delyse had so often told her – that she should believe in miracles – seemed like it was true.

'What's the matter, Kali Ma?' Usha asked, suddenly getting up and walking over to the bed.

Imtiaz raised her head, questioning.

'She's upset. She says the lullaby stirred her up, like it was deep in her. She thinks she might know the tune from when she was a baby.'

Imtiaz nodded. 'Your great-grandma Sara, who stuffed the conch with Lucky's sari piece and was weird with your Kali Ma about listening to it – she must have heard Lucky, too?

We've got to find out about her. To think poor Lucky's voice has been trapped in the shell all this time.' Imtiaz shook her head, pulling the conch away from her ear and feeling the heavy weight of responsibility settling on her shoulders.

Free my story
To free this house

Lucky's conch voice, although calm, was forceful, like an insistent wave lapping against a rock that will not stop until the tide turns.

'Usha, do you think she's talking about the documents your parents have to find? It feels like she's making a bargain with us. *Niagrab* – that's one of the words in the Promise Book, isn't it? She came to your Kali Ma and she didn't help her. Now she's trying to get through to us. It feels like the deal is, if we both want to stay in this house, we've got to find out what Lucky wants, but now I'm wondering about your mum . . . We need to find out if Lucky visited her too. Maybe she knows something.'

Usha scowled, feeling suddenly defensive.

'Why don't you ask Lucky? If we've set her voice free and if she knows where the documents are, why can't she just tell us?'

'I can ask!' Imtiaz tried several times but all that came back in the ear of the conch was the lullaby and the same words.

Laying the shell on the floorboards between them, Imtiaz and Usha sat cross-legged, facing each other. 'Looks like we've got to find out what Lucky's story is first. If she's tried before and never managed to get anyone to listen, why should she trust us to help her? She's testing us. If your great-grandma Sara blocked her voice, why should she believe in us? You have to earn people's trust.' Imtiaz looked pointedly at Usha.

She nodded. When they'd woken from their sleep in the anchor den Usha had been hopeful that they might start a new day feeling better about each other – trusting each other – and they did, a bit more, but she supposed deep trust took time.

Imtiaz waved the sari piece in the air. 'In my dream, there were three missing pieces. This one stuffed in the conch is the first. I think Lucky wants us to find the other two, and if we do, it seems she'll keep her side of the bargain about setting the house free. How long did you say your parents have got to find these papers?'

'Not long. They're under a lot of pressure . . .' Usha glanced behind her and edged closer to Imtiaz, lowering her voice. 'The other thing is, Kali Ma feels like she's getting weaker every day she's here, like she's losing her heat. Kali Ma's not sure but she says it feels like Lucky's relying on what's left of her passing-over energy . . . She suspects that one of them couldn't be here without the other.'

Imtiaz shivered at the thought.

'If I can't see your ghost and you can't see mine, we're going to have to believe in each other. How long do you think she's got?' Imtiaz asked.

Tears pooled at the rims of Usha's eyes. 'How do I know?' Usha shrugged. 'Days, maybe?'

'We've got to get on with it, then,' Imtiaz said.

'But how?'

'You need to tell me everything that's happened up to now.'

It was so hard at first for Usha to tell the story that, for a moment she thought about letting Imtiaz read her diary instead, until she remembered what she'd written about her. But as she spoke, Usha felt the relief of sharing the burden of living with her Kali Ma's ghost. 'You say I spooked you out today, but the weirdest thing for me was seeing that poster Delyse gave you of the whale and what you said about the whale's eyes, because that's how Kali Ma came back to me.' Usha hesitated, fearful that Imtiaz would laugh at her.

'Go on,' Imtiaz urged.

'I know how wild it sounds, but she came surging through the water on the back of a whale.'

Imtiaz yawned heavily. 'I'm sorry, Usha. I feel a bit sick with tired. I've got to lie down.'

Usha nodded, yawning herself as they headed for their beds, leaving their sail screens open.

Imtiaz lay down, arms folded behind her head, staring at her poster. Her brain ached with the effort of piecing together how Usha had behaved on her first day. Scattered fragments of the last few days floated towards each other in her mind's eye. From the first time she'd seen Lucky at the swimming pool before she'd moved in, to the cat at the window when she'd dropped in the card, to the fact that Spirit had gone and Lucky had arrived, in her dreams and in the conch, and was now sitting by her side, intently watching and waiting.

'I thought you were playing a trick on me when I woke up and saw Lucky. I thought you were pulling out all the stops for your grand finale of spooking me.'

'I know,' Usha whispered. 'But maybe Lucky was waiting for you to come along for us to do this together. Do you believe me now, Imtiaz? Because I believe you.'

'That's like what Lucky says, "Your belief in me sets my voice free,"' Imtiaz reflected. 'At least we've started talking to each other.'

'Well do you believe me or not?' Usha insisted.

'Yes!' Imtiaz sighed.

With that tentative truce they lay awake to feel the beginnings of a new dawn glowing through the Globe Window. *Weird, how I didn't really hear that navigation clock before!* Imtiaz thought. As the sun rose the ticking of the chronometer announced again and again and again, *no time, no time, no time.*

Independence

'My beautiful Tanvi!' Kali Ma exclaimed, waking Usha from a sleep teeming with ghosts and a dream-warning she was determined to act on. To rip up the pages of her diary where she'd vented about Imtiaz.

'I've managed to get an appointment at the optician's for you,' Tanvi whispered, kissing Usha on the forehead. 'Sorry it's so early, but Dad and I have a lot to do today.'

Usha blinked and opened her heavy eyelids. 'I don't need to go. My headache's gone now.'

'But they've been coming and going. Best to get checked out. You look like you've hardly slept at all?' Tanvi sighed, glancing over to where Imtiaz's breathing had grown into a light snore.

'She snores like Ma!' Tanvi giggled.

'The cheek of it!' Kali Ma interrupted. 'I've never snored in my life!'

Usha giggled too, placing her finger over her own mouth.

'Good to see you laughing. How did you two get on, then?'

Usha shifted uncomfortably, feeling suddenly crowded out by her Kali Ma and her never-ending worry monologue about how exhausted Tanvi looked.

'Yeah, we've been talking,' Usha said.

'That's good. Come on, get dressed, quietly. Let Imtiaz sleep. I'll leave a note to say where we are. See you downstairs in five minutes – your appointment's at 8.30.'

'You want to come with me, Kali Ma?' Usha whispered as she got dressed behind the wardrobe door.

Kali Ma yawned, returning to the bed and laying her head on her pillow. 'If you don't mind, darling, I'll stay here. I'm feeling a little fragile today. Ever since Lucky spoke to Imtiaz through the conch, I've felt a bit shaky, like her speaking has weakened me.' Kali Ma began to cough and held her hand to her throat; her voice did sound sore. Usha felt sorry for her and guilty that somehow finding the Promise Book and unblocking the conch might have had something to do with all this happening, when it was so obvious that Kali Ma just wanted to float away.

'Mum's planning an outing all together. If you could choose, where would you go?' Usha asked.

Kali Ma didn't hesitate for a second. 'The Victoria and Albert Museum, of course! I'd love to roam the galleries one last time.'

'Your wish is my command, oh Kali Ma!' Usha smiled as the words slipped out.

'Was that a joke?' Kali Ma laughed, peering over at Imtiaz. 'You know what, Myush, I think you two – chalk and cheese though you are – could be quite good for each other!'

Tanvi tucked her arm firmly through the crook of Usha's as they walked down the front steps and out into the street. Usha glanced up at the balcony, where she was surprised to find Imtiaz peering down at them. Kali Ma stood at her shoulder, waving. Perhaps Lucky was nearby too. Tanvi followed her gaze upwards as a plane rose through the clouds, painting a vast white feather across the pale blue sky.

'Merve and Delyse will be in the air now!' Tanvi said.

'I've been thinking. Isn't it a bit mean not to let Imtiaz be in touch for a whole month, unless it's an emergency?' Usha asked. 'She's already missing Delyse.'

Tanvi shook her head. 'Delyse knows what she's doing. She thinks it's the right way for Imtiaz to settle, and learn to come to me or your dad if she needs us. Shall we give her a wave?'

'I'm not five any more, Mum, waving at the man in the moon and random planes!'

Tanvi laughed and pointed up to the roof garden. 'No, Ush! I meant wave to Imtiaz!'

Usha did as she was told and waved.

'We're off to the optician's. Go on down to The Hearth if you like. Lem's got breakfast out and Nilam's there. We shouldn't be too long,' Tanvi called up and waved a bit too enthusiastically at Imtiaz.

'Do you have to shout, Mum? I thought you said you left a note!'

Tanvi sighed. Usha watched her mum closely for any sign that she saw either Lucky or Kali Ma but there was not a flicker.

Squeezing Usha's arm, Tanvi said, 'It's going to be an exciting summer for you two. So much to discover about each other! But we'll have to lay down a few ground rules.' Tanvi looked up at the wispy high clouds. 'Especially as it's forecast to be a heatwave. You can camp out on the roof, go on a few trips. Delyse says Imtiaz is pretty independent! Knows her way around the area and I think at eleven you're old enough to get out and about together as long as you' – her mum grinned as she took an iPhone out of her pocket – 'keep in touch! Here you go. It's my old one.'

'Wow! Can we get online?' Usha asked, taking it from her mum.

Tanvi shook her head. 'You know the score about keeping the top deck tech free! There's zero data allowed. If you want to go online, use the computer in The Hearth or go to the library. But you can take photos, record yourself singing or make little videos. Anyway, it's yours and Imtiaz's to share.'

'Thanks,' Usha mumbled. Staring at the red man at the pelican crossing, she felt a brooding jealousy building in her after her mum's talk about 'independent' Imtiaz. She wasn't proud of it, but there it was. 'And how would you know if I'm independent or not?' Usha blurted out.

'Don't take it like that, Ush. I just meant if you're out and about together, you can keep in touch, that's all. No big deal. Come on, green man!' Tanvi said, attempting to take Usha's arm again, but she flattened her elbow hard against her waist so there was no way for her mum to get close.

A message pinged into Tanvi's phone and she stopped dead. 'Mum! I thought you said we were in a hurry? If you've got so much on, why do we have to go to the optician's today? Isn't it a bit rude to leave Imtiaz on her first morning?' Usha sighed as she leant back against the park railings and waited.

'Hang on a minute. This is urgent, Ush,' Tanvi said, tilting the phone away as she replied to the text. Her forehead had wrinkled into deep worry lines by the time she slid the phone back into her pocket.

'Is it about the house again, Mum? Have you found the documents you need yet?'

Tanvi closed her eyes for a moment to compose herself and breathed deeply before walking on.

But Usha planted her feet on the pavement. 'I'm not going anywhere till you tell me what's happening. It's my house too, Mum. Don't you think I've got a right to know?'

Tanvi returned to Usha and placed both hands on her shoulders.

'It's all very dry, official stuff.'

Usha glared at Tanvi.

'OK! You know that we have to find some legal papers to prove we have the right to run The Hearth as a charity downstairs.' Usha nodded. 'Well, from what I understand, your great-grandmother Sara, Kali Ma's mother, inherited this house out of the blue from some distant relation, and it came with some conditions that the downstairs be kept for community use and public good.'

'Well, we are using it for that!' Usha butted in.

'I know, but we need to find these papers to prove it was part of the will, and that we can keep The Hearth on the ground floor. Your great-grandmother Sara told Kali Ma once that the papers are somewhere in the house. That's why your dad and me are a bit distracted turning the house upside down. Councillor Puttock – you know, who lives on our road – seems to be pushing for us to find the official documents or relocate The Hearth somewhere else. And if we have to move The Hearth I'm afraid we'll have to sell the house too.'

'We're not doing that! Imtiaz loves it already . . .'

Tanvi stroked Usha's arm and nodded. 'At least we don't have to disturb you two up top because the documents haven't been seen since your great-grandmother was alive and your top deck wasn't built then, so . . .'

If there's a time to ask Mum what she knows about Sara or if she's ever seen Lucky, it's now.

But just as Usha was steeling herself to ask, another message pinged into Tanvi's phone.

'Well?' Usha prompted her mum, watching her scowl soften.

'We're making progress. I managed to get a meeting with a housing lawyer later, who's going to try and get us access to the archives. There must be a copy somewhere. You might have to keep yourselves occupied today. Maybe take Imtiaz to the library to get her card?'

Usha shrugged. 'I don't think she likes reading much. She didn't bring many books.'

'No, but she's keen to use a computer. Delyse said she was outraged by our top deck screen embargo!' Tanvi paused outside the optician's and sized up Usha. 'One thing, though. Don't worry Imtiaz with any of this house business. She doesn't need this sort of insecurity.'

Like I do! Usha thought. *Too late for that, anyway.* She leapt aside as brakes screeched and a floppy-haired boy, eyes almost completely covered, swerved, only seconds away from crashing into her.

'What? You don't own the road!' he yelled as he corrected a skid. The tiny flags in his spokes spun so fast that all Usha could see was red wheels flashing and sparking. They stood and watched as he careered along the road, veering wildly, as he looked over his shoulder at them.

Tanvi shook her head. 'Not even wearing a helmet!'

When Usha and Tanvi returned, Imtiaz was tidying art boxes in The Hearth with Khalid, a quiet little boy she'd already befriended. 'You don't need glasses then?' Imtiaz asked, looking up. But she was on her feet within seconds, backing away, placing a protective arm around Khalid, who spontaneously started giggling and clapping his hands.

Imtiaz skewed her mouth in confusion.

'You all right?' Usha asked.

Stunned, Imtiaz took a deep breath and shook her head, watching the child follow Lucky who hurried to the front door, her arms outstretched as she greeted three women in white saris like long-lost friends. Behind them, Imtiaz caught sight of the swishing of skirts and more women, this time wearing high-necked blouses. They entered the house and paraded up the staircase as if they knew exactly where they were heading.

'I think I'm the one who needs glasses,' Imtiaz whispered.

Usha shook her head as she picked up a sketch of a conch. 'Did you do this?' Imtiaz nodded. 'It's really good!'

'Thanks!' Imtiaz leant into Usha and whispered, 'You can't see the other ghost women who came in with you, can you? Some of them are wearing saris like Lucky. I think the three of them, settling themselves at this table' – Imtiaz pointed out the seats – 'could be Lucky's family or friends. She looks really happy to see them, like it's a reunion.' Imtiaz looked nervously through to the hallway and pointed up the stairs. 'But there are lots of others too, like they're from a different time to Lucky.'

'How do you know?' Usha asked.

'Well they walk really straight-backed and they're wearing long skirts and high-necked blouses. I've never seen people who look a bit like us in outfits like that before, you know, in history books and stuff.'

Usha peered around herself in amazement. 'I can't see anyone. Is Kali Ma upstairs?'

Imtiaz raised her hands in exasperation. 'I don't know, is she?'

Usha looked at the little boy holding out both hands to an invisible space above him. He seemed to be playing a clapping game with thin air.

'Thanks for entertaining Khalid, Imtiaz,' Nilam said, smiling. If only Nilam could see the four ghost women sitting around the table, entertaining Khalid, who began to hum a familiar tune.

'Lucky's lullaby?' Usha whispered.

Imtiaz nodded. One thing she felt certain of now was that whoever Lucky and these women were, they had something to do with caring for children.

'I can't believe it. Khalid hardly ever speaks, never mind sing! Delyse told me that you have a way with little ones!' Nilam silenty clapped Imtiaz and nodded to Usha. 'If you two could come down and help out you'd be very much appreciated, especially now it's the summer holidays we'll have more young ones around. It really does make it easier for the parents having their appointments,' Nilam explained, indicating two doors. Above the lintels were faded wooden plaques, one with the name 'Dr Sara Gopal' on it and above the other, 'Dr Parvinder Gopal'.

'Your great-grandparents?' Imtiaz whispered, pointing to Usha's great-grandfather's plaque. 'So he's the Dr Mistry of the Promise Book.'

Usha nodded. 'This was their old surgery.'

'Why don't your parents put their own names up?' Imtiaz asked.

Usha shrugged. 'Don't know. I've never asked them. I suppose they like being part of the history . . . because this house has been in our family since my great-grandparents' time.'

Imtiaz nodded, wondering what it would be like to have that feeling of belonging. 'Did you get to ask your mum what she knows about Sara? If she ever saw Lucky?' Imtiaz asked.

'Not yet.'

Just then Tanvi and Khalid's mum came out of the room with Sara's plaque above the door. 'As I say, Amrita, we're trying to get you into emergency accommodation as a first step while we wait for your asylum claim to be processed and we're looking into some counselling for Khalid,' Tanvi explained. But Amrita sank into a chair and hid her head in her knees so that it was hard to tell if she was praying or crying. Lucky and the other ghosts swept in and gathered around her protectively.

'OK, thank you. I only want safety for my son.' Tears

filled Amrita's eyes and as she began to sob, Khalid shielded his own face from her and began scribbling all over the drawing of the conch that Imtiaz had given him. As his mother's voice rose and fell his squiggles emerged like waves of sound floating from the conch ear. Amrita lifted her head forcing herself to open her heavy eyelids as if so exhausted she could fall asleep right there, but Khalid climbed on to her knee and thrust the conch picture in her face.

Amrita forced a smile through her tears as Khalid cupped his hands, pursed his lips and blasted a trumpet sound into the room. Imtiaz looked up as Lucky and her ghost friends raised their hands to their mouths as if they were blowing the conch too. Amrita kissed her son's head, whispering what sounded like a story in his ear.

Khalid grinned, holding his hands into a shell shape. 'Vishnu conch!' he said clearly.

Nilam, Amrita and Tanvi looked to each other in surprise.

'These are his first words in English!' Amrita explained, smiling through her tears.

'What story did you tell him?' Imtiaz asked Amrita.

'I told that Lord Vishnu will protect us, that here in these hands' – she took her son's little hands in her own – 'we have the power to hold Lord Vishnu's conch. It brings life out of the sea and speaks of truth.' Khalid pulled away from Amrita to trumpet his imaginary conch again.

'Shhhhhhhhh!' Lem's door opened. 'I'm on hold to the council. Can you just keep the noise down a bit . . .' He stopped in his tracks to take in the sight of Khalid standing on the table trumpeting with all his might.

'Lem! Khalid just spoke!' Tanvi laughed. 'I'm not telling him to be quiet now! Seems like Lord Vishnu's paying us a visit.'

'Vishnu?' Lem asked, confused.

'Protector of the universe? I think Imtiaz's conch drawing inspired him,' Nilam added.

'You better share your secret, Imtiaz. None of us have even got as much as a peep out of him! Carry on then, Khalid of the Conch!'

Lem and Tanvi smiled at Imtiaz and she felt herself flush with happiness. 'Whatever you did, Imtiaz, carry on.' Lem ruffled Khalid's hair as he handed some notes to Tanvi, who cringed and held her forehead. 'I think that headache of yours is catching, Usha,' she said and slowly walked upstairs.

'I'm going up too,' Usha said, scraping her chair back from the table.

Not, 'Do you want to come too, or . . . sure you don't want me to stay with you, with all these ghosts around?' thought Imtiaz as she waved to Khalid, who was now snuggling into his mother, sucking his thumb and humming Lucky's lullaby.

Imtiaz tentatively followed Lucky and her three friends up the stairs and almost tripped on to the first landing when she saw through the open doorway Tanvi at her table surrounded by ghosts, sitting calmly with her as if they'd been invited. As she stumbled, Tanvi and another woman sprung up to help her.

'I'm fine!' she said, her heart racing.

'Come in, Imtiaz.' Tanvi smiled.

She would freak if she could see that all the chairs are taken! Imtiaz thought as she hovered in the doorway, spotting a TV in the corner, as the women turned as one in her direction like they were curious to meet her.

Tanvi followed her gaze. 'Usha's never been that keen, but you can come down here to watch TV sometimes if you like.' Imtiaz nodded her thanks. 'Delyse called from the airport before she left, to see how you're getting on, and sent her love. I told her you're doing fine.' Imtiaz bit the inside of her mouth. 'Are you? Settling in OK?' Tanvi asked.

Here's my chance! Imtiaz thought. 'Yeah! I love the house. It's well old, isn't it? Do you know anything about like, the history, 'cos I'm into that?'

Imtiaz watched as the ghost women smiled to each other, sitting up taller as if they too were keen to hear what Tanvi knew. Now she was closer she saw that one of the women reminded her a bit of Mala, who had worked at Acorns. She was from Mauritius. The women nodded in her direction. They seemed peaceful and caring but just like Lucky, what disturbed Imtiaz the most was their silence. As they sat quietly around the table it was like they were trapped birds, and this house was their cage. The thought made Imtiaz feel trapped too. Lost in her daydream she'd almost forgotten that she'd asked Tanvi a question.

'I'm ashamed to say I don't. It's Victorian, I think. I asked my ma about the history once and she didn't know much, but I happen to know there's this local history exhibition our friend Charles is planning at the library – Usha's going to take you later. If you find out anything, let us know! But remember, Imtiaz, any concerns or worries about anything at all, no matter how small, Lem and me – we're here for you.'

'Thanks!' Imtiaz smiled and the ghost women nodded back as if they too were here to help.

***

Imtiaz found Usha at the Helm, twisting knots, the conch cradled in the space between her crossed legs. Lucky and her friends were already making themselves at home among the long grasses.

'Your Kali Ma OK?' Imtiaz asked.

Usha nodded without looking up and continued tying a knot that when she pulled on it, became a long piece of rope again.

'Slip-knot!' Usha whispered.

She really has spent way too long on her own up here with her grandparents, Imtiaz thought.

'Lucky's over there with a few of those other women. I think they're her friends. The rest are downstairs.'

Usha looked bewildered. 'How many are there?'

'About fifteen! The other women are sitting with your mum around her table.'

'Why do you think they've come?'

Imtiaz contemplated Lucky's ghost friends as they admired the roses. 'I guess to keep her company. It looks like they've all got her back! Like, whatever she needs us to discover, they do too. The way they're dressed, even the ones who look more old-fashioned, they're wearing some kind of uniform like they're carers . . . or' – Lucky's lullaby played through Imtiaz's mind – 'nannies. They were so good with Khalid and he could definitely see them . . .'

Lucky walked over the rope bridge. It did not sway as she stepped on. Pausing at the centre of it, she looked directly at Imtiaz and touched her fingertips to her third eye.

'I'm right!' Imtiaz lifted up the conch and listened again, but Lucky's voice had grown no louder and there were no new whisperings.

'I don't think she'll tell us anything more until we find the next sari piece.'

Imtiaz grabbed the rope from Usha.

'Forget your slip-knot. Sitting here's not going to help us. Usha, we've got to get out there. If we don't, we're going to lose all this!' Imtiaz's hand swirled around the top deck.

'Where's Kali Ma anyway?' asked Imtiaz.

Usha smiled at the familiar way Imtiaz spoke her

grandmother's name. 'Sleeping again. She didn't even wake up when I came in,' Usha replied.

'OK. Come on, let's go out.'

'Where?'

'I asked your mum about the history of the house on my way upstairs just now, but she didn't know much. Said we should check out some history thing at the library. Let's start there.'

'OK!' Usha mumbled, accepting Imtiaz's helping hand.

'Hang on a minute, let me test something.' Imtiaz paused in among the grasses. 'Excuse me, Lucky. Are these your friends? Are they part of your story?'

The four women linked arms with each other and smiled.

'Yes! And what about the women downstairs? Do you know them?'

Imtiaz followed Lucky as she sped inside, past Usha's bed to the chronometer where Lucky was cartwheeling her hands in an anti-clockwise direction. Imtiaz frowned, straining to understand, and Lucky's gestures grew more frantic.

'You said this is a navigation clock, right?'

'Yes, why?' Usha asked, catching her breath as she now stood at Imtiaz's shoulder.

'Because Lucky's turning her hands backwards!'

Imtiaz switched her attention to Lucky. 'Are they from another time, before you? Did they live in the house too?'

Lucky twisted her hand this way and that, as if to say, 'That's half-true.'

Imtiaz sighed in frustration. 'Whatever it is they want us to discover it seems like it's linked to this house somehow. Let's see what we can find out.'

Usha and Imtiaz ran downstairs together, both as relieved as each other when Imtiaz confirmed that, apart from Lucky, the other ghost women had stayed behind. Feeling in her pocket, Usha took out the mobile phone. 'I forgot to tell you – we've got this we can use between us!'

Imtiaz's mouth fell open. 'How could you forget that! I've been asking Delyse for one for ages! We can look up loads on it.'

Usha shook her head. 'Don't get too excited. There's no data. In any case, no screens or anything allowed up there! Mum and Dad are strict about it,' Usha said, shrugging and slipping it back in her pocket.

'I don't get it. When there's Wi-Fi in the house, why can't we have data? What's the point of having an iPhone then?' Imtiaz sighed.

'That's what I said!' Usha shrugged.

As they reached the bottom of the staircase, Lem was lifting the front wheels of a bike over the front door threshold, a huge grin on his face. 'Here we are, look what's been delivered back, just like Kali Ma willed it – her and Pops Michael's tandem, for you girls.'

'Wow,' Imtiaz exclaimed. 'I've never actually seen one of those in real life before!'

Usha beamed, running her hands over one of the leather seats. 'Thanks, Dad,' she said softly.

Lem nodded. 'It hasn't brushed up too badly – a little paint job on the rust, new wheels and it was good to go! The frame's a bit heavy, but I'm sure you girls will manage. Delyse said you're a good cyclist, Imtiaz, so it shouldn't be too hard to get used to this.' He indicated for Imtiaz to climb on to the front. 'Get on then, see if the seats are the right height!' His enthusiasm was infectious.

They climbed on and wobbled, steadying themselves against the hallway mirror. For a moment, Imtiaz stared at the reflection of the two of them with Lem behind. To anyone who didn't know, they would look like sisters with their dad.

'Luckily you and Usha are about the same height!' Lem held the handlebars and waited for them to dismount. 'It came out of the hell-hole!' He pointed to an understair cupboard. 'It's a bit tight, with our old bikes in there, but see if you two can get it back in. We can't have visitors to The Hearth falling over it.'

Imtiaz ducked as they pushed the tandem into the gloomy, cramped cupboard, backing up the wheels a few times. Manoeuvring inside they knocked the handlebars against the understair walls and a pocket of plaster crumbled and fell to the ground. Tanvi walked down the stairs and held the cupboard door further open.

'Everything all right in there?' she asked, concern in her voice at the sound of shards of wall shifting.

'Sorry!' Imtiaz muttered, bending to pick up a chunk of plaster and attempting to place it back where it came from.

'Oh! Don't bother yourself,' said Tanvi. 'The décor under there is the least of our worries! Once you're in, it's hell getting out!'

It was true. Imtiaz and Usha were crouched inside and, having leant the tandem against the wall, were struggling to clamber over it, back into the light. As Usha stood up, the phone slipped out of her pocket into the hallway. Tanvi bent down and picked it up.

'You could have used the torch! Here! Look!' Tanvi said, clicking on the function to show them. 'Remember our numbers are in here and you've got unlimited texts. So – no excuse not to keep in touch,' she said, handing it to Imtiaz, who thanked her and placed it in her jacket pocket.

'Oh! And you should have your own keys.' Tanvi took a set from a metal box attached to the wall and placed them in Imtiaz's palm. 'Usha's already got hers, so here you are. In the daytime the door's nearly always open, but just in case . . .'

Imtiaz pocketed the keys and nodded to Lucky, who stood patiently at the door.

'Lucky's waiting,' she whispered, but as they walked down the steps, Imtiaz felt Usha curl in on herself again. *Maybe she thinks I'm taking over her life? Maybe she'd prefer it if I didn't have keys to her door?*

History Speaks

Give her space, be patient . . . OK, Delyse, OK.

Delyse's advice buzzed in Imtiaz's ear, and she managed to follow it for a while, but the air prickled with tension as they trailed up the road. *Just my luck to have a silent sister.* Lucky turned around, beckoning them to hurry. *A silent sister and a house full of silent ghosts.*

'If you're annoyed with me for having the phone, here – you can take charge of it.' Imtiaz offered it to Usha.

'I'm not.' Usha shrugged and made no attempt to take it from her.

'Or is it about the keys?' Imtiaz tried again.

Usha shot Imtiaz a you-are-so-way-off look. 'Nothing like that. I feel guilty for leaving Kali Ma. What if she fades away while we're out?' Usha said as they reached the end of King Edward Road. 'I'm worried about her.'

So that's what's up. 'But Lucky's friends are there to keep her company.' Imtiaz looked ahead where Lucky was backwards-walking, smiling in agreement as she listened. 'Lucky thinks so too. It's like you could trust them with your life.'

'Or your dead gran,' Usha shot back.

Imtiaz flattened her palms over her mouth to stop herself from laughing.

'Sorry! But you've got a wicked sense of humour!'

Usha smirked. 'No one's ever said that to me before!'

The library was only five minutes from the lido and it was so small that Imtiaz almost walked straight past what looked like a scaled-down version of Usha's house. Outside it, a bike that Usha vaguely recognised was secured to the railings.

As they entered, a tall boy with a mane of dark hair trailing from under a back-to-front cap, stood at the front desk. Usha thought she might have seen him before, but couldn't place him.

'I didn't realise you were into poetry, Cosmo?' said the librarian. 'I can show you lots more if you like this!'

The boy checked self-consciously behind him at Usha and Imtiaz's arrival. But Imtiaz was surprised to see Lucky stepping forward and opening her arms as if she knew him. From this distance Imtiaz realised that the boy wasn't staring at them at all but straight at Lucky. His hands shook slightly as he flicked his cap around, tipping the rim to shade his face. 'The poems are for my Grandma

Valini!' he mumbled, shifting awkwardly from foot to foot.

'Then why don't you ask her to come in and see if she can contribute to our little history exhibition? Your family's an important part of it all.'

'I'll ask her. Don't hold your breath, though. I should go,' he said, glancing nervously once more towards Lucky, who had lowered her hands but still smiled at him. *Maybe Lucky's made a mistake and she doesn't know him after all. But how come he can see her?* Imtiaz mused.

'I was very much hoping your grandmother might record some memories for us,' the librarian continued.

Cosmo shook his head emphatically. 'Nah! She wouldn't want that – won't even be photographed these days. Anyways, she doesn't stray far from the canal now,' he explained, looking over at Lucky, the corners of his mouth curling into a smile.

'Why is he staring?' Usha muttered.

'Not at us! He can see Lucky!' Imtiaz whispered.

'OK, Cosmo . . .' the librarian conceded, patting him on the shoulder, 'but tell your grandmother she's always welcome.'

Cosmo nodded and backed out of the library door. Turning at the last minute, he walked straight up to Usha. 'Where are all the others who nearly had me off my bike this morning?' he asked.

'Sorry, I don't know what you're talking about,' Usha replied, stepping away from him.

'Suit yourself!' He shrugged and carried on out.

'How do you know him? What's he on about?' Imtiaz whispered.

Usha breathed deep as it finally clicked where she'd seen him before and grasped Cosmo's meaning. 'I think he saw the other ghosts when we were coming back from the optician's. I didn't know they were there, did I? I thought he was just showing off weaving around on his bike, but he must have been avoiding bumping into them,' Usha whispered back, feeling all stirred up as she remembered the red flags sparking on his wheels like flint.

The librarian wore an old-fashioned tweed jacket and a name badge that announced that he was 'Charles' and a volunteer.

'Don't mind Cosmo. He has his moments, but he's one of my best customers!' Charles smiled. 'Welcome, I've been expecting you. You're Usha's new sis—' He hesitated, nudging his loose glasses further up his nose. To hear the 'sister' word he'd almost said felt like a stretch for Imtiaz too, no matter how hard she had wished it to come easily. 'Tanvi's already called in with your details. There's your card, Imtiaz.' She thanked him and picked it up off the counter.

'No, thank *you*! I won't be able to keep my little endeavour going if numbers dwindle further. Now, you make yourself at home and just shout if you need any help. As you can see,

I'm not exactly in demand in here today. You've got the run of the place. When you've chosen what you want to borrow I'm sure Usha will show you the ropes – how to register loans in and out on the computer over there.'

'It looks more like someone's front room than a library,' Imtiaz commented as she took in the place.

'It is! Charles used to work at the Central Library. He set this community library up in his house when he retired,' Usha explained.

Charles gestured to the bookshelves and showed them through to another crammed room that contained a row of computers and display boards taking up half the space. Behind them, tucked away in the far corner was an old passport machine. Beside this, a narrow desk, scattered with photos and shoebox stacks, skirted the walls.

'Sorry about the mess in here. I'm halfway through setting up a little local history display – hoping to get a few more people through the doors this summer.'

Imtiaz edged behind the display boards to a photo booth. 'What's this for?' she asked.

'Ah! Well, you may ask! It's a defunct passport photo-taking machine! One of my big ideas, from way back, was to get all these archive photos digitised and have them' – Charles twirled his finger around, closing his eyes in concentration as he struggled to find the right words – 'on a loop rather like a Rolodex display.' Imtiaz and Usha both looked blank. 'OK! I haven't explained it very well. Picture this!' Charles persisted. 'One of you . . . step inside the photo booth.' Charles held out his palm and gestured towards the machine.

'What? Actually?' Imtiaz laughed.

'Yes! Actually.'

Usha giggled as Imtiaz pulled a 'what next?' face and stepped inside.

'Close the curtains. Good! Now imagine sitting there, plugging in your earphones and listening to people telling you their local history stories while watching all the photos and documents in those archive boxes scrolling around the screen in front of you. Your very own personal experience in the passport booth of history!'

Imtiaz swished back the curtains, grinning. 'That sounds brilliant!'

'Yes . . . but to be honest, I need a bit of help with the technical execution. Every summer I think I'll manage it. At one point I had ambitions for every library in the land to have one . . . but now I'd just be happy to get *one* off the ground! I'm no good at tech and I'm afraid I've never progressed far beyond the shoebox-and-pinboard phase of evolution! But you've got to start somewhere. The theory is, if people bring in pieces of their own story, it'll draw them, their families and neighbours into the library and get the whole community involved. But if I don't get it done this summer, I'm told the collection will have to be returned to the archive. Fair enough, I suppose. They've entrusted it with me for long enough. "Professor of procrastination", my wife used to call me!'

'What's he on about?' Imtiaz whispered as she watched Lucky step inside the booth, staring at her reflection on the screen as if it was a mirror. Stepping out again she inspected the examples of unsmiling faces on the outside of the booth and turned to Imtiaz with a lost expression. *I wish you could tell me what's wrong, Lucky. Why do these passport photos upset you?* Without words to rely on, Imtiaz tuned into Lucky's ever-changing moods and right now felt the urge to comfort her, but didn't know how.

'Actually, we are interested in finding out about the history of our house and the street,' Usha said, 'because Imtiaz has just moved in and she wanted to know about it and even Mum and Dad don't have that much of a clue.'

'Don't know much about history!' Charles sang, but stopped abruptly when he registered the vacant look on both girls' faces.

'Tanvi said the house is well old, is it like, Victorian?' Imtiaz added.

Charles laughed. 'Not like! *Actually* Victorian! Yes, and I'm sure it's got an interesting history. I haven't come across anything yet but I'm afraid I've only managed to log one of the small boxes so far – I've still got all that stack to go through.' He gestured despairingly to a variety of sizes of boxes on the table; some of the larger ones were scuffed at the edges. 'It's a mammoth task and if I don't get some help,

I'll be nothing but a puff of dust myself.' Charles tapped the old-fashioned writing on the lid of one of the identical larger boxes. 'Just like Dawson's Department store.'

'He does go on a bit!' Imtiaz whispered under her breath.

'Anyway, you girls take a look and see what treasure you can find, but handle with care. See if you can sort it into some kind of order for me as you look through. That'd be a help.' Charles smiled. 'I'll tell you what. If you get into it, you could be my curators! Help me decide how to organise the audio and the visuals. Any good at tech?' he asked Imtiaz.

'Actually, yeah!' She nodded. 'Can we get online, too?' Imtiaz asked, glancing over at the computers.

'Just log on with your ID. You don't usually use them though, do you, Usha? More of a bookworm!'

'Haven't got much choice in our house,' Usha replied as Charles ambled away back out towards the reception area.

'I can't believe we're not even allowed a TV in our room,' Imtiaz complained.

'I know!' Usha nodded, feeling the heat flush her cheeks. *Imtiaz thinks I'm nerdy enough without any encouragement from Charles,* she thought as she looked through the old photos. Some were in colour, like the ones in her Kali Ma's albums, stuck behind the plastic yellowing sheets of cellophane, stained by time. But it was the black and white ones that attracted her attention most.

'No way I'm going to spend the whole summer organising all this!' Imtiaz said, but Usha and Lucky seemed so engrossed in the pictures that she joined them. 'Did Charles know your Kali Ma?' Imtiaz asked.

'Yes, and Uncle Merve and Pops Michael when he was alive. He came to Kali Ma's funeral.'

Imtiaz nodded, following Lucky along the display of old photos. Lucky's search-light eyes darted here and there, her forehead furrowed in concentration. She seemed to recognise a curved street with old-fashioned cars with stick-out headlights like eyes and a bus passing a shop called Dawson's on the corner. People in long coats walked along the pavement. Another brown-edged photo revealed a canal and an old factory with a metal advertising hoarding in blue and white that said 'Hovis'. In the next picture a butcher stood outside a shop with – Imtiaz looked closer – rabbits and hares hanging from hooks. The girls turned to each other with the same grossed-out look on their faces.

'We're wasting our time here.' Imtiaz sighed, starting to edge out from behind the display boards towards the computers. 'Come on, let's get online. We're not going to find anything to help save your house in this lot, are we?'

But the intent look on Lucky's face made Imtiaz pause again, and now Usha seemed frozen to the spot, staring at the same photo.

'What?' Imtiaz asked.

'You found your Kali Ma and Michael with their tandem then!' Charles paused in the doorway.

'Did Mum bring this in?' Usha asked.

'No, surprisingly enough, your family is not the source.' Charles smiled. 'Actually, Cosmo just donated it. I was chuffed to hear at Kali's funeral that Lem was planning to get the old tandem fixed up for you two so I mentioned it to Cosmo, because' – Charles pointed to the photo – 'the Bike Barge has been his family's business for generations. But I gather from Tanvi the work's already done. It's a shame as I do like to put the custom Cosmo's way.'

Charles shook his head, looking from Usha to the photograph. 'You really are the spitting image of your Kali Ma at that age. I have an idea!'

Imtiaz rolled her eyes.

'How about you bring in an updated photo by the barge with you two in it, and maybe Cosmo too?' Charles leant forward as if confiding in them. 'Tanvi says you'll be starting at the new school after the holidays, well that's where I helped Cosmo to apply for too. It would be good for him, for all of you, to get to know each other . . .'

A bell rang on the desk. 'Excuse me!' Charles said, hurrying out.

Usha peered closer at Kali Ma's little-girl face: her broad, open smile and long, black hair tied over one shoulder. She stood beside an unsmiling boy with wide, wondering eyes, a halo of Afro hair and a satchel slung over his back.

'Is that your Pops Michael?' Imtiaz asked, gently nudging Usha's shoulder. Lucky smiled at her encouragingly.

'Yes,' Usha confirmed.

'You know the way Cosmo could see Lucky and the other ghosts?' Usha nodded. 'Well, I think he must have something to do with this because Lucky knew him. It feels like this is leading us somewhere.'

'What's Lucky doing now?' Usha asked.

'Sitting by one of those big department store boxes. Beckoning us over.'

Imtiaz slung her jacket over a chair and they settled themselves on the floor opposite each other. 'How brilliant would it be if the documents were in here!' Imtiaz whispered.

Together they removed the lid, carefully unfolding the tissue paper underneath.

Leafing through the random collection of photos and clippings felt like searching for something in a pack of cards but not knowing what numbers or sets you were looking for. *Diamonds, clubs, hearts* . . . Curious, Lucky leant forward as Usha inspected a photo and placed it in a pile she'd loosely categorised as 'street life'.

'Hang on a minute!' Imtiaz said, picking it up. It showed children with scraggy clothes and hair looking straight into the photo lens, standing next to a barge. 'Is this the same barge as in the tandem picture? Cosmo's Bike Barge?'

'Could be? Hard to tell, it's so grainy.' Usha nodded, peering behind the children at the washing line where bright-coloured skirts and a white sheet hung wafting on a breeze. A random wheel leant against the barge side.

Lucky pointed repeatedly from the photo to Imtiaz's pocket.

'Usha! For some reason, she wants us to take this one,' Imtiaz whispered.

Usha bit her lip, glancing through to Charles. 'We can't! I want the one of the tandem too, but they're not ours to take.'

Imtiaz turned the photo over. Printed in swirly writing on the back were the words, *DONATED BY: VALINI.*

'Valini – that's Cosmo's grandma's name,' Usha said.

Imtiaz attempted to return it to the table but Lucky shook her head firmly. She was so tiny and slender, like a little bird, but the brightness in her eyes and the tight, determined set of her chin made Imtiaz feel that she was not about to take no for an answer.

'What if she needs you to show it to your Kali Ma? What if she knows something about it? Charles won't miss it and we can bring it back tomorrow. There are so many photos here. Oh! Hang on! I forgot . . .'

Imtiaz took the phone out of her pocket. 'We could just get a photo?' She took the picture and held it up to show Lucky, but she looked straight through it. Imtiaz waved it around in front of Lucky, but her expression remained blank.

'It's like she can't see it through the screen. Hasn't got a clue what this is.'

'Why would she?' Usha said.

As Lucky became more distressed, Imtiaz felt the need to stand up and join her, pacing up and down the tiny back room.

'What's she doing now?' Usha asked.

'Telling us to hurry up! Trying to show me how much she desperately wants me to take the original photo. It's horrible how upset she is. She's got her hand over her mouth as if she's been gagged. Now she's holding her other hand over her ear and pointing from me to you like she's pleading for us to listen. Come on, Usha. Let's take what we've found back to your Kali Ma. Maybe she can help.'

Usha gnawed at her lip. 'I really need to get back to her, see how she is.'

Imtiaz hesitated, then placed the photo in her pocket, desperately trying to push Delyse's thunderous face to the back of her mind. *She would kill me if she saw me stealing anything.*

Just then, Charles pushed a trolley past the doorway and smiled at them. Imtiaz's spine tensed. 'Look at you two, thick as thieves! I told you it was compelling stuff.'

Imtiaz's cheeks flushed hot with guilt as she observed Lucky, whose hands hovered over a large envelope. 'We can't go yet. It really feels like she's guiding us now!' Imtiaz whispered as she picked up the sealed envelope, and read the cover. '"Empire Day, 1957". This looks interesting. The ship Delyse came to the UK on was called *Empire Windrush*,' Imtiaz commented as she carefully broke the wax seal.

'Do you think we should ask if we can . . .' Usha's voice trailed off; Imtiaz was already taking photos and documents from the envelope.

'Charles said we could look! No one's even bothered opening this one.' Imtiaz's newspaper blanket flashed through her mind as she carefully picked up an old clipping with a photo of a house on it. 'Wow. This is ancient! From the *Hackney Gazette*, 1921!' she said.

Huddled close together, Usha read the clipping aloud.

'Ayahs' Home Relocates. Ayahs will be a familiar sight to the good people of Hackney. But this week marks the new opening of the Ayahs' Home at number four King Edward Road, only a few hundred yards from the previous house at number twenty-six. The Ayahs' Home, with its many rooms, divided by nationality of the women, is designed not only for Indian ayahs, but also for nursemaids—'

'I knew it!' Imtiaz punched the air. 'Those Victorian ghosts at your mum's table probably came to visit from up the road!'

Lucky nodded, gently smiling.

Usha placed her hands to her lips.

'Sorry, Usha! Carry on!'

'Nursemaids . . . from other countries such as China and Mauritius, who were similarly brought over by British families who failed to secure homebound journeys and so the women required assistance in order to return.

'The Home is not merely a hostel for displaced ayahs, but a venue for missionaries with a zeal to convert the ayahs to Christianity. Demand has risen following the war, as travel by sea has been curtailed and so regrettably there have been many more stranded ayahs during these years.' Usha looked closer at the faded photo beneath the article and felt her heart race with anticipation. Here were the two pillars of her house. The sign above the door – 'London City Mission. Ayahs' Home' might not be there any more, but the railings and the windows were the same. Usha shivered as she stared at the strange collection of people standing on the front steps that she walked up and down every day. In the front row were two women in white saris.

'Imtiaz? Are either of these women Lucky?'

Imtiaz peered from the photo to Lucky and shook her head.

'But this is definitely our house,' Usha whispered. 'That's why the ayahs' ghosts are there.

'Because it was their house too, in another time!' agreed Imtiaz. 'Did you live there, Lucky?'

Imtiaz mimicked Lucky's movement, almost joining together her thumb and first finger.

'I think she's saying . . . for a little time,' Imtiaz whispered, hugging her own chest. 'I feel all worked up! Like I want to run away.'

'You're feeling what she's feeling? Weird, isn't it? It's like that with Kali Ma.'

Imtiaz nodded. 'At least *she* can talk, though,' she said, following Lucky's restless search leading Imtiaz to another photo of women sitting around a table. She handed it to Usha. 'These are the ayahs who were sitting around the table upstairs in your mum's room. It's like they're all in this together,' Imtiaz whispered, looking at the old-fashioned clothes of the women and behind them the decoration in the room with the vintage wallpaper.

Lucky sat cross-legged by Imtiaz's side, pointing to some thin blue pages of uneven type. Imtiaz scanned the lines, then, shaking her head like she didn't trust her own eyes, got out the phone.

'You think we can record on this? Delyse could on hers.'

Flicking through the functions, Imtiaz searched for one that would let her record and clicked on it. Gesturing to Usha to be quiet, she started reading.

'Oral history: transcribed for "Empire Day" local history exhibition. Gladys Garskill, 1890-1949. Domestic Worker, House of Ayahs.

'Well, I'm not exactly educated but I have got some things to say about the ayahs because I think they've missed out. Anyway, what I know about them is they were the nursemaids who came over to Britain with the children of the British Raj, you know from Queen Victoria's time. Not just from India, but I'd say most of them were. They would look after the children during the long journeys travelling to and fro. Children spent so much time with their ayahs that they were more like mothers to them. Would you credit it, some families had them bring their children over and then didn't look after the ayahs, didn't even pay the return journey. Some were left to fend for themselves out on the streets. My mam, used to work at number twenty-six ... that's how I got the job when number four opened up, she said she'd seen these poor women in her time roaming about, not a penny to their names, selling bits of postcard art or sewing, hardly earning enough money to eat, let alone to get home. So that's why the missionaries got involved. Strange house it was. How they used to split them up by nationalities and religions although to my mind they all got on just fine. To be honest, I preferred the ayahs to the missionaries, always looking down their noses, treating them like children when most were mature women who'd travelled the world and seen a few things.

'I worked at number four for twelve years in all, so I got to know a few of the ayahs who were always interested to chat to me about my own children, Seth and Clara, and I felt sorry for them, just sitting there in that house waiting to go home. Still, better than being on the streets.

'Like I say, the ayahs were mostly older, but there was this younger one, Mina, more my age, and I tried to make friends. But Matron didn't want us to mix. Told me to get on with my work. Matron called her Millie, don't ask me why the missionaries gave the women all new names – pet names. Insulting, I thought.

'The ayahs would sit around with bibles or sewing, looking like they would rather be doing something else—'

Imtiaz's mouth fell open. 'Usha, that's what they were

doing sitting around your mum's table!'

Usha pointed to the phone to remind Imtiaz that she was recording and to continue.

'Sometimes in their rooms I'd find the ayahs praying in their own languages to their own gods. I liked Mina's candles and perfume but incense was banned so she gave her sticks to me. Oooooh, I thought the smell was lovely. You can get hold of them these days - joss-sticks but I call them joysticks! It was a joy to be friends with Mina. I remember one day Clara, my daughter, was ill and I had to bring her to work and Mina looked after her. Do you know, when we got back home she was singing in Lucky's Bengali language. After that, every time Clara passed the house she would cry to come in and see her. I wanted to invite her to ours for tea but Matron was having none of it. When Mina finally got her passage home, me and Clara went to wave her off at the docks and she gave me her little goddess statue. Funny-looking thing with lots of arms. She did laugh when I said all them hands would come in useful for cleaning, because a woman can never have enough! But she was a poetic one, Mina. Said the statue was something about doing away with darkness and bringing light, so I keep it over my fireplace. I'm Quaker by religion, myself, so I've never prayed to the goddess, but I think on her and then I think about Mina and wonder what happened to her. For a while I had this fancy that me and Clara would go and find her in India. But you know, it soon faded. (Gladys laughs.) A woman like me, no savings, I would have had to be a reverse ayah to get that chance! Strange really, how they came and went year after year like ghosts who mostly we never got to know living on our street. But this call-out for stories got me thinking – you never do really get to know about what us working-class women do, even when we travel across the world!

'I do miss that house, how it made my life bigger, like I was travelling somewhere ... I wouldn't have minded seeing the world. You know, I met some of the ayahs two or three times, they liked the adventure. They must have had good sea legs! But they didn't all go back. There was this other woman came just before Mina left. I remember because there was a brief but happy reunion between those two. Her name was Lucky.'

'She knew you?' Imtiaz turned to Lucky, whose face was serene as if she was meeting an old friend.

'Don't stop!' Usha gasped, gesturing impatiently for Imtiaz to read on.

'There were a few others she was friends with, I can't recall their names. They said they knew each other from the long passage too but they both found families who needed ayahs to go back with and Lucky was left behind. She wasn't a favourite with Matron because she refused to pray or sing the hymns. One day, I turned up for work and there was a right scene! Lucky was giving matron what for! Telling her, in her own quiet way, to stick her rules, that she wouldn't be paraded around anywhere like an exotic bird to show how charitable the missionary ladies were. She was having none of it. "You might call us human birds of passage, but we can't fly, can we! I have friends here and I'd sooner never go back than be treated like this!" - words to that effect. She left, slamming the door, tiny little thing she was, but strong. I'm telling you, she shook that house when she left! I went after her.'

Wishing Delyse was here by her side, Imtiaz paused and clenched a respect fist towards Lucky's in solidarity before reading on.

'She said she'd decided that she'd rather never have a passage home than stay in that house. In any case, she'd made some sort of promise to the child she'd brought over - 'Swati' something or other was her name. She loved that child like her own. Swati was a 'half-caste', she told me - Indian mother, English father - and she hadn't been able to keep a promise to look after the child as she'd wanted because she'd been thrown out. I was thinking of inviting her to mine ... but I don't know how it would have gone down with my other half. She said she had friends among the Roma, down on the canal. I used to walk that way sometimes, looking for her, but never came across Lucky again.

'I suppose I was missing Mina because we were

friends, more than friends really, and I still miss her.

'*Amar mishti bon* - that's what she called me when I waved her off on the ship. Later, I found from the Indian doctor who set up the surgery in the old Ayahs' Home that it means "my sweet sister".'

Imtiaz's voice choked with emotion as she ended the recording and wiped her eyes, smiling through her tears, as she caught Usha wiping her eyes too.

'Too much!' Usha whispered, feeling like her brain was scrambling. 'That doctor was my great-grandad! Parv!'

'So the ayahs on the top deck right now are the friends you travelled to Britain with?' Imtiaz asked Lucky. 'Is one of them Mina?'

'She's nodding.'

Usha held her head in her hands. 'I can't believe these ayahs used to live in our house and we didn't know anything about them!'

Imtiaz glanced over to Lucky, who was smiling at her, fingertips once again touching her third eye. 'Feels like we're on the right track now . . . So if Lucky went to stay on a barge with Roma people . . . We've got to find the Bike Barge where Cosmo lives. We known your Kali Ma went there – that's why Lucky wants us to take the photo to show her. And who knows, maybe' – Imtiaz turned the photo over to read the name on the back – 'Valini, Cosmo's grandmother, can help us too.'

Usha laid out all the documents from the envelope and

sighed. 'For a moment I thought what Mum and Dad were looking for might be in here too. About the house being used for the community . . . because if it was the Ayahs' Home and then the surgery and now The Hearth . . .'

Imtiaz shook her head. 'That's all there is.'

Picking up the photos, Usha peered into the ayahs' faces. 'You can see they're not happy. Looks like someone's forced them to pose in the doorway . . . like exhibits.'

Imtiaz felt light-headed from all the information swirling through her mind – Lucky's lullaby, the conch clues and Gladys's voice – 'amar mishti bon'. She repeated Mina's words in her head. *My sweet sister.* They didn't fit yet and she doubted that they ever would.

Suddenly all this felt bigger than them, like the women in the photo were about to break from their frozen poses to speak. Imtiaz's heart pounded with anticipation. 'I need to listen to the conch again. We haven't found another sari piece, but it feels like we're getting closer.'

'And I need to see Kali Ma.' Hurriedly they tidied up the shoeboxes and placed the photos and envelopes back inside. Turning over the 'Empire Day' envelope, Usha noticed some faint, faded writing in the bottom left-hand corner and pointed it out to Imtiaz.

Documents found at 4 King Edward Road, Hackney.
Donated by Dr Sara Gopal.

'The name over the door in The Hearth,' Imtiaz said,

peering over Usha's shoulder.

'My great-grandmother again,' Usha said.

Imtiaz nodded. 'Her name keeps coming up. Your Kali Ma said she wouldn't talk about her family and she was weird when she went to India. Why would she take the conch away from your Kali Ma when she heard Lucky's voice? Unless she'd heard it too? What if Lucky looked after your great-grandmother? Gladys called her a . . . "half-caste"?' Imtiaz wrinkled her nose at the term. 'But why would she hide that? And if she donated this envelope, she knew all about the Ayahs' Home. But it seems like she didn't want anyone else to.' Usha, who felt like her head was going to explode, leant in closer to Imtiaz. 'I need time to think. If Lucky wants you to take that photo, I really want to show Kali Ma this. The original – she'd love to see it.' Usha pulled the photograph of the tandem down from the display. 'Can you put this in your pocket with the other one?'

Imtiaz backed away, feeling suddenly fiery. 'Why? So only I get into trouble? No, *you* want to show it to her, so if we're in this together, *you* do it!'

'I've never stolen anything before,' Usha whispered.

'And you think I have? We'll bring them back.'

'Sshhhh!' Usha peeped through the gap in the display boards to see Charles busily replacing books from a trolley on the shelves. She stared at Imtiaz for a moment, determined to show her that she was up to the challenge. Turning round, she slipped the photo into her bag.

158

As they legged it down the road, Charles appeared in the doorway. 'Bye, girls! Thanks for your help!'

They waved back, sprinting towards home. The home they shared with the ayahs – and now they knew why.

Ayahs' Home

Swinging around the edge of the railings, Imtiaz and Usha were too out of breath to speak, but both held the same photograph in their mind's eyes of the ayahs standing right here on their doorstep. Once inside, Lucky headed straight for the 'hell-hole', placing a finger over her mouth and ushering them to follow her. Light fell in slanted shafts through the cracks from the staircase floorboards above.

'What are we doing in here?' Usha asked, confused.

'Following Lucky.'

Imtiaz clicked on the phone's torch, shining it deep under the stairs where Lucky was now crawling between the tandem pedals, towards the back of the cupboard, beckoning for Imtiaz to follow her. Usha closed the door quietly behind them while Imtiaz observed Lucky's concentrated expression as she traced her hands over the plaster work.

'What are you trying to tell us?' Imtiaz whispered. 'Is there something behind here?' As she tugged the tandem backwards to get by, it scraped against the wall, once again loosening a cascade of powder dust as it crumbled. 'There's something around here she wants us to see,' Imtiaz whispered as the girls froze, stilling their breath momentarily at the sound of Lem and Tanvi's voices in the hall.

'How can they expect us to believe that? Official records destroyed in a fire before they could digitise them. Our only hope to save The Hearth's to find the originals now and time's running out. I bet Puttock knew there were no replicas all along,' Lem said.

Cramp seized Usha's foot as she shifted slightly. Her jacket buckle caught on the back wheel of the tandem and as she unhooked it the spokes began to spin.

Swinging round to stop the whirring sound, Imtiaz dislodged the handlebars of another bike that came crashing down towards her. Imtiaz clung to the wall, her fingers finding the frayed edges of exposed wallpaper that came away in her hands. She shone the torch on it, brushing off the powdery surface. Usha's nose itched and she attempted to muffle a sneeze.

'Usha!' Imtiaz whispered. 'This is the same pattern that was in the photo of the ayahs sitting at the table . . . It must have been all over this house. It's like Lucky wants to prove to us that everything we touch here, even behind the paintwork, is part of her sto- sto- STORY!' Imtiaz let out an explosive sneeze and began coughing and spluttering.

'What on earth?' Light blasted into the cupboard as Lem

peered inside and Usha watched the plaster dust curl into the light and spiral up the staircase.

'Whatever are you doing hiding in here? I thought you two were at the library!'

Usha crawled out first. 'We were, but we wanted to have another look at the tandem and the door closed behind us.'

Imtiaz climbed out, brushing the dust from her face.

'You two look like ghosts!' Lem joked. 'Go and clean yourself up and get some fresh air. While you were out, I set up the tent for you to camp out tonight. We'll bring you up some pizzas later. How does that sound?'

'Great! Thanks!' they chorused, racing upstairs. Usha headed straight over to Kali Ma and breathing a sigh of relief to see her propped up on her pillows, took the photo out of her pocket to show her while Imtiaz grabbed the conch.

'I'm going out to the tent with Lucky. Ask your Kali Ma to come too. Bring her Promise Book, the photos. We've got to piece together everything we know.'

Out on the top deck, Imtiaz crawled into the tent, which had been decked out in brightly coloured cushions and a patchwork quilt. Lucky sat opposite her cross-legged. Imtiaz nodded as Lucky pointed to the woman next to her. 'Are you the Mina that Gladys talked about?' Imtiaz asked. The woman smiled and inclined her head as Lucky's two other friends settled around the edges of the tent as if they were witnesses to the unfolding story.

Imtiaz locked eyes with Lucky as she listened to the

conch. There was no doubt about it – through the surge and surf of waves and Lucky's sweet lullaby, her voice was becoming clearer and growing in strength.

> *Your belief in me sets my voice free*
> *Promise to piece me together*
> *Or my story's lost for ever*
> *To find peace in this house*
> *Sew my patchwork*
> *Of forgotten promises*
> *Pomegranate pieces*
> *Bargains broken*
> *Secrets unspoken*
> *Free my story*
> *To free this house*
> *Save my memory*
> *Set my spirit free*

Breath held, Imtiaz listened close through the whispering waves. *Please let there be more . . .* she willed.

> *Find my Kalighat art*
> *To open hearts*

Just two lines, before looping back to Lucky's lilting lullaby.

As Usha opened the tent-flap, Imtiaz gasped at the sight of the ayahs who had been sitting downstairs with Tanvi, crowding around them.

'What's the matter?' Usha asked.

'All the other ayahs are here too.' Imtiaz sighed. 'Standing around the tent like guards. Is Kali Ma with you?' Usha nodded and Imtiaz quickly closed the tent-flap.

'Anything new in the conch?' Usha asked.

'Just two lines – find my Kalighat art, to open hearts.'

Kali Ma clapped her hands. 'Well, we were going there anyway, weren't we, for my swan-song!' Usha looked blank. 'My grand finale outing?' Kali Ma said. 'The Victoria and Albert – that's where the Kalighat art is. It's my favourite gallery. I took you once, remember?'

Usha shook her head.

'Share, please!' Imtiaz said, scowling.

'Kali Ma knows where the Kalighat art is. It's at the Victoria and Albert Museum. She's going to show us. Mum asked what we wanted to do tomorrow so . . .'

Imtiaz sucked her breath in. 'Good. OK. Lucky's happy too. I thought we didn't have much more to go on, but we'll see.' Imtiaz nodded to Usha. 'Let's do this.'

'Kali Ma! We need you to look at what we've found out and then tell us everything you know.' Turning to Imtiaz, Usha explained, 'I told her a bit when she was waking up just now. She's shocked though – she just can't understand why her mum didn't tell her about the ayahs when she heard Lucky in the conch or why she would give away the evidence that they lived here?'

Imtiaz shook her head as she laid out everything they'd

164

found. 'It feels really crowded here,' she said, as the ayahs on the outside of the tent leant in closer to listen, their shadows and the swaying grasses looming large through the canvas.

Imtiaz reached into her pocket and took out the phone.

'If I record this like we recorded Gladys's story, we can play it all back as many times as we want. We might miss something if we don't.'

Usha nodded slowly.

'Just make sure Kali Ma tells you everything!' Imtiaz checked herself. 'Sorry! I don't mean to be bossy, we just can't mess around. You heard what your mum and dad said about time running out.' Imtiaz picked up the photo of the children by the barge. 'Ask her about this first, because we need to take them back tomorrow. They belong to that boy Cosmo.'

'What do you want me to ask her?'

'It's not what *I* want, is it?' Imtiaz snapped, her eyes flitting around the tent of ayah ghosts. She wiped the sweat from her forehead. 'Sorry, I'm feeling a bit pressured here. At least you've only got one ghost, of someone you actually know, to deal with. Just ask your Kali Ma to talk – anything and everything that comes into her head and then we might be able to work out what Lucky's got to do with your great-grandmother.'

Usha hesitated. Imtiaz supposed that for someone who usually spoke so little, this must be a big ask. 'We can take it slow,' Imtiaz said encouragingly as she pressed record.

'OK . . . Well Kali Ma recognises the photo by the barge . . . It's where she and Pops Michael went once to get their tandem fixed but she says the old woman who sat on the deckchair scared her with all her questions.'

'These people could be Cosmo's ancestors. We've got to find out where his barge is. Charles might know. What else?' Imtiaz nudged.

Usha picked up the photo of the tandem and listened to her Kali Ma. 'She's a bit emotional talking about how Pops Michael was bullied at school because of wearing his beaten-up old satchel.' Usha peered at the photo. 'Look, he's got it strapped across him because he used to get it pulled off his back . . . Now she's going off on one a bit about their school days, how tough it was . . . something about rivers of blood and a refugee crisis where a lot of people came from Kenya . . . She says there was a lot of racism, so she and Michael looked out for each other. She remembers there was a politician whipping up hatred. She saw him on TV round at Michael's and his mum said, "That man has hate in his eyes, but we'll show him . . . rivers of love are stronger than rivers of blood." It still didn't stop the racist bullies at school, though.'

Rage-heat rose from Imtiaz's belly. 'Shame on them. Delyse said that too, about growing up. That's why she's so angry. She said she never thought she'd be treated that way again.' For a moment, Imtiaz felt as if she was confiding in Kali Ma directly.

'How long did she see Lucky for after Dr Sara took the conch away?' Imtiaz asked, and, pausing to listen, Usha answered, her voice fusing to sound like Kali Ma's.

'A little while, maybe six months. She would appear sometimes, pleading for me to follow her out on to the streets, to train stations, along the canals, even to the Victoria and Albert Museum. Now I think of it, it was Lucky who introduced me to the Kalighat Collection.'

'That's definitely where we'll go tomorrow,' Imtiaz exclaimed, picking up the Promise Book. 'Ask your Kali Ma if her mum knows about any of this?'

Usha only had to raise the question in her eyes to prompt an answer. 'No. I never wanted her to. When Tanvi was born, I decided not to tell her what I'd been through. She was always such a confident little soul. I didn't want another haunting. So perhaps Lucky skipped a generation. Maybe it takes an outsider to see what's happening.'

'Thanks!' Imtiaz bristled at the word 'outsider'.

'It's not me saying all this!' Usha reminded her.

But it had soured Imtiaz's mood because for a moment she had felt right at the heart of the family's story, as if it belonged to her too.

They fell silent and Usha's voice lowered to a soft whisper. 'Kali Ma says she feels a bit lighter in spirit now.'

'Good for her! I don't and nor does Lucky.' Imtiaz's jaw

clenched. 'Talk in her voice. I like it better when you talk in her voice.'

Usha felt the bite of Imtiaz's resentment but carried on anyway as she picked up the photo of Kali Ma and Michael by the barge. 'She wants to talk about this!'

'What's stopping her then?' Imtiaz jabbed.

'This brings back some memories. That was the thing about Michael and me, we always accepted each other's quirks. Even though he couldn't see Lucky, he used to ask after her!'

Usha wiped her eyes, feeling Kali Ma's emotion. 'She says we now know more about Lucky and the ayahs than she did. Kali Ma wants to be set free too and she's truly sorry for not trying harder to help Lucky because now she knows what it feels like to be trapped . . . coming?'

Imtiaz followed Usha, who was now crawling out of the tent after Kali Ma. The wind lifted suddenly, buffeting the canvas sides, as Imtiaz emerged to find that the listening ayahs had slipped away. Standing, she felt as if she was dream-walking as she watched Lucky, Mina and her friends join hands and begin to twirl around in a slow, rhythmic dance. The top deck swirled with white rose petals drifting over the balcony edge and floating on airstreams along the road and out across the city.

Lem brought the pizzas up and the girls ate hungrily, afternoon slipping seamlessly into evening as they lounged on their beds, sail screens flung open, listening to the recordings they'd made of Gladys and Kali Ma.

'So weird to hear ourselves speaking other people's stories,' Usha commented. But Imtiaz found the strangest was to feel Lucky's voice fuse with her own as she recorded all she heard in the conch, ending by humming the lullaby. When she'd finished she looped the recording to memorise Lucky's chant.

'You've got a good voice,' Usha said, yawning.

'Thanks!' Imtiaz yawned too. 'Is Kali Ma listening?'

Usha turned to her side and shook her head. 'No. She's snoring in my ear!'

'Delyse said I snore, am I loud?'

'Not as loud as Kali Ma.' Usha smiled. 'But the two of you together do rattle the place!' Imtiaz giggled.

Tanvi's footsteps clicked on the staircase, drawing nearer.

As the door handle turned, Imtiaz fumbled around to stop the recording.

Crossing the room, Tanvi planted a kiss on Usha's forehead and walked over to the Globe Window to close the latch, but stood with her hands against the glass and stared into the garden.

'What is it, Mum?' Usha asked.

'Nothing. Thought I saw Spirit out there for a moment, but it was probably just a reflection,' she said, looking up at the sky. 'I'm sure she's back home safe, wherever she came from.'

Usha and Imtiaz exchanged a glance.

'It's a beautiful starry night. Why don't you get set up properly for an all-night sleep-out some time this week? Lem's right. It's a bit too windy tonight.' Tanvi headed over to Imtiaz, smoothing over her covers.

'So, have you and Usha discussed where you want to go tomorrow for our family outing?'

'We thought the Victoria and Albert Museum? Usha's told me about Kali Ma. How it was one of her favourite places,' she added.

Tanvi looked over to Usha and smiled. *Do I want her to kiss me goodnight? No! Not yet* . . . Tanvi hovered over Imtiaz for a second but, sensing her discomfort, stepped away. 'The museum idea's so thoughtful,' she whispered, closing Imtiaz's sail screen.

'Sleep tight, girls.'

'Night!' they echoed.

Porcelain Dance

Usha woke to the sun blasting through the Globe Window. Kali Ma was already sitting waiting, her hair coiled in an elegant swirl.

'It won't be open yet, Kali Ma,' Usha said out loud.

'Lucky's standing by the door too. She can't wait for us to get going,' Imtiaz told Usha, quickly brushing her teeth.

When they had both dressed, Imtiaz stashed the photos from the library in her pocket.

They were downstairs by nine o'clock. Breakfast eaten and ready to go. Mina and Lucky's other friends had followed them down and settled around The Hearth table beside Nilam, as if readying themselves to help.

'Come on then, culture vultures!' Lem laughed as he swigged his coffee. 'I was thinking more Brighton Pier than V&A, but anyway!'

As they passed the library, Imtiaz looked meaningfully at Usha.

'I've just got to collect my computer card,' Imtiaz made her excuse as planned. 'Won't be a minute!' Lucky stepped inside with her.

Glancing around, relieved not to see anyone, she slipped straight through to the computer room and nearly jumped out of her skin when she found Cosmo and Charles sitting at the screens.

'Morning, Imtiaz! Can I help?' Charles enquired.

'No, it's all right! I was going to email someone. I'll come back later . . .' Imtiaz's voice trailed away. Cosmo looked past Imtiaz and stared straight into Lucky's eyes.

'Well, we won't be too long now, will we, Cosmo? I was telling the girls that you'll start secondary together after the summer.'

Cosmo nodded.

Imtiaz hid the photos behind her and backed away. If she could get to the desk by the display boards, she could drop the photos and leave.

'You two hurried off the other day before I could thank you for your sorting. You made a good start. Oh, and I meant to call and ask – Cosmo here donated a photo that belonged to his grandma. It appears to have gone astray.' Imtiaz had already let the photos slip from her hands and out of the corner of her eye saw them waft under the display boards.

'The thing is, I didn't tell my gran I was taking it,' Cosmo said, quickly standing up and walking behind Imtiaz, glancing to where the photos had fallen.

'What a coincidence! It appears to have appeared again. Here they are on the floor!' Cosmo exclaimed, lightly mocking Charles's voice as he picked up one photo and seemed to be genuinely taken aback to find the other. Looking from his grandmother's name to Imtiaz in confusion, he put the second quickly in his pocket.

Imtiaz blushed, caught out in her lie.

'That's strange. I thought I'd scoured the place!' Charles said, frowning but nodding reassuringly at Cosmo. 'I told you it would show up.'

Cosmo raised his eyebrows at Imtiaz. 'At least I don't have to tell my grandma that *it's* lost.' Cosmo smiled, his eyes sparking with humour, glancing from Lucky to Imtiaz. 'Yeah! Well. Gotta go!' she said as she rushed out. Lucky hung in the doorway, looking at Cosmo as if she would have liked to spend more time with him. As Imtiaz gestured for Lucky to hurry she joined her palms together and inclined her head in Cosmo's direction by way of goodbye.

'Great to see you making friends already.' Tanvi smiled in Cosmo's direction, where he stood waving to Lucky. 'Aren't you going to wave back?' *I can't exactly tell her that he's waving at a ghost*, Imtiaz thought and half-heartedly raised her hand in the air so as not to look unfriendly.

'Ridley Road Market's been here for well over a hundred and fifty years. They've changed the fruit and veg, though!' Lem joked as they meandered between stalls on their way to catch the train.

Usha groaned. 'Imtiaz doesn't want a tour guide, Dad!'

'Not what I heard! A little bird told me you're interested in the history of the area!'

Imtiaz nodded and Lem pulled a 'told you so' face at Usha.

Lucky paused at a fruit stall and refused to move on. Pointing to a pile of pomegranates, she reached towards the display as if begging Imtiaz to take one.

'I can't, Lucky! I nearly got caught once today. People will think I'm a thief,' she whispered as they approached the station.

·················

'It must be years since I've been here,' Lem mused as they passed through the colonnades into a huge courtyard, pausing to read a plaque on an original stone wall. 'Says they've kept the damage from World War Two, so people don't forget.'

But Lucky hurried on and was already pulling Imtiaz up the steps into a huge entrance room with a vast white floor.

'I thought we were coming here because of your Kali Ma, but Lucky's desperate to see the place too,' Imtiaz whispered in Usha's ear. 'How's your Kali Ma behaving?'

'Looks like she's here on a day trip. Tired but pretty relaxed.' Usha leant in to Imtiaz. 'She says she's on home turf!'

'A sea of porcelain,' Tanvi uttered as she paused to admire the wide stretch of tiles but Imtiaz was already heading into the centre of the vast room, where Lucky now twirled around and around, as if she heard music playing.

'If only you could see Lucky dancing now,' Imtiaz said

174

when Usha had made her way through a huddle of tourists to join her. 'She reminds me of the pictures in the Promise Book.'

'How . . .' But Usha's question hung in the air as a little girl, letting go of her dad's hand, took a running skid into the middle of the room, and began to dance with Lucky. Watching their daughter, her parents laughed, applauding as they captured the moment on their phone. They did not see Lucky take a low bow and place her hand over her heart as she watched the child run off.

Imtiaz peered at all the people around her, busying themselves deciding which galleries they would visit. Suddenly it felt as if she was walking through a secret, invisible portal she had never even known existed. It was as though Lucky was charged with the energy of the art, culture, colours and patterns of the building, as if being here among these people from all over the world was bringing her to life.

Usha nudged Imtiaz. 'What are you thinking?'

'Tell you later!' Imtiaz grinned at Usha and beckoned her over, pointing to the sign for the South Asia Gallery.

'This is where Kali Ma's taking us,' Usha explained.

'You girls want to explore on your own and come back and meet at the café in an hour?' Lem asked. 'Is your phone charged?'

Imtiaz nodded, feeling for it in her pocket.

'OK, see you later,' they called to Lem and Tanvi and waited till they were out of sight, then entered the gallery in the old part of the building. Lucky sat on a bench to admire the beautiful patterns on the vaulted ceiling.

'Where's your Kali Ma now?' Imtiaz asked and Usha indicated the same bench that Lucky was taking a rest on.

'Then they're sitting together!'

Usha laughed. 'Kali Ma's giving us a specialist tour.'

'Hang on!' Imtiaz whipped the phone out and pressed record. 'We don't want to miss anything. Just talk into here,' she ordered, holding it close to Usha's mouth.

'You see now where I got my inspiration for my prints. I love the simplicity of line, lack of fuss.' Usha's hands batted the air back and forth in an over the top gesture so unlike her that it made Imtiaz laugh . . . but it seemed like Usha was being given no time to draw breath. 'Brings back such lovely memories of our honeymoon in Kolkata. I remember it like it was yesterday when Michael bought a little book of postcard paintings for me, just like these.

'What's that?' Imtiaz interrupted.

'A ghat? A little jetty by the river. Michael joked that it was "coals to Newcastle!" them selling a Kalighat painting to Kali on a ghat! So you see why I always think of this as my gallery.' Usha pushed the phone away, grinning. 'She's loving this!'

'Lucky isn't. She looks miserable.' Imtiaz sighed. 'Where's this all taking us?'

Usha shrugged and raised her arm in the air, pointing to where Kali Ma had broken off to admire a painting.

'You said Lucky spoke about Kalighat art in the conch and Kali Ma did say it was Lucky who brought her here for the first time. So I suppose we have to be patient. If we follow where she goes maybe . . .'

Usha tracked across to the opposite side of the gallery and Imtiaz reluctantly followed.

'I do actually like this art,' Imtiaz said, inspecting the paintings closer. 'It's good how they're not too posh, of ordinary people and things. The way they're just done on paper. I could have a go at painting something like these!

'But I wonder why so many of them say "artist unknown"?' Usha listened for a moment then reported back. 'Kali Ma's saying that it's because they were often made by amateur artists to sell to the British or other tourists at a profit. Kali Ma thinks you should keep up with your drawing Imtiaz, apparently you've got a good eye for the line. She saw your drawing of the conch on The Hearth wall.'

'Tell her thanks!' Imtiaz smiled, feeling a warm glow inside.

'Kali Ma says that's all she can help us with. She's off to see the textiles now,' Usha announced when they reached the far end of the gallery.

Imtiaz shook her head. 'I'm staying here with Lucky. She's back-tracked to the beginning of the postcard paintings. She wants to stay here, so . . .'

Usha nodded. 'I'll meet you here in twenty minutes then.'

Without distractions now, Imtiaz followed Lucky's every move as she progressed through the gallery and finally came to a standstill. Suddenly the expression on Lucky's face turned to thunder as she crossed over the security rope and reached up to a painting as if about to grab it off the wall.

At the sight of her distress, Imtiaz's mind filled with Lucky's conch voice that now echoed through her louder and louder.

Your belief in me sets my voice free! Lucky's words blasted her brain as she jumped over the rope to where Lucky's trembling fingers pointed at the painting. It was a close-up of an Indian woman in a white sari, the ends of a veil covering her hair. To one side of her was a white swan and on the other a little girl whose hand she held. In the child's right hand was clasped a giant ruby-pink pomegranate fruit, just like the one embroidered on Lucky's sari piece.

'Is this yours, Lucky?'

Lucky nodded. Her eyes were wide and pleading as Imtiaz read the information on the wall.

The symbolism in this painting represents Saraswati, goddess of knowledge, art, wisdom, and nature. The pomegranate she holds is commonly understood to be the fruit of love. Found during renovations of Wilmington Manor Care Home, Hertfordshire. Gifted to the V&A. Artist unknown.

Lucky's face contorted into a silent howl so upsetting that Imtiaz's reaction was to reach up to touch the painting, as if that could comfort her.

'Did you paint this? Is this yours?' Imtiaz asked, as she spotted the initials L.R. in tiny letters in the bottom left-hand corner.

Lucky nodded sadly.

Imtiaz was filled with a deep well of sadness too, as she remembered Gladys's description of Lucky facing up to the matron. 'You weren't always silent, were you, Lucky? I'll fight for you, don't worry. I won't give up. We'll go to this Wilmington Manor place and find out what happened to you, I promise.'

'Stand back!' A security guard warned, looming over Imtiaz, taking her by the arm he guided her over the rope.

'That painting belongs to someone I know. I was just looking,' Imtiaz protested, shrugging off the guard's hold.

A woman in a smart navy-blue suit and with short white hair who had been chatting to the security guard strode on over. 'Thank you, Lovik, I'll take it from here,' she said. 'Young lady, your behaviour is most irregular, but if you're making inquiries into the provenance, you're in luck; I'm the one you need to speak to. Follow me.'

Imtiaz nodded, even though she hadn't a clue what the woman was on about. But Lucky walked by her side and her growing calm stilled Imtiaz's nerves a little.

Stepping into the hallway on her way back to the first gallery, Usha was just in time to see Imtiaz being led through a small oak door with a stained glass window. She peered closer, thinking she must be mistaken, but then confirmed that the design on a background of sea-green, blue and turquoise glass was of a flesh-coloured conch shell. Through the glass she could just make out the shape of Imtiaz's short, bobbed hair.

Usha pointed to the door. 'Imtiaz is in trouble, Kali Ma!'

'Maybe not. That girl can handle herself.' Kali Ma folded her arms, sat on a bench and waited. 'The funny thing about Imtiaz is, she reminds me a bit of me! Not just the snoring, either. She's a fiery little soul.' Kali Ma yawned and winced as she held her hand against her heart.

'You feeling OK, Kali Ma?'

She nodded but her voice grew weaker with every word. 'How's a ghost supposed to feel? It's been a wonderful day, Myush, but I'm definitely here on borrowed time.'

Dr Devi

'Do you have anyone you would like to contact?' the woman asked, offering Imtiaz a seat at her large glass desk that also served as a display cabinet. Lucky hovered over it, peering at the exhibits as if searching for something.

'Er! Not really.' Imtiaz shook her head, reading the woman's name badge.

Dr Devi
Conservator (Kalighat Collection Specialist)
South Asia Gallery

'Now, you know my name, so what's yours?' Dr Devi asked gently.

'Imtiaz,' she mumbled, following Lucky's tour around the tiny room. Its walls were painted in deep blue and covered in hundreds of mounted prints of the Kalighat paintings.

Dr Devi leant forward, clasping her hands together. 'I

181

won't lie, Imtiaz, it's of interest to me that you claim to know the owner of one of these paintings.' Dr Devi leant forward.

Sitting in this room, with the stained-glass-conch-panelled door, facing Dr Devi, Imtiaz felt as if this was the moment. She was definitely on the cusp of finding something here. Of all the people who would know about the painting and how it got here, this Dr Devi would. *Say something that will get her to talk, even if it* is *made up as I go along,* she coached herself.

'A relation of mine used to paint those and when I saw it said Wilmington Manor I was like, shocked, because she lived there once. She was an ayah, an Indian nursemaid.' As Imtiaz let the story flow she studied Dr Devi's face and beside her she felt Lucky relax.

Dr Devi's eyes shone with excitement, as if she'd been gifted a present. 'How fascinating, because it's so hard to trace the original artists of these precious little paintings. It's been my life's work, really.' Scanning around, Dr Devi located the print of Lucky's art on her wall. 'They do vary in quality but I've always thought this one is particularly accomplished. Something in the expression of the ayah's eyes always makes me feel like she's following me around, Mona Lisa-like.' She chuckled. 'But perhaps I've spent too long in these galleries. Sometimes when it's quiet, I imagine Queen Victoria herself wandering around the place!' Imtiaz smiled at Lucky. *What would you do, Dr Devi, if you could see the ghost at your shoulder?*

'Unusual subject too, for Kalighat art. This seems to be a

self-portrait. Interesting story about the ayahs, you should look into it. I've written a few books on the subject. What was her name, this relation of yours?'

'Lucky,' Imtiaz said. 'I don't know her surname, though. I know a bit about ayahs because I've moved into the house.'

Unable to contain her enthusiasm, Dr Devi clapped her hands. 'Number twenty-six or number four?'

Imtiaz held up four fingers.

'Curiouser and curiouser!' Dr Devi nodded. 'You know, Lucky was possibly her ayah name so the L might not be her initial. Tell you what – I'll dig around and do a bit more research myself. If you find out anything else, be sure to let me know, and vice versa!' Dr Devi said, handing Imtiaz her card.

'I will. Thank you.' Imtiaz was about to stand up, but Lucky shook her head as if she had unfinished business here. 'I was wondering, when the people from the care home gave the painting to you, did they say anything about the artist?' Imtiaz hesitated, feeling as if she was walking in the dark.

'Well, every submission comes with documentation, but I'm afraid that's private archive material . . .' Dr Devi glanced behind her at a cabinet of thin wooden drawers.

'But if it's my family . . . you can't just take—'

Dr Devi raised her hand. 'I know, it's all very complicated, this business of what belongs to whom, but it's a tangled old web and I've spent a great deal of time trying to untangle it. Now! I'm sorry . . .' Dr Devi paused. 'Imtiaz. I have to get on. Let's take from this the lesson not to step over the red rope again.' She winked. 'But between you and me, I'm rather glad you did!'

I can't leave now. How can I get her to talk? Imtiaz racked her brains for an answer. She'd already done what Delyse would call 'pushing this woman's buttons', but maybe she could still find out more. Lucky nodded her encouragement. It was worth a try. Imtiaz reached for her phone, placed it on the desk and selected the conch recording she'd made last night. 'This is from a book of hers we found,' she lied and pressed play before Dr Devi could stop her.

Your belief in me sets my voice free
Promise to piece me together
Or my story's lost for ever
To find peace in this house
Sew my patchwork
Of forgotten promises
Pomegranate pieces
Bargains broken
Secrets unspoken
Free my story
To free this house
Save my memory
Set my spirit free
Find my Kalighat art
To open hearts

Dr Devi's brow began to unfurrow as she listened. 'Extraordinary! Fascinating!'

Imtiaz nodded, adding, 'We found Lucky's book after our grandma died. There's art too.' Now that she was in the swing of it, the lies knotted together easily.

Dr Devi breathed in deep at the mention of art and sat back down. 'You can buy a postcard of Lucky's painting in the museum shop but I think you should have this one for free.' She took one out of her desk drawer and handed it to Imtiaz. 'This business of reparation has been much on my mind. I've written about the subject but no one's actually asked me for something back. I can't give you the painting, but there is something that came with it.' Dr Devi tapped the table in concentration. 'I remember filing it away myself because it arrived in such a neat material package – an embroidered handkerchief – and I wondered who'd sewn it. Now, let me see . . .' She turned around and started leafing through a drawer. 'Apparently a builder found it shoved between bricks in a wall they were plastering. I argued for it to be exhibited alongside the painting, because of the pomegranates in both, but I was a junior then. Ah! Here it is! Hasn't seen the light of day for years!' Dr Devi pulled out a square of material from the drawer, wafting her hands to disperse the dust through which emerged the second of Lucky's sari pieces. Imtiaz gasped as Lucky turned to her. Holding her palms together in thanks, she straightened her shoulders, seeming to grow taller.

Dr Devi ran her fingers over the embroidery letters of Lucky's name. 'I wonder what story's stitched into this?' She sighed. 'There's so little documentation of these women's lives! I was right to want this seen. The next time you come here, I'll have this handkerchief displayed next to the painting and it will be credited to your great-grandmother Lucky. How about that?'

'Thank you,' Imtiaz said, struggling not to sound too disappointed.

Dr Devi ran her fingers over the pomegranate fruit. 'This was obviously her tag!'

At that moment Lucky fanned out the folds of her sari and Imtiaz saw the exact place it had been cut out from.

'One little request! If you do come back, I would love to see the book you spoke of.'

Imtiaz stared at Dr Devi, sizing her up. *It's all I've got left.* 'You give me the handkerchief that no one else even knows about and I'll bring you the Promise Book and anything else we find.'

Dr Devi leant over the table towards Imtiaz, her eyebrows raised in amusement. 'Are you striking a bargain with me? I can't just go giving away precious arti—'

'Here's proof!' Imtiaz said, laying the first sari piece on the table. 'And if that's not enough, guess where I found it!' She pointed to the stained glass door. 'In a conch shell!' Imtiaz squared her shoulders and waited.

For a moment Dr Devi seemed lost for words, then she

leant across the table and whispered, 'And you promise you'll come back and tell me what you find? This has to be our secret . . .' Dr Devi raised her finger to her lips, unaware that by her side Lucky's gesture echoed her own.

'I promise.' Imtiaz met Dr Devi's eye as she placed the sari piece flat in Imtiaz's hand. Pausing, palm against palm, it felt to Imtiaz like she and Dr Devi were sealing a contract.

Detour – Elizabeth Garrett Anderson Hospital

Imtiaz came out of the conch room charged to talk, showing Usha a postcard of what she was convinced was a self-portrait of Lucky and desperate to get Usha on her own to tell her all that she had discovered behind Dr Devi's conch-panelled door. As they walked through the park, Lucky stared up at the statue of Queen Victoria and Imtiaz slipped the two sari pieces from her breast pocket. Glancing up, Imtiaz had the feeling that Queen Victoria was witness. 'I wonder if she knew about you ayahs,' Imtiaz mused. Lucky shrugged and turned away from the stern expression on the statue's face as a flock of pigeons came to settle on the queen's shoulders.

Lem hurried ahead, taking phone calls every few minutes. Now Tanvi hung back, waiting for them and began to chatter on.

'Lem's got to have a meeting. Councillor Puttock's coming

over to chat things through. I think it's best if we keep out of the way. We could pop in on Charles at the library? He said you've been helping him out with his exhibition. Anyway, hope you enjoyed our first outing?' Imtiaz was about to answer but Tanvi gabbled on not waiting for a response. 'Maybe one day we'll save up to go to India and to see Delyse and Merve in St Lucia . . . Sure we'll have lots of adventures together!'

Imtiaz smiled at the thought of epic journeys like that – the furthest she'd been was Euro Disney.

'I bought this,' Imtiaz said. 'I might send it to Delyse,' she added, handing Tanvi the postcard.

'Kalighat art! Ma's favourite!' Tanvi smiled, peering closer. 'The little girl reminds me a bit of my grandma Sara when she was little. I've got a photo of her somewhere. When everything's settled down I'll see if I can find it. It's in one of the albums.'

'Dr Sara – the one with the plaque above your door?' Imtiaz asked.

Tanvi nodded, raising her eyebrows as if surprised by Imtiaz's interest. 'I tell you what, instead of going to the library . . . let me take you to see something special. We've got some time on our hands and it's a lovely day so we can walk. It'll take just under an hour!' Tanvi said, checking her phone app. 'And it's a scenic route.'

'Where?' Usha asked.

'You'll see!' Tanvi smiled. 'I'd almost forgotten, Kali Ma took me when I was your age, wondering what I'd be when

I grew up . . . I think she half-hoped I might become a doctor too one day! I should have taken you before, Usha.'

Tanvi linked arms with Usha on one side and Imtiaz on the other, oblivious to Kali Ma and Lucky's presence.

———

'Mum! You sure you want to go?' Usha asked Tanvi who yawned for the third time as they ate their sandwiches and watched a juggler balancing on a low tightrope in the Covent Garden Piazza.

'Yes! Sorry, girls, I didn't get much sleep last night. I had the strangest dreams. I was sitting on the driftwood bench talking to a doll I lost when I was little. It was a miniature of a woman dressed in one of Kali Ma's designs that she brought back from a trip to India. Silly really but I used to imagine she was trying to talk to me. Well, last night I dreamed the driftwood bench floated out on to water and I looked over the balcony and saw the doll in a tiny boat waving to me.' Tanvi shook her head. 'Dreams are so random, aren't they?'

'Just a bit,' Imtiaz agreed, turning to Lucky, who nodded in agreement as they walked down the road. *So Lucky did try to get through to Tanvi when she was young too. Poor Lucky, trapped in that house for so long, desperate to find a way to get each generation of children to listen to her.*

'Mum, do you know anything about ayahs . . . ? They were like old-fashioned nannies who used to live on the street?' Usha tested.

Tanvi scowled and shook her head as she tilted her phone to

find her bearings. 'No, but I *can* tell you something about how our family came by our house and The Hearth, generations back. You've noticed the plaques above mine and Lem's doors.'

Imtiaz nodded.

'Well, Dr Sara was my grandmother and she's the one who bought our house. Who knows, maybe this detour to see her will bring us luck. I hope so because my feet are killing me. It's a bit further than I thought,' Tanvi admitted as they finally arrived at the Euston Road.

'We saw all these photos of old streets at the library. I wonder what this looked like in olden times? ' Usha said, imagining that they had faded into one of the black and white pictures. It felt to Usha as if they could easily bump into Dr Sara.

'Here we are, what used to be the Elizabeth Garrett Anderson Hospital. This has always been a place of girl power!'

'Mum!' Usha groaned. 'Don't go on about your feminist stuff now!'

Tanvi laughed and squeezed Usha's arm. 'We come from generations of women who will not be silenced, Usha Joseph, and I'm not about to start now! This was the first hospital to train and champion women doctors, including your great-grandma. Be proud!'

Usha raised her eyes to the sky and Imtiaz stifled a giggle. As they walked up the steps of the museum dedicated to the old hospital, Tanvi mused. 'I've been thinking recently how unusual it must have been for Sara to have had the money to buy her own house.'

Once inside the hallway, Tanvi pointed up to the marbled walls covered in long wooden panels, with golden names and dates inscribed on them.

Imtiaz followed Lucky's gaze, scanning down the rows. 2000s, 1990s, 1980s, 1970s, 1960s . . . Following Lucky's gaze upwards, Imtiaz spotted a name partly covered by a red velvet curtain. Peering behind it and straining her neck, she read the name, 'Dr Saraswati Wilmington, 1959.'

'That's her.' Tanvi placed her hand over her chest and breathed deep, tears clouding her eyes. 'Sorry, girls. Sleepless nights have taken their toll! I think I'll take a pew. Excuse me a minute.' Tanvi sat down on a bench opposite the plaque. 'Why don't you two go over and look in that cabinet?' Tanvi suggested, pointing to the far wall beyond the plaques. 'From what I remember, there were a few bits and pieces about her in there too.'

Usha smiled to see Kali Ma sit next to Tanvi, mother and daughter together. Kali Ma wore a look of deep concern on her face.

'Wilmington!' Imtiaz whispered to Lucky. 'That surname's the same as the manor house where they found Lucky's painting.'

Lucky nodded and sped ahead to the cabinet. Imtiaz's chest tightened, feeling Lucky's desperation as, nose to the glass, she stared at a collection of trophies and objects inside. Imtiaz's eye was caught by a photograph of a wedding day. The bride's head was thrown back, laughing through a cloud of rose petal confetti. Alongside it was a fading, yellowing newspaper clipping.

20th June, 1959
Dr Saraswati Wilmington and Dr Parvinder Gopal of Calcutta, India, were married at Hackney Town Hall, followed by a reception given by the Elizabeth Garrett Anderson Hospital, where Dr Wilmington was one of the first Asian women doctors to qualify. The couple plan to work as National Health Service GPs serving the East End of London, if a practice can be found.

Tanvi came up behind them, placing her arms around both girls' shoulders. 'Sorry about that! All a bit nostalgic today, remembering coming here with Ma.' Tanvi smiled as the girls and their ghosts parted to let her look into the cabinet. 'I know all this probably feels like ancient history to you.' Kali Ma pushed her way to the front to see and Imtiaz noticed that Lucky looked as emotional as Tanvi as she stared at the newspaper clipping.

'Yes, Ma always said she was a bit of a mystery woman, my grandma Saraswati.'

'Why didn't I know she was Indian?' Usha scowled.

Tanvi raised her eyebrows in surprise. 'Didn't you?'

'But I thought her name was Sara?' Imtiaz frowned and as she did, Gladys's voice filled her mind. Imtiaz felt a tangle of disconnected wires fuse in her mind and spark. Lucky's painting was something to do with the goddess Saraswati. What was the name of the baby Gladys said Lucky looked after? It wasn't Saraswati. Now Imtiaz was desperate to hear the recordings again and see if there was anything they'd missed.

Tanvi shrugged. 'People probably found her full name too difficult to pronounce. Sara Swati!'

Swati! That was it! Not that *difficult*, Imtiaz thought, peering into the picture. 'That's an Indian name, isn't it? She doesn't look it?'

'She was fair-skinned, from the photos we have of her.' Tanvi explained.

There was not much conversation as they travelled on the Tube towards home, both girls, their ghosts and Tanvi following their own thought-tracks.

Once they were alone on the top deck, Usha and Imtiaz settled themselves on the driftwood bench with the conch, Lucky's two sari squares and the Promise Book laid out on the decking between them. Lucky and Kali Ma stood by the rose balcony watching on as they began their ritual of conch listening.

Imtiaz was about to pick up the shell when Lucky shook her head and gestured for her, instead, to offer it to Usha. '*She* can't hear you, Lucky,' Imtiaz said. But Lucky insisted.

'She wants you to try!'

At first Usha heard nothing except the sway of the sea, but then, as if suddenly plugged into headphones, a woman's voice emerged. *Too close.* Usha shifted uncomfortably, momentarily pulling the conch from her ear.

Imtiaz grabbed Usha's arm as she watched her eyes widen in amazement. 'Say what you hear! Exactly what you can hear!' Imtiaz ordered. 'I know it off by heart.'

Imtiaz strode restlessly up and down the deck, speaking the words she'd memorised at the exact same time as Usha, like a chant. As their words flowed and swelled together the joint force of their voices sounded like they were making a vow, sealing a promise . . .

Your belief in me sets my voice free
Promise to piece me together
Or my story's lost for ever
To find peace in this house
Sew my patchwork
Of forgotten promises
Pomegranate pieces
Bargains broken
Secrets unspoken
Free my story
To free this house
Save my memory
Set my spirit free
Find my Kalighat art
To open hearts

Out of words, Imtiaz stopped but Usha carried on.

Turn the wheels of time
Where the waters meet
On the old barge track
That flows to the manor
Matron took my faith away
Restore me now
Please, I pray
To right a wrong
And write me in
Save my memory
Set my spirit free
To sail across the cosmos

'You hear her too!' Imtiaz laughed, tapping her third eye and grabbing the conch from Usha, who was too stunned to speak.

Lying in bed, their sail screens open, holding one fragile sari piece each, Usha replayed the recordings they'd made without interruption till they were done. 'That's all we've got so far,' Imtiaz sighed.

Usha stroked the fine embroidery and, feeling torn between Lucky and her Kali Ma, tears welled in her eyes. 'I'm sorry for Lucky but this is horrible for Kali Ma too. She's so weak now, but it feels like she's being held here till we find the last piece.'

'That's why we've got to go to this Wilmington Manor. The baby "Swati" that Gladys talked about was Saraswati, your great-grandma Sara. She was the one who denied that she heard Lucky in the conch even though it's pretty obvious Lucky was her ayah. Remember your mum said the girl in Lucky's postcard looked like her?'

'She did.' Usha nodded.

'What's Kali Ma doing now?' asked Imtiaz.

'Nothing. Just listening.'

'Go on, then, Usha. Let's put our heads together! Third eye time! You start.'

Usha paused as she collected her thoughts. 'I've been thinking about Dr Sara. Trying to work out why she was so complicated.'

'Just a bit, by the sound of it!'

'I think I know how she felt though. I mean, I hated what Gladys called her – "half-caste",' Usha said. 'I know it's probably what people said back then and Gladys didn't mean anything insulting but it got me thinking. When anyone asks me where I'm from and I want to say London, but I know what they really mean is where are my family from, so I say India and the Caribbean even though I haven't even been to either yet.'

'What?' Imtiaz laughed. 'Say your Basian British then! Don't take any notice. We're all just humans! Girls at my school thought I'm Bangladeshi. I don't know for sure . . . I *could* be. Delyse says if I want to, one day I can do a test to find out, but I don't really care now. Being brought up by Delyse, I feel more like her culture and Merve's and your dad's. But I get it's confusing . . . it does seem like Saraswati was covering up who she was.'

Usha mused, 'Gladys said Lucky went to live with Roma people on the canal; she even talked about the postcard art ayahs used to sell . . . Ask Lucky if she ever sold any of her Kalighat art.'

Lucky shook her head.

'No, she didn't . . . and what Lucky said in the conch . . . *Sail across the cosmos.* That must be a clue for Cosmo. We've got to get on with it now. You saw how your dad looked when we got back, like it was all hopeless. It's obvious the only hope we have of saving this house is finding Lucky's story. One thing I believe about her is she's not the sort of person to break a bargain. I trust her.'

Usha nodded, drying her eyes. 'It's just, I'm not tough like you.'

'I'm not. I just pretend I am,' Imtiaz admitted.

'What I don't understand is why it's up to us to sort out a promise made so long ago?' Usha mused. 'Shouldn't promises die with people – instead of being carried on and on, through history, like some kind of never-ending nightmare?'

'You're only saying that because you're thinking about your Kali Ma, but you heard for yourself how much Lucky needs her story told. How do you think your Kali Ma's still got a voice? You remember her and there's evidence about her life wherever you look, the same for your great-grandma too. Their history's out there, but Lucky and her ayah friends were almost forgotten. Nearly silenced for ever.' Imtiaz gasped as it dawned on her that if it wasn't for them the ayah's story could fade away completely. 'Remember how weak Lucky's voice in the conch was at first and now we can both hear her. Usha, we *have* to do this. Uncovering this story is bigger than us or even saving this house.' Imtiaz felt breathless as she lay on her back speaking into the dark, her chest burning with emotion.

'Are you all right? You sound upset.' Usha asked, propping herself up on her pillow.

Imtiaz shrugged and swallowed back her tears. 'I don't know. Maybe because all this is shaking things up for me. No one knows who my mum or dad were, or anything about my birth family. I've never thought about them that much before, but this has kind of made me.' Imtiaz sighed. 'It's just I *know* it's the right thing to do to help Lucky. If you think your Kali Ma's spirit should be set free, we can't let Lucky's be trapped for ever, can we? Things must have to be equal at least when you're dead?'

Usha smiled at the strangeness of their conversation. 'I'm not arguing. You're right,' Usha admitted. 'But how are we going to get to this manor house?'

'So annoying. If we had your mum's mapping app we could just look up the address and it would show us the way, *if* the place still exists.'

'We could creep downstairs, to The Hearth computer?' Usha suggested.

Imtiaz shook her head. 'We don't want your parents checking our search history and getting suspicious. No, let's go to the library first thing, then see if we can find out from Charles where the Bike Barge is and what Cosmo's got to do with this.'

Usha bit her lip. 'Or we could just come clean and tell Mum and Dad what's been going on and get them to take us to Wilmington Manor?'

Imtiaz checked with Lucky, who sat cross-legged on the floor, hands held together in prayer, shaking her head.

'We can't do that. You think they'll let us go anywhere if we tell them about our ghosts? They might even decide to split us up or something and . . .' Imtiaz paused. 'I wouldn't want that.'

'Me neither!' Usha answered, without a hint of hesitation.

In the darkness Imtiaz wiped her eyes with Lucky's sari square, Gladys's words scrolling through her mind. *Amar mishti bon. Is this what it feels like to have a sister?*

Helmets On

'Why are you wearing a suit?' Usha asked her dad as they backed the tandem out of the cupboard.

'Believe me, it's not through choice.' Lem cringed, loosening his tie a little. 'We've got a hearing at the council today. Nothing to worry about!'

'Dad,' Usha groaned, 'we both know *all* about it!'

'OK, well, just so you know, whatever the outcome, we'll face it together, as a family – OK?' Lem held the tandem as the girls climbed on. 'I was hoping to take you for a test drive around the park, but let's see how you go. Have a ride up and down the pavement. Helmets on! Who's going to be captain first, then?'

Usha stood back and let Imtiaz take the handlebars.

'Well, Delyse and me used to ride all over London on our bikes, so . . .' Imtiaz bit her lip as she concentrated hard.

After three faltering attempts, they finally managed to set off, veering this way and that, dangerously close to careering over the kerb on to the road, they came to a halt, laughing, just as a man in a smart suit came out of his door. As he stepped on to the pavement, he caught Imtiaz's eye. 'Fancy bumping into you again! The clue's in the name. This is a pavement and that is the road. It's illegal to—'

'Oh, why don't you just bog off?' Imtiaz shouted riding straight at Councillor Puttock so that he had to stand aside.

'Imtiaz, don't be rude,' Lem called. 'They're just practising on it, till they're safe.'

'And what about everyone else's safety?'

Lem ignored the councillor, gesturing for the girls to carry on.

'OK, I think you've got the hang of it, but not on the roads. Have a good blow-out in Victoria Park, over the Downs or London Fields . . . wherever you want.' He held his hand to his ear. 'Keep in touch!'

Dismounting and pushing the bike ahead of Lem, they overheard his conversation.

'I imagine, Mr Joseph, that we're walking in the same direction? We can at least tolerate each other. Care to walk together?'

'No, Mr Puttock, I would not. I have no interest in solely tolerating people. What I'll be arguing for today is honesty, trust, kindness and community spirit and a decent neighbour. Unless, of course, you can start walking in *that* direction . . . ?'

As they pushed the tandem down the road, Imtiaz and Usha felt bolstered by Lem's words.

'This is the first time we've been out on our own!' Usha whispered. 'Without our ghosts, I mean.'

They both looked back at the balcony.

'Your Kali Ma there?' Imtiaz whispered.

Usha nodded. 'Lucky?'

'And her friends! Like they're rooting for us,' Imtiaz said, peering up to where Lucky, Mina and the other ayahs, whose names she wished she knew, stood among the white roses.

Charles was just opening the library when they arrived on their fact-finding mission. He made a fuss about taking a photo of them on the tandem and, as they'd forgotten to bring a lock, insisted that they wheel it inside.

Sitting side by side at the computers, Imtiaz's and Usha's hands hovered above the keyboards as they typed in 'Wilmington Manor' at exactly the same time, bringing up identical screens.

Wilmington Manor, Hertfordshire. Was privately owned by a wealthy landowning family of the same name. Built in 1850 from wealth accrued through the Silk Route to India. From 1920–1945 the house was run as a small boarding school for girls. It was sold into private ownership in 1968 and in 1985 became Wilmington Manor Residential Care Home, run by Hertfordshire council.

'My Kali Ma has a book about the Silk Route,' Usha said.

'Forget about books now Usha! I was worried that

Wilmington Manor might have been demolished like that department store Charles was on about.' Imtiaz sighed with relief. 'But how are we going to get there?' Imtiaz clicked on 'distance finder' and typed in the postcode. 'It's not that far! According to this map, we could bike it in a day.'

'I'll ask Charles if we can use the printer,' Usha said.

'OK. Just don't let him see what you're doing,' Imtiaz warned.

When Usha had left the room, Imtiaz logged into her email and was surprised to find a photo of Delyse and Merve walking on a beach and a message.

Dear Immy,

In case you can't wait till the end of the month!

Here safe and sound. So happy to hear from Tanvi and Lem that you're getting on so well.

I'm taking a leaf out of your book and keeping this short and sweet.

Wishing you all the very, berry best!

Delyse

Imtiaz wiped her eyes. Even in that tiny note she could hear Delyse's voice. Her chest ached with the same raw pain she'd felt on the night they'd said goodbye. Delyse was right – they should try not to contact each other too often.

Dear Delyse,

You know me! I couldn't wait! But you broke your own rule first! I'll tell you about everything when we speak at the end of the month. But the main thing is I want to say thank you for not letting me shred my story book. I've changed my mind and I really want it back now. Please look after it for me.

By the way, I'm thinking about your dealing-with-things tips all the time and I know I used to get annoyed with you for going on a bit but the whale's-eye view thing's actually helping me and Usha to get on with each other (mostly), so thanks.

Hope you like your new life.

Immy

Does that last bit sound bitter and twisted? Imtiaz wondered and she was just about to delete and rewrite her last words when Charles appeared in the doorway. Flicking the keyboard by mistake, she heard the funnelling 'joom' as her email sent.

'Come on, Imtiaz. You two should get some fresh air on that stupendous tandem!'

'Yeah! Coming! I'm done now.' Imtiaz logged off and walked through to help Usha carry the tandem down the steps. Imtiaz paused on the way out. 'We were wondering if you had a card for the Bike Barge, you know, the one that boy Cosmo works on?' Charles raised his eyebrows. 'It's just that there might be something a bit off with the balance!'

Charles smiled. 'That'll be a good jaunt . . . through

London Fields and out on to the towpath – you can't really get lost . . . Follow the signs for Regent's Canal. It's about half an hour tops! But have a practice first. You don't want to fall in!'

'It's all right, I'm a good swimmer!' Imtiaz reassured him as they lugged the tandem out into the street.

Charles laughed. 'Just don't go testing the water. Hang on a minute!' he called, returning from his reception desk with a card. He tapped the back of it where an address was printed that took both their breaths away.

THE
BIKE BARGE
· Fixing wheels since 1880 ·

The Sara Kali, Regent's Canal,
Underneath the Hovis sign: 'AS GOOD TODAY AS IT'S ALWAYS BEEN!'

In Tandem

'Maybe the balance *is* off,' Imtiaz shouted in Usha's ear as they pedalled because at first the tandem seemed impossible to ride. Swapping over who was captain didn't seem to make any difference either.

When Imtiaz was in front, they went too fast and once almost careered off the park path into a tree, collapsing into giggles as the bike toppled to the side.

With Usha as 'captain', whenever they coasted they wobbled dangerously.

'Kali Ma's tandem tales made it sound so easy,' she complained.

The hardest thing was setting off. They discovered that if Usha placed her left leg and Imtiaz her right leg down, then counted three, two, one and kicked off at the same time, they stood half a chance of keeping straight.

Usha was on the cusp of giving up, when they finally got the hang of it along a wide path. Now that they were on their way, neither of them wanted to stop. As they pedalled together, Usha felt closer to Imtiaz than she had since she'd arrived. Watching their knees rise and fall and their feet turn the pedals, Usha felt Imtiaz's determination, her courage and something else she had not sensed before . . . like a deep, deep ache. At that moment, Imtiaz turned round and signalled for them to slow.

Usha stopped pedalling and Imtiaz pressed on the brakes until they came to a standstill at a park bench. Usha took off her helmet. Her hair was wet with sweat where it had pressed against her face.

'I've been working it out,' said Imtiaz. 'Dr Devi said she got the Kalighat painting in 1968 and that's when Wilmington Manor was sold. Come on, Usha. Now we've got the hang of this and a map, why don't we take a ride out there today?'

'We can't, Imtiaz. Mum and Dad have only just let us out to the park! They'll come looking for us. Anyway, doesn't Lucky need to come with us?'

'That's true,' Imtiaz conceded. 'But we can't hang around.'

Usha nodded, taking a deep breath. 'Looking at the map I printed, it's near a station. We should get a train. Remember how Kali Ma said Lucky used to hang around stations?'

Imtiaz nodded. 'OK, so we'll plan it. Tonight we'll camp out on the roof garden . . . tell Lem and Tanvi we're bonding or something, and we want one night and the whole of the next day upstairs on our own, not to be disturbed. Then we'll have to creep out and get to the station. If we leave early morning, we can be back by late afternoon and no one would have to know we'd gone anywhere! I've got some money Delyse left with me. Enough for us to get a train.'

Usha's chest swelled with a mixture of excitement and fear. 'What if Mum and Dad came up and found us gone?'

'They're busy and stressed out. It'll be a weight off for them! We'll tell them we really want be on our own to get to know each other better. They'll buy that!'

Usha nodded tentatively, biting her lip.

'We've got no choice! If Lucky's bargain is what she says, this seems like the only hope of saving The Hearth. Haven't you ever done anything you weren't supposed to?' Imtiaz asked, irritated by Usha's caution.

'Sorry, I didn't mean to snap,' she said sighing heavily. She sat next to Usha on the bench and took her own helmet off, scruffing up her hair. *We're right here, facing where my story started. If this is the only way I can get Usha to understand about trust . . .*

Imtiaz stared at the bench opposite, the bench that when she had ridden past it earlier had caused them to wobble so hard on the tandem that they'd almost crashed. The bench that Delyse had brought her to after she'd begged to see it. The very place where once a mother who had just given birth had left her baby wrapped in newspaper. *My mum and maybe dad too. There is no escaping history. It's in the land.* Imtiaz heard the waves in the conch play through her mind. *It's even in the sea*. The thoughts that would not be pushed aside since Delyse had gone away struck Imtiaz now with the clarity of a truth-bolt.

She moved closer to Usha. 'I've been thinking. Maybe your family owe Lucky. Like I owe Delyse for looking after me even if she says I don't. I've got a record of everything that's happened to me in a book and just before I moved in with you, I nearly shredded it. I, like, tried to get rid of my past because of being angry with Delyse for going away and I thought – why shouldn't I just have a whole new start as well?'

'You think my great-grandma was doing something like that too? Maybe that's why she didn't want to talk about her family. It could be why she gave away the envelope about the house history too?' Usha asked.

Imtiaz nodded. 'But with all that's been going on, it's made me get what Delyse said, that if I *had* destroyed the sad bits, I would have shredded the evidence of all the good she did for me too.'

'You mean if Saraswati hid something that made her sad, then maybe she had to block Lucky's story as well,' Usha whispered.

Imtiaz gestured at the bench and the bin opposite. 'Right there is where Delyse found me, wrapped in newspaper.'

Usha turned to her, eyes glassy with tears.

'True! Famous at birth! In the news and everything!' Imtiaz attempted to lighten the atmosphere. 'Delyse says I've got trust issues. I think Lucky has too and she must have her reasons. It's not that easy to trust people, is it? I've never shown anyone but Delyse this place before.'

Usha shook her head and placed a tentative hand on Imtiaz's arm. 'Thanks, for telling me.'

'Our secret, OK?'

'OK,' Usha whispered as they replaced their helmets.

'Come on! We've got to find Cosmo.' Imtiaz held the handlebars straight, feeling shaky after telling her story. She rallied herself. 'Right, your turn up-front!'

'I can't!' Usha fiddled nervously with her helmet catch.

'Brace, balance, three, two, one, kick off!' Imtiaz shouted. Finally their feet left the floor at the same time and, pedalling slowly, they fell into an even rhythm.

I was wrong about Imtiaz. She's not tough, she's brave and asks questions and she's right about me. What have I actually done *before?* Usha pondered as she steered the tandem, discovering that it was easier to pedal than cruise.

'Faster!' Imtiaz laughed, tapping Usha's back – they were on the straight now – pressing harder on the pedals as they picked up speed.

Usha felt the tears stream down her cheeks as her heart went out to the baby who was Imtiaz, and the thought came to her. *What if Lucky chose you to discover Imtiaz's story because she was abandoned too.*

Something inside Usha unlocked as they sped along. *This feels like the first day of my life*, she wanted to scream at the top of her voice. Here I am with my sister, trusting, daring and free.

211

The Bike Barge

'It's so much harder to go slow,' Imtiaz complained as they steadied the tandem, giggling with relief to have avoided a pile of dog poo and veering off into the grime of the canal.

Here the towpath narrowed, forcing them off their saddles to walk. They followed the path of a family of ducks gliding through the mossy film that reflected the afternoon sunlight.

'Everything slows down by the water, doesn't it?' Imtiaz said. 'That's why I love swimming so much – time flows at a different speed. Why are you looking at me like that?'

Usha smiled. 'I don't know . . . it's like I can see who you are. I never imagined you would think something like that!'

'I can be deep too!' Imtiaz knocked against Usha's arm. 'Only joking.'

They ambled along in silence for a while, admiring the newly painted barges, reading out the names – a combination of smart plaques and hand-drawn signs.

Even Home

BETTY'S CREW

Skylark

KINGFISHER HAVEN

They walked under a bridge with crumbling red brickwork decorated in street art and almost bumped into a sleeping woman with lilac flowers in her hair.

It always made Imtiaz sad when she saw someone so young living rough on the streets and she wished she had some money or food to leave her.

They pushed the tandem on, past the corrugated rear wall of a factory, under a second bridge.

The canal path widened now and the barges were moored further and further apart. The buildings that backed on to the canal began to change. Some were tumble-down, with the odd white or purple butterfly bush sprouting from cracks in the brickwork. *Maybe this is where the girl under the bridge picked her flowers,* thought Imtiaz.

The mobile rang and they halted the tandem as Usha answered.

'Hi, Mum! Everything OK?' Tanvi's voice sounded strained and distant. 'What's wrong? Are you crying, Mum?'

'Let me take it.' Usha heard her dad intervene. 'Hi, Ush. Can you and Imtiaz head home? We've got news about the house. Can't talk now. Hurry back though.'

'OK.' Usha hung up, her heart sinking. 'It doesn't sound good. We'd better go,' Usha called to Imtiaz, who had pushed the tandem on and was pointing to an old-fashioned rusted metal advert.

Usha checked the business card against the slogan written in faded blue paint on the brickwork: 'As good today as it's always been'.

'Hovis! We're here! If there's anything in this, we've got to find out now. Shouldn't take long,' Imtiaz said, pointing to a barge ahead. It danced with blue and green flags with a red wheel in the centre. The same as on Cosmo's bike.

'The *Sara Kali*!' they both read together, as a whirring sound came from beneath a tarpaulin roof canopy.

'You nervous?' Usha asked.

'Bricking it. That name can't be a coincidence, can it,' Imtiaz commented as they wheeled the tandem along the towpath to the wine-red barge.

So strange to be standing exactly where Kali Ma and Pops Michael once stood in the photo, Usha thought.

Now, by the side of the barge Cosmo came into view, watching them through the turning spokes.

'How are we going to explain why we're here?' Usha whispered.

Imtiaz shrugged. 'Tandem needs looking at, doesn't it?'

Usha nodded.

'Hi! Charles from the library gave us your card . . . We just want to check the balance is OK,' Imtiaz said, as they wheeled the bike down a ramp towards him.

'Cut the crap, you two! Gran, they're here!' Cosmo shouted, setting off the bike wheel he worked on. It whirred faster, releasing a low humming sound.

A tiny door opened from below and a woman about Kali Ma's age, wearing a silken yellow headscarf, looked out. She spoke to them directly in a language Usha thought she understood a scattering of words of.

'They don't understand Roma, Gran. She thinks you look like you're of us – especially you.' Cosmo pointed to Imtiaz, tapping his own cheek. 'You're Indian background, yeah?'

Imtiaz smiled at Usha, remembering their conversation and nodded.

'Well you know we come from India too way back? Are you like sisters or what?'

'Yes!' Usha said firmly. 'We are . . . like sisters.'

Imtiaz's jaw ached in an effort not to grin. It felt as if she was coming home.

Cosmo nodded. 'This is my grandma, Valini.' He lowered his voice. 'She wants to know about the ghosts you walk with,' he explained, then began to tinker with the bike. 'She's been on at me to bring you to see her since I told her about them and the photo you knicked that she donated years ago.'

Valini broke in speaking directly to Cosmo, gesturing up to a deckchair at the front of the barge.

'Gran's disappointed you didn't come with your ayah.'

Imtiaz and Usha frowned at the strangeness of the situation, reading each other's thoughts.

'She stayed at home today to look after Usha's Kali Ma,' Imtiaz explained.

'Alive or ghost? Your Kali Ma,' Cosmo asked Usha.

Usha blushed. 'Ghost.'

It was disconcerting the way that Valini stared, like she was looking through them. Imtiaz and Usha glanced around nervously at the flower pots, scarves and flags strung on the washing line above the bright yellow and blue deckchair.

'We shouldn't be too long. We've got to get back!' Usha whispered, feeling suddenly rattled.

Cosmo shrugged. 'Stick around if you want to know what's going on but I'm warning you, Valini's time runs with the tide. She won't be hurried. Look around if you want? Just don't sit in that chair or my gran will give you an earful.

As they wandered around Imtiaz muttered to Usha, 'So this is the *Sara Kali* . . . where Lucky must have come to after her argument with the matron of the Ayahs' Home.' They were quiet for a moment as they listened to Cosmo chattering on to Valini in Romani. It sounded to Usha like a piece of music she couldn't understand the lyrics of, but knew the tune all the same. After a while Cosmo stood up and called to them. 'You're in luck! She'll talk to you!' he said, gesturing for them to follow him.

Valini offered Usha her hand as she led her down the footworn steps into the narrow barge. They were both amazed to see everything here – a table with bright cushions, a tiny wood-burning stove in the kitchen and sofa beds at either end. But the thing that struck them most was the bright and hand-painted swirly, flowery decoration on every surface.

Maybe it's because I'm so used to the top deck that I feel like I know this place, Usha thought.

Imtiaz sniffed the air. 'Smells like Lucky's rose oil!'

'It's beautiful!' Usha gasped.

Valini surveyed the barge proudly. 'It is.' She wore a red silken blouse and around her long neck were heavy beads of painted walnuts the size of Kali Ma's jade skull necklace. Her belt, thick and embroidered with fruit and flowers, gathered in a full, bright orange skirt that came down to her ankles. On her feet she wore soft brown leather boots. Her skin was weather-worn, with ruddy cheeks and her dark eyes sparkled.

Imtiaz and Usha gazed in awe at the wooden panel that bordered the whole barge with its colourful paintings of pomegranates.

An enormous enamel kettle began to screech on the gas hob, making both girls jump. Inviting them to sit down, Valini poured them tea and pushed a plate of warm bread rolls towards them that smelt of oranges and cinnamon.

'Thanks,' they echoed.

'Eat then! Now my Cosmo tells me you are to be in the

same school.' Valini paused to watch them eat and listen to her grandson working on the bike and lowered her voice. 'I know why you're here.' She gestured around the barge. 'But one thing I ask – do not tell anyone else that Cosmo saw your ghosts. His ability as a seer, as you two are and' – she gestured to herself – 'as I am, has taken him by surprise and he's sensitive about what people assume about us Roma. There's enough prejudice and nonsense spoken as it is. He's already nervous about going to school and he doesn't need such stories spreading. Do we have a bargain?'

'Understood,' Imtiaz said, gulping down the last of the cinnamon bun. Now Valini turned to Usha for her agreement.

'Promise,' she whispered, and the word 'Esimorp' on the cover of Kali Ma's book flashed through her mind.

Valini smiled and the lines fanned across her face. 'If I'm not mistaken, you two are here about a bargain. Am I right?'

Imtiaz and Usha were open-mouthed as Valini stood up, reached into a tiny cupboard and took out a conch shell, placed her mouth to it and blew. The deep, low sound reverberated through them, swirling deep, seeming to pulse through their blood.

Like sonar whale song, Imtiaz thought as the resonant note-strains hung heavy in the air.

'See how the music of the past plays through us. Lakshmi taught me and my mother to play the conch,' Valini explained.

'Lakshmi?' Imtiaz asked.

'Perhaps you know her as Lucky.'

Imtiaz pinched Usha's arm under the table and both reached for the sari squares they'd kept close to their hearts in the breast pockets of their jackets.

Valini smiled at the sight of them, running her fingers over the pomegranate embroidery. 'Of course. I remember now she used to sign her name as Lucky.'

'We have a conch too and we hear her voice in it,' Imtiaz explained, picking up a sari square. 'There's one last piece she needs us to find. The first one was . . .'

Valini nodded. 'No need to speak more.' She held the conch to her ear. 'We're tuned into the same channel! I'm here to help you find what you need.' She sighed and began to hum the tune of Lucky's lullaby.

'She hums that to us!' Imtiaz gasped.

Valini smiled as if all that was happening was just as expected. 'Lakshmi used to sing it to me too when I was a baby.'

The phone buzzed in Usha's pocket and Valini backed away, affronted by the interruption.

'Sorry.' Usha hastily switched it to silent. Valini closed her eyes and breathed deep, collecting her thoughts.

'So, according to the conch rhyme, Lucky wants me to take you to the manor house, where our family found her.'

'When . . . ?'

'How . . . ?'

Usha and Imtiaz's questions clamoured out but Valini raised her hand to stop them in their tracks.

'Go home now, girls and tell Lakshmi I received the message loud and clear and I am longing to welcome her spirit again on the *Sara Kali*.'

Usha and Imtiaz were both struck silent.

'Tomorrow we will make the journey together.' Valini smiled without opening her eyes. 'Tonight, prepare your questions and return at dawn with everything you've found. All the patchwork pieces . . . yes?' Valini blew into the conch once more.

Cosmo opened the door at the top of the steps and beckoned them up.

'You should leave the tandem here, for an excuse to come back,' Cosmo said, matter of fact.

Usha hesitated for a moment.

'What's the matter, don't you trust us?'

'We do!' they said at the same time as they walked up the ramp, adrenaline rushing through them.

Usha switched on the phone to find a thread of messages.

How far away now?

What's keeping you?

Imtiaz read the texts over Usha's shoulder as they walked back along the towpath. 'Say we've had a puncture and . . . the brakes are faulty. Tell them . . . we found somewhere to fix the bike, so it'll take us longer because we're walking, and . . . sorry it got put on silent but we're not used to having a phone yet.'

Usha laughed. 'You're good at this!'

220

When they approached the bridge they found the homeless girl sitting cross-legged. As they passed her she took a flower from her hair and offered it to Imtiaz.

'May it bring you butterfly freedom and good luck!' she whispered as Imtiaz took it from her and they hurried on home.

Lem and Tanvi peered over the balcony gesturing for them to hurry. Lem was pacing up and down by the time they'd sprinted up the stairs to find everyone: Lucky, Mina, their ayah friends, and Kali Ma, waiting impatiently. Both got a stern telling-off for not checking the phone, but sympathy for the their tandem trials.

Imtiaz raised her eyebrows at Usha as if to say, 'See, we handled that.'

With forced calm, Lem and Tanvi recounted the experience of their unsuccessful visit to the lawyers and how it looked as if, without the papers being submitted before the end of the week, they were going to have to close The Hearth. Lem explained that they were left with no choice but to sell the house and seek new premises for their Hearth and home, somewhere they'd be more welcome. Lucky and her friends and Kali Ma crowded around, making it hard to concentrate on Lem and Tanvi's news that before the girls started secondary school they would have to move out of the ship house.

'We'll do our best to make sure we can stay in the area, so

you can go to the same school,' Tanvi reassured them, her eyes red and sore with crying.

'It's OK, Mum.' Usha hugged Tanvi close, catching sight of Imtiaz shaking her head as if to say, 'Don't say a word.' It was all Usha could do to stop herself from telling her mum that maybe, just maybe, there could still be hope.

'Is there anything you girls would like to do before we have to start packing up?'

'Can we have our own, like, survival camp up here, just me and Usha? So I can take it all in before we have to leave,' Imtiaz asked.

Tanvi nodded. 'Not a bad idea, a great way for you to get to know each other better. We could set it all up with a box of food to fill the mini-fridge so we wouldn't need to bother you.'

'Good call! We should enjoy all this as much as we can,' Lem said, sighing as he and Tanvi wandered around the garden as if attempting to memorise every detail. 'We'll take the ship's wheel and the driftwood bench with us and we can plant a new garden,' Lem soothed as he picked a rose and handed it to Tanvi. 'We'll leave everything outside the door,' said Lem, looking up at the sky. 'A beautiful harvest moon tonight. Make the most of it, the forecast's for rain tomorrow. Just come on in if the weather changes. It's not a test!'

Imtiaz looked to Usha and smiled.

'We don't care what the weather's like,' Usha said. 'Just

promise you'll leave us to . . .' Usha searched for a word that would convince her parents. '. . . bond.'

Imtiaz's eyes shone with approval.

'And you're sure the tandem's in safe hands?' Lem asked as they headed for the Globe Window.

'Charles at the library recommended the menders,' Imtiaz chipped in, tapping the phone. 'We've got their number. When we've finished camp we'll go and get it.'

'Seems like you're all sorted then!' Lem smiled at them both.

As soon as the adults had gone, Lucky and her friends surrounded Imtiaz. Sitting on the driftwood bench, Lucky fanned the folds of her sari, revealing the last torn square.

'This is it, Usha. She's showing me the last empty space. If we find the missing piece and Lucky keeps her side of the bargain, it could change everything. Not just for us, but all the people at The Hearth.'

Home Truths

'So we leave at dawn with Lucky.' Kali Ma listened intently as Usha filled her in on their plan of travelling to Wilmington Manor on the barge with Cosmo and Valini. 'Will you be all right?' Usha asked, her forehead a worry-furrow.

'I'll be fine here with Lucky's friends. Just make sure you don't wake me up when you leave – I need my beauty sleep!' Kali Ma smiled, weakly. 'Seriously though, I don't have the strength for another outing, Myush.' Kali Ma held her hands over her heart. 'You girls go with Lucky, and come back as soon as you can.' She yawned. 'I'm happy to stay here, having my driftwood dreams of Michael.'

In silence the girls ate Nilam's still-warm samosas and puri from the hamper left outside the door. Their minds raced with all that the next day might bring. Afterwards, they packed a small rucksack containing everything they had found out about Lucky. Despite all the upheaval, something inside Imtiaz felt settled as they worked together.

'I'm so tired,' Usha sighed. 'I can't believe we've got to wake up at dawn. I haven't even been getting to sleep till then.'

'Are you scared?' Imtiaz asked.

'Terrified!' Usha admitted.

Imtiaz sat on the end of Usha's bed as she rummaged in the wardrobe, looking through a box for Kali Ma's jade necklace.

Usha held up the green skull beads and Imtiaz pulled a face. 'Seriously goth!'

'Kali Ma gave them to me on the night before she died,' Usha whispered.

'Sorry, no offence meant.'

'It's OK. They freak me out a bit as well. And this is the Kali statue Merve gave me, just before Kali Ma came back to life,' Usha said, placing it in the rucksack too.

Imtiaz scrolled through the photos. 'We'd better not risk taking the phone or they'll know we're gone!'

'How?' Usha asked.

'Delyse was always losing her phone and tracking it.'

'I don't think Mum and Dad would do that,' Usha said.

'Bet they would, if they had to. In any case, you saw Valini's face when it rang!'

'Yes! But what if we get into trouble and need to be in touch?' Usha asked.

Imtiaz shrugged. 'We'll find a way. We're in this together, aren't we? In any case, we're off to Hertfordshire, not India!

Don't worry all the time. If we get some sleep, we'll be fine.' Imtiaz yawned. 'Want to know what I used to do when I was little, to get to sleep?'

Usha nodded.

'Delyse played this tape of whale song – sounds a bit like Valini blowing the conch. Anyway, it helped me.' Imtiaz pointed to the poster on the wall. 'Delyse says it relaxes you because it sounds like what we hear before we're born.' Imtiaz prodded her own stomach. 'In here! I've grown out of it, but if I'm struggling I sometimes just imagine I'm listening to it. Maybe after all this we could get hold of some? Random, I know but . . .'

'Thanks! I'll try that.' Usha smiled, tapping the rucksack. 'I think that's everything except for the Promise Book!' Usha peered around the wardrobe door to where Imtiaz now rested, momentarily hypnotised by the ticking mechanism of the chronometer. 'Can you pass it to me out of my drawer?'

'What?' Imtiaz asked, propping herself up.

'The Esimorp Book!'

She's starting to trust me. Imtiaz smiled as she reached into the drawer and lifted the Promise Book out. Underneath was the small, green cloth-covered book that, now she looked closer, she realised was the one Usha had been writing in on her first night.

'Thanks,' Usha said, taking the Promise Book from Imtiaz and stowing it in the bag. 'I'm off for a shower,' she announced and headed to the hallway bathroom.

Listening out for the water flow, Imtiaz quietly opened Usha's drawer and removed her notebook. *What does it matter what she's written, now we're close? Anyway, it might help me understand her better*, she reasoned. By the cautionary scowl on Lucky's face she did not agree but the more she warned Imtiaz off, the greater her urge to read.

It was too late, her stomach churned. Every word she read felt as if she was swallowing poison.

I'll tell Mum and Dad I don't want Imtiaz here. This is one enormous mistake. We'll never get on. I wish Merve had never met Delyse, then none of this would be happening.

Imtiaz felt raw wounds gnawing at her insides. Flicking forward, she found more writing that looked like a diary entry. Her chest convulsed, holding back the sobs as she registered the title: 'Imtiaz Invasion'.

I've seen enough! Imtiaz ripped out the pages and shoved them in her pocket. *I'll face Usha up with this in my own time*, she thought, closing the book and replacing it in the drawer.

'You want a shower?' Usha offered, as she emerged from the bathroom with her hair wrapped in a turban towel.

'You saying I stink or something?' Imtiaz snapped.

Usha stopped dead, shocked at the changed tone in

Imtiaz's voice, the vicious light that sparked from her eyes. 'What's the matter?'

'Nothing I can't handle,' Imtiaz sneered. 'I'm off to sleep outside with the ghosts! Wouldn't want to invade your beauty sleep!'

Usha curled up with her Kali Ma. *Maybe it's the stress of everything that's been going on. Even worse for Imtiaz than for me. I'm probably being oversensitive,* she reassured herself as she tried to focus not on Imtiaz's offhand mood but her kindness in sharing her whale-music story and the fact that she'd trusted her enough to say how her baby-self had been saved by Delyse. Usha closed her eyes and pictured them riding the tandem around and around the park, the breeze in her hair and the feeling of flying.

She woke to her alarm and crept out of bed, so as not to wake a wheezing Kali Ma. Opening the portal door, she found Imtiaz already sitting among the long grasses.

'I don't think Kali Ma's going to be with us for much longer. She's so weak,' Usha said, looking back inside.

'Yes, you've said that before! We'd better get on with it then.' Imtiaz watched the ayahs stream back inside. 'Lucky's friends are staying to support her, like true sisters.'

Let it go. She must be nervous, Usha told herself, clinging on to Imtiaz's closeness last night. There had been so many times when they'd misread each other. 'And how's Lucky?' Usha asked.

Imtiaz turned to where Lucky stared out over the rooftops, her chin tight with concentration as she nodded towards her and climbed over the balcony rail to the spiral staircase.

'She's leaving!'

Imtiaz leant over to watch her go, mesmerised by the swift swish and sway of her sari disappearing down the steps in a swirl of ever-decreasing circles.

'Got the bag? Come on then!' Imtiaz said, indicating the rusty staircase.

'We can't go down there. It hasn't been used in years. It's not safe!' Usha warned, grabbing hold of Imtiaz's arm. 'You'll fall!'

'What do *you* care? It's a fire escape, isn't it?' Imtiaz snapped.

Usha sprang back.

'Lucky's down there, waiting for us,' Imtiaz mumbled. 'Seems like she can't wait any more. Let's go.'

'Wait!' Usha hurried over to the Helm and untied a length of rope from a hoop. Returning to the balcony's edge, struggling to still her shaking hands, Usha looped the rope over the top of the ladder. In her panic her knot-tying memory failed her and she had to start again, every so often glancing warily at Imtiaz, who refused to meet her gaze. Finally, she secured a mooring knot and, leaning back with all her might, pulled it tight.

'Are you sure you're all right?' Usha asked, catching sight

of Imtiaz's white knuckles clinging on to the rambling rose. 'Watch out for thorns,' Usha warned.

Imtiaz laughed flatly. 'I'm used to thorns.'

Another jibe! There was so much bitterness in her voice it made Usha recoil.

'Let *me* go first. At least I've climbed it even if it was ages ago,' Usha whispered. 'Give me the bag. Just wait till I'm at the bottom.'

'Yes, Captain!' Imtiaz sneered.

Usha carefully climbed down, the metal creaking heavily at every rung. But the fire-escape staircase, which had seemed like a tower to the sky when she had walked up it with Pops Michael when she was little, held firm. Now, she was already half-way down the side of the house. *It's not that far to the ground . . . Either the staircase has got smaller, or I've grown,* she thought.

Waiting above, Imtiaz suddenly felt a hot flash of rage, reached in her pocket, scrunched Usha's hate-words into a ball and lobbed them at her head.

'What are you doing?' Usha's hands gripped the staircase as she dodged the bombardment of missiles.

'See how far you get without me and Lucky!'

'Shhhh.' Usha placed her finger over her mouth. Staring up at Imtiaz, she caught a ball of paper and opened it, horrified to read her own words – 'Imtiaz Invasion'. Words she had meant to destroy.

'And I thought we were getting close,' Imtiaz hissed, climbing over the rail.

'No! Imtiaz, it won't take our weight together!'

'No room for both of us! Yes, received loud and clear!' Imtiaz muttered to herself, the hurt of rejection and abandonment flaring through her as she tore down the steps, hardly knowing where she placed her feet. A haunting moan of whale song came to her from far away as the mooring knot gave and the rusty staircase cranked away from the wall.

'It's not strong enough!' Usha warned, scrambling down the final few steps to the ground.

'Ah well. *You're* safe – that's all that matters!' Imtiaz peered down and her vision began to spiral.

'Don't look down!' Usha held her hand over her mouth to stop herself from screaming as Imtiaz missed her footing and froze, clinging to a vine. From the ground, Usha clearly heard her whimpering and weeping. The sound of Imtiaz's distress shot through her. Her whole body braced, Usha turned to the staircase. Jaw clenched, every muscle tensed, with one giant shove she attempted to push the staircase back against the wall but still it swung in mid-air. Closing her eyes, she willed Lucky by her side. 'Help us. Please help!' But as she blinked her eyes open, not Lucky but a lion-sized snarling Spirit appeared, braced, as if about to pounce. Spirit reared up on to her back legs and lunged forward with her giant front paws, forcing Usha forward too, her Spirit-charged body giving one last push against the staircase. With a heavy thud, Spirit was gone and the staircase returned to the safety of the wall.

Usha's whole body trembled with exhaustion now and her voice shook too. 'You've got to trust me, Imtiaz. Come down before Mum and Dad catch us! You can't stay there. I can hold it still now. I promise you,' Usha coaxed her, every muscle tensed to breaking point, as she held the staircase against the wall.

Imtiaz slowly descended the steps, sobbing and shaking as she whispered her own name, feeling Delyse close and comforting. 'Immy, Immy, Immy.'

'You're safe!' Usha held out her arms and Imtiaz allowed her to hug her close. They stayed there for a while, gulping breath, gulping life. 'Those things I wrote about you. I don't think any of that now. I'm sorry, I'm sorry I wrote it.' Usha sobbed.

Imtiaz was still too shaken to speak as she stared up at the heavy metal staircase.

'How did you do that? You saved my life!'

'I think it was Lucky . . . she leant me her spirit,' Usha whispered in shock herself as they slowly disentangled from each other. Over her shoulder she watched in awe as an ordinary-sized Spirit melted into the silvery, moon-washed pavement.

Wilmington Manor

It was the floating time between night and day, when the moon and rising sun live together in the sky. Imtiaz kept a tight hold of Usha's hand, pulling her along to keep up with Lucky as she sped away from them through London Fields, heading for the Regent's Canal. Finally they reached the water's edge and doubled over to catch their breaths. On lifting their heads, they were amazed to find they had already reached the canal path.

As they approached the *Sara Kali*, Usha and Imtiaz slowed, hearing a sound so deep and strong that Imtiaz thought it truly was whale song. Valini stood beside the deck-chair blowing her conch and the sound of her echoing *auuuuuuuuuuuuuuummmmm* reverberated along the earth-banks and under the waterways. Inside the *Sara Kali*, the tiny curtains opened and Cosmo, sleep-blurred and hair tangled, appeared at the window.

Imtiaz paused beside Lucky as she placed her palms over her heart at the sight of the barge.

'Gran! Lakshmi's here!' Cosmo stood back as they boarded.

Valini was a vision, dressed for the occasion of Lucky's welcome in a purple silk sari and crimson blouse. Ignoring Usha and Imtiaz too, hands held together in a namaste, Valini bowed low and led Lucky on to the deck-chair. *Looks like she's ready to steer the barge home*, Imtiaz thought. When Lucky was seated, Valini stood at her shoulder and called to Cosmo to 'set sail'.

'Are you two going to give me a hand or what?' Cosmo asked, passing Imtiaz the barge-pole and instructing her to push against the bank, where Usha still stood, as the barge slowly pulled away.

'Go on! Take a leap of faith! Leave it any longer and you're staying on shore!' Usha leapt across the widening space and almost knocked him off his feet. 'Good jump!' he laughed as he grabbed her arm to steady her.

As they sat on the deck feeling the growing warmth of the morning on their skin, Valini moved around in the cabin below.

'Your gran looks beautiful in her sari,' Usha commented, as her blush receded.

'Only wears it on special occasions,' Cosmo explained as he steered the barge. Imtiaz kept checking on Lucky but her eyes focused firmly into the distance, seemingly set now on one course only.

'Can *I* have a go?' Imtiaz asked. Cosmo stood aside and handed her the tiller.

'Done it before?' Imtiaz shook her head and raised her eyes to the sky.

'Right, well! You've got the tiller and' – he pointed into the water – 'there's the rudder. Now! The way you turn the tiller is the way the back of the barge moves. If you want to turn the front to the right, you pull the tiller left, OK?' Imtiaz shrugged off his help and Cosmo crumpled into laughter as he watched her switch the tiller stick back and forth in panic.

'It's not that easy!' Imtiaz conceded as Cosmo took charge.

'Want to have a go, Usha?' he asked, handing over to her. 'That's it. Think about the middle of the barge as a kind of pivot point. If the back of it rotates one way the front rotates the other.'

'You could have told *me* that,' Imtiaz complained.

Usha couldn't help feeling a small glow of pride when Cosmo announced that she was more suited to barge speed! As they took it in turns to steer, the upside down tandem wheels spun faster. Time and again, Valini sounded the conch from the bowels of the barge as they travelled along. Ducks swam at their side and further on, a swan glided leisurely, gracefully, peering up at Lucky so often that Imtiaz was convinced that the graceful bird could see her too, as it guided the *Sara Kali* all the way along the River Lea and into Hertfordshire.

'Reminds me of the swan in Lucky's Kalighat painting,' Imtiaz said. Valini nodded as she joined them, her eyes too following the swan's progress. 'Saraswati always comes as a swan! The goddesses are gathering on the *Sara Kali*,' Valini announced as, once again, she headed down the steps to the lower deck.

'Is the barge named after my Kali Ma and my great-grandmother Saraswati?' Usha asked as she settled into steering.

Cosmo laughed. 'No! The whole world doesn't revolve around you! Sara-la-Kali is our Roma goddess. Don't you know anything?'

'Sorry!' Usha muttered.

Imtiaz smiled to herself as she imagined what Delyse's 'moderate your voice' advice would be to Cosmo. *He reminds me of me!* she thought. *Maybe I've met my match!*

A sweet, syrupy smell wafted around the barge. Imtiaz noticed Lucky sniff the air. 'Lucky looks blissed out!' Imtiaz commented as she watched her close her eyes and the breeze lift the ends of her sari.

'My gran always says the reason why Lakshmi's never been forgotten by us is because the only land we claim to own is grown from stories. That's what makes us rich.'

'What do you mean?' Imtiaz asked, but Valini's voice blasted out at them as she opened the door below and set to arguing with Cosmo. 'That's me told!' Cosmo shrugged when Valini retreated back inside. 'She says I'm not to tell you anything until you've fulfilled Lakshmi's bargain. Not until you return to the yog with Lucky's treasure is the story yours.'

236

'What's a yog?' Imtiaz asked, crinkling her nose.

'A fire. We'll build it in the woods, near your manor house. We're not far off now.'

It felt so strange to Imtiaz and Usha that they had lived with Lucky, desperately trying to work out her story, when all the time Cosmo's family held missing pieces of it too.

'You going to give me a hand on the lock?' Cosmo asked. 'Close the gates and I'll let the water out.' Usha and Imtiaz jumped off the barge, pushed the gates shut and watched the water level plummet.

Cosmo laughed at the looks on their faces. 'It's not a miracle or anything. It's just the way to even out the land levels.'

Valini brought them pomegranate cordial but refused to answer any questions about Lucky and the pomegranates. Imtiaz studied Lucky closely and reported to Usha that the nearer they drew to their destination, the more serious and strained her expression became.

'I have this odd feeling,' Usha confided in Imtiaz, as they listened to the wheels of the tandem turning slowly in the breeze. 'Like we're winding back in time.'

As they approached some dense woodland, Cosmo moored the barge and stirred them to action.

'The story is already written that while we wait here and build the yog, you will restore whatever your people took from her.'

'What do you mean *our* people?' Imtiaz asked, bristling.

Cosmo shrugged. 'That's how the story's told. Don't shoot the messenger!'

At that Valini gave Cosmo another mouthful for talking too much.

'OK, OK, Gran!' Cosmo turned to them. 'Just look for the yog smoke on your way back. Make your way through the wood and along the one straight road and you'll come to Wilmington Manor. It's about twenty minutes' walk away. On the bike it'll take maybe ten at most,' Cosmo told them.

Lucky had already set off through the wood by the time the girls disembarked.

It was heavy going wheeling the tandem through the dense woodland, struggling to keep up with Lucky. Finally they emerged on to a long, narrow single-track country road with railings on either side. Bright yellow rapeseed crops ripened in the fields. Imtiaz crinkled her nose at the sickly smell as they climbed on the tandem. Steadying themselves before pushing off, they soon got in sync.

Following Lucky, it felt for the first time as if neither of them were leading or trailing behind. Both focused on one path, for the same reason. Delyse's voice filled Imtiaz's mind. As they sped along, her whale's-eye view notion didn't seem such a wild idea any more.

Slowing down, they approached some tall metal gates and a sign that said: 'Wilmington Manor Residential Care Home'. Riding, cautiously now, along a bumpy, weed-spattered driveway they reached an austere-looking building in grey-brown stone with small towers and turrets on either side of lead-latticed windows.

'Lucky's shaking. She's afraid of this place,' Imtiaz whispered.

'I don't blame her!' Usha said, staring up to a window where an old woman peered from behind a curtain and waved.

'I just hope she's alive.' Imtiaz shuddered as they both raised their hands to wave back. 'I can't take any more ghosts!'

Dismounting, they walked around a fountain with a statue of a mermaid in the centre, holding an enormous clam-shell. It looked as if it might have once produced a waterfall but now the stone edges were covered in algae and the stagnant pond slime pooling in the bottom smelt stale and rotten.

Imtiaz drew close to Lucky, whose arms were wrapped around herself, knotted tight in an attempt to keep warm. Her lips trembled and under her breath she began to pray.

'It's OK, Lucky. We'll get in and out of here as fast as we can.'

As they approached the cracked but grand sweep of front steps, a huge studded door opened and an old man came out, chatting to a woman in a white plastic apron. She reminded Imtiaz of Mala from Acorns and one of the ayahs she'd seen sitting around Tanvi's table at their house.

'Thank you, Maritesse. I'll be back to see Fleur next week. I like to think that somewhere inside that shattered memory of hers she knows I've been here. Ah! Looks like you've got some young visitors!'

Maritesse seemed taken aback but smiled at Usha and Imtiaz and instructed them to wait inside while she helped 'the gentleman' to his car.

The dark wood panelling in the hallway looked like it hadn't changed in years.

They waited on a worn velvet chaise-longue, both feeling suddenly out of their depth. But Imtiaz followed Lucky's gaze as she stepped closer to an enormous oil painting.

It showed a family in the very room they sat in. Peering closer, Imtiaz realised that the sofa was the same as the one they were sitting on, but in their place sat two unsmiling women in the process of passing a baby to another woman. She sat on the floor in a white sari. To her side was a tall man with kind eyes who stared out of the painting as if dreaming of a distant place.

Imtiaz pointed at the woman in the sari. 'That's Lucky! Don't you think she looks like her self-portrait in her Kalighat postcard, except they changed the colour of her eyes. Look! Both brown!'

Usha nodded, gazing at the painting. 'What's Lucky doing now?' she asked.

'Staring at the painting. She has tears in her eyes, rocking back and forth as if she's comforting herself as well as that

240

baby.' Imtiaz stepped closer to the painting. 'Lucky, is that Saraswati?' she asked tenderly.

Imtiaz wiped her eyes. 'It is, Usha!' she whispered.

Both breathless, Usha and Imtiaz moved closer to read the plaque at the bottom of the frame.

'Homecoming 1921. Wilmington Family. Commissioned by Louis Wilmington, on the occasion of bringing his daughter Saraswati Wilmington home.'

Usha held her hand over her mouth. 'This proves it. This baby was my great-grandmother Saraswati. Dr Sara!' Usha gasped. 'This must have been painted just after they came here from India by ship. And that is Louis – my great-great-grandfather.'

'Sorry to keep you waiting!' Maritesse said, closing the front door and joining them by the painting. Imtiaz now stood close to Lucky, trying to comfort her. She seemed to grow more fragile by the minute now she was coming face to face with her own past.

'I found that in the tower when I moved in. Apparently it's the original family who owned the house.' Maritesse pointed at Lucky in the painting. 'The nursemaid reminded me a bit of me! Except I look after the elderly. Now, who have you come to visit?'

Usha took Lucky's Kalighat postcard out of her bag and handed it to Maritesse, pointing to Lucky in the painting. 'This is the same ayah as in the painting. She used to live here. This postcard is her work. We've just found out that when the care home was renovated, the builders found it hidden in a wall here and the owners sent it to the Victoria and Albert Museum.'

Maritesse seemed fascinated. 'That's strange. A professor from the V&A is coming to have a look around next week,' she said. 'I told her there's a lot more to interest her in the tower!'

Imtiaz pushed against Usha's arm and chipped in. 'We're part of her work experience team.'

Maritesse looked doubtful.

'Dr Devi asked us to do a reccy before she came because we live just up the road. We rode our tandem here.'

Usha let her hair fall over her face so that Maritesse couldn't see her smirking as she remembered Kali Ma saying how clever Imtiaz was.

Maritesse walked over to an appointment book on the desk, looked up at the girls and nodded. 'Ah! Yes, "Devi", that is the professor's name! I always thought this house feels a bit like a museum. Too many old objects hanging around above my head in that tower. I did ask if it could be cleared when they did my room up, but not a priority . . .' Maritesse shrugged, raising her palms to the sky. 'Come on, then, I'll show you.'

The words from Kali Ma's Promise Book flew around Usha's mind as they followed Maritesse along a carpeted corridor. 'Sterces, esimorp, niagrab,' she muttered.

'Sterces, esimorp, niagrab to you, too!' Imtiaz whispered

back, feeling Lucky's sense of urgency set her own heartbeat racing.

Maritesse led them past room after room of elderly people and their carers, nearly all women.

'They look a bit like modern-day ayahs,' Usha remarked.

Reaching the end of the corridor, Maritesse opened an arched doorway that led into a tower. 'Here we are. I'll leave you to it,' she said, pointing to the staircase that Lucky was already climbing.

'Lucky knows exactly where she's going, but I've never seen her looking so sad,' Imtiaz reported.

As they climbed further up the tower, the narrowing stone walls became dusty, leaving a white powder on their hands and the air grew distinctively chilly. Finally, reaching the top, they arrived at a heavy stone-framed door.

'Looks like the entrance to a church or something,' Imtiaz said, hopping from foot to foot impatiently as Usha failed to budge the door that had lost its handle.

'Here let me!' Imtiaz leant her shoulder against it and, together, they gave it one huge shove, almost falling into the gloomy loft space lit only by a small circular window that reminded them both of a miniature Globe Window.

Cobwebbed, crumbling plasterwork fell from the door lintel as they entered, eyes darting around at the furniture junkyard that smelt of damp, and another smell too . . . roses.

Imtiaz nodded distractedly as she followed Lucky, who was clambering over a pile of chairs towards the window. Now she stood on an old bed to see the view across the fields to the woodland.

Usha joined them and pointed to where a faint wisp of smoke was already rising from the tree canopy. 'Cosmo and Valini waiting for us,' she said. 'Was this Lucky's room, Imtiaz?' she asked, looking back inside to where a wave of dust surfed on a sun shaft.

'Seems like it.' Imtiaz nodded, stepping down from the bed to track Lucky, whose hands traced over the far wall. To get to her Imtiaz pulled aside boxes, crates, paintings and photographs.

Sneezing at the dust, Usha clambered closer and picked up some black and white school photos in long, narrow frames showing girls in uniform, standing in neat rows. Usha's mind cast back to their library research as she remembered the house history. It had been a school for a time. Here were pictures of the same girls in different years, like a record of them getting older. Her heart fluttered as she scanned the faces and picked out her great-grandmother as a little girl, just as Lucky had painted her in the Kalighat postcard. She stood out, with her enormous, dark-lashed eyes and long plait, but mostly because in the photos of when she was younger, she clung to a woman in a white sari. 'Lucky and Saraswati are here together,' Usha gasped.

'And here and here.' She worked her way through photo

after photo. 'But look at this one . . . 1947 – she looks about our age and Lucky's already gone.'

In place of Lucky, a stern-looking woman in a blue uniform stood next to Saraswati, as if standing guard. Usha's chest tightened. For the first time she felt like she wanted to reach into the photo and hug the child that had once been her great-grandmother.

'She must have been about our age in 1947. Lucky's already gone in this photo.'

Imtiaz rummaged in the rucksack and took out the conch. Her hands shook violently as she offered it to Usha. 'Lucky wants you to listen again! Quickly, Usha. She's upset, like Khalid's mum was that day in The Hearth – traumatised. Her lips are moving all the time, like she's praying. I feel so sorry for her.'

Taking the conch from Imtiaz, Usha placed it to her ear.

Your belief in me sets my voice free
Piece me together
Or my story's lost for ever
To find peace in this house
Sew my patchwork
Of forgotten promises
Bargains broken
Secrets unspoken
Free my story
To free this house

Save my memory
Set my spirit free
Find my Kalighat art
To open hearts
Turn the wheels of time
Where the waters meet
On the old barge track
That flows to the manor
Matron took my faith away
Restore me now
Please, I pray
To right a wrong
And write me in
Save my memory
Set my spirit free
To sail across the cosmos
Speak my story
Here from this tower Matron cast me out
Made me leave my Saraswati
Made me break my promise to Lata
Broke my heart
Changed my name
Tried to hide my faith away
Find my prayer box
To sail my passage
Home

Usha repeated it all to Imtiaz as they clasped each other's arm for support and Lucky's emotions surged through them both.

'So it's her prayer box we're looking for.' Imtiaz frantically scoured through the crates.

Usha joined her, turning over more photos and old school books but found no prayer box.

Imtiaz sighed as they caught their breath. 'Lucky's looking, too. This is hopeless. She doesn't know where it is and she's in a real state.'

'Calm down, Lucky! Remember how you led us to the envelope in the library?' Imtiaz hovered her hands over the crates to remind her. 'See if you can do that again now!' Imtiaz followed Lucky's tentative path towards a wall. 'That's it, Lucky, as soon as we have what you need we'll get out of here.'

Usha and Imtiaz held each other's hands and breathed deep. After a few minutes Imtiaz trailed after Lucky encouraging her.

Now Imtiaz traced her hands where Lucky laid her head and sniffed the air. 'I can smell roses?' Imtiaz said, pushing against the plaster and the wall eased open. 'Sterces . . . a secret door.' Stunned, Imtiaz beckoned Usha into a cupboard.

Once inside a thick smell of incense hung in the air. 'Smell that?' Imtiaz asked as Usha breathed in the heady scent. Huddled close, shoulder to shoulder, they discovered a large oblong box containing small drawers. Carefully Imtiaz lifted it off the shelf.

'Your prayer box. Is this what you were looking for, Lucky? Let's get it into the light!' she said as they headed out and over to the round window with it. Using the ends of her T-shirt, Imtiaz wiped the thick layers of dust from the top and found that the box was hand-painted in beautiful bright colours.

'Did you paint this, Lucky?' Imtiaz asked but Usha had already found a pomegranate on the lid.

'She left traces of herself on the prayer box, all over the *Sara Kali* barge . . . everywhere,' Usha whispered. 'Is this what Lucky's brought us here for? I don't understand. How can the documents for our house be in here?'

'The last sari piece must be in here,' Imtiaz said as Maritesse called from down the staircase. 'Girls! Dr Devi's been on the phone!'

'Now we're in trouble. We'd better make a run for it. No time to look inside now!' Imtiaz said as she held open the rucksack. They placed the prayer box beside the conch and climbed over the obstacle course of furniture. On her way out, Usha grabbed one of the school photos of Saraswati and Lucky.

'And you had a go at *me* for stealing!' Imtiaz exclaimed.

'It's not stealing if they belong to our family!' Usha reasoned, stuffing it in the bag. 'In any case, we're doing this for Lucky and the people in The Hearth as well as ourselves. We've got to see what's in that box.'

Imtiaz smiled at Usha.

'What? Why are you looking at me like that?' Usha scowled as they hurried down the steps.

Imtiaz shrugged. 'I thought you were a bit gutless. But turns out I was wrong.'

'Thanks. I think!'

Maritesse was waiting for them at the bottom. 'Find anything interesting?' she asked.

'There's a lot up there!' Imtiaz replied.

Maritesse nodded. 'I just thought I'd check in with Dr Devi to tell her you're here.' Usha bit the inside of her lip, waiting for Imtiaz to make her move. 'Which one of you is Imtiaz?'

'Me!' Imtiaz said, her voice half-choked.

'Well, Dr Devi asked me to remind you of your promise.'

Imtiaz nodded.

'What promise?' Usha asked.

'Tell you later.'

Maritesse wrinkled her nose. 'I suppose every house has a smell, but that scent of roses is getting stronger,' she said almost bumping into an old lady standing in the middle of the corridor. 'Oh dear, Fleur, have you lost your way?' She guided the lady gently by the arm, turning to Usha and Imtiaz and waving.

Once out of the corridor, Usha and Imtiaz ran at full pelt, Lucky by their side, past the family portrait and out of the house to the waiting tandem. They fled through the gates of Wilmington Manor, towards the woodland where the smoke trails rose above the tree canopy and merged with bulging charcoal clouds.

Dismounting, panting for breath, they pushed their way towards the scent of wood smoke.

Imtiaz laughed. 'Lucky's dancing through the trees!' she told Usha as they wheeled the tandem forward and caught sight of the flames, shimmering between brown bark. Through the clearing they found Valini and Cosmo sitting by the fire quietly chatting. Valini stood as soon as she saw them, her face searching Lucky's and theirs.

'Lakshmi looks happy. Have you got the final sari piece?' Valini asked.

'We think so!' Usha pointed to her rucksack as a deep roll of thunder swelled the sky. The wood felt charged with the energy of the ancient trees and those spirits both living and dead who sheltered beneath wildly swaying branches.

Valini's sari swirled around her as she ordered Cosmo about. Without explaining what he was doing, he grabbed armfuls of earth and began to dampen the fire. Usha and Imtiaz joined him, feeling the earth in their hands while above them great heavy raindrops began to fall and steam sizzled up between the trees. Valini signalled for them all to follow her back to the *Sara Kali*, where the darkening surface of the water danced with rain.

Valini's Truth-Telling

Their journey home along the Regent's Canal, clothes steaming by the wood-burner, drinking hot soup and pomegranate juice, was one Usha and Imtiaz would never forget for as long as they both lived.

As soon as they were on the barge, Valini spread a cloth on the table and asked Usha and Imtiaz to lay the prayer box and all the pieces of their story out. Imtiaz watched as Valini settled Lucky on her bed and plumped up the cushions to make her comfortable.

'That's right, dear Lakshmi, you can rest now.' Returning to the table, she added the photos she had donated to Charles's exhibition. Valini pointed to the washing line in one of the photographs, on which a sheet – Usha looked closer – a *sari* hung.

'One of Lucky's?' asked Usha.

Valini nodded. Smoothing the folds of her own sari-skirt, she pointed to the eldest child among the group.

'And that's me! Open the prayer box. Let's see what else is here.'

Slowly, with shaking fingers, they lifted the lid and the scent of incense grew stronger. The top section contained spent candles. In the drawer beneath were some spare night lights.

Usha opened the next to find a tiny black and white photograph of a mother and father, smiling proudly as they held their baby.

On the back was written, 'Lata and Louis Wilmington, on the birth of their daughter, Saraswati.'

'So this is Saraswati's mother, my great-great-grandmother?' Breathless and unable to pull her eyes away from the faces of her ancestors, Usha gestured for Imtiaz to carry on. Tentatively she opened the next narrow drawer to find fragments of browning paper on which she made out eyes and lips torn apart. Cringing, Imtiaz reconstructed the familiar gentle features to find Lucky's face. Over on the bed she nodded her encouragement. Picking up the scattered words Imtiaz began to join these together too.

'They destroyed your travel documents too, like Delyse's,' Imtiaz said. *So that's why she was so upset,* Imtiaz thought, remembering the look of dismay on Lucky's face when she had stepped into the photo booth. 'This is your passport, Lucky!' she cried. 'And your real name?'

Lucky nodded and closed her eyes, holding her hands together in prayer as Imtiaz whispered the last words they had heard echoing through the conch. 'Broke my heart, changed my name, tried to hide my faith away.'

Usha fiddled with a drawer at the bottom of the prayer box and found what she had hoped would be there – for Lucky's sake at least – the third sari square. There were no other documents.

Valini nodded and placed her hands together as if she had been waiting for this moment. 'I think, Cosmo, we're ready to set sail. You take the tiller and I'll steer the story!'

Cosmo nodded. 'I've heard it at least a hundred times but I never thought I'd actually get to see the prayer box!' he said, shaking his head in disbelief as he climbed the steps.

Valini closed her eyes, and picked up Kali Ma's jade skull beads, feeling their weight and turning them over in her fingers.

Removing the two spent candles from under the lid, Valini replaced them with night lights and ceremoniously lit them.

Imtiaz turned towards the bed where Lucky lay peacefully, meditating. Valini felt under the table and opened a drawer. Picking out a circle of embroidery, she unhooked a needle from the back and held it up to Imtiaz and Usha to reveal an almost complete embroidered pomegranate. 'Just a few seeds to add before I'm finished. Lakshmi taught my grandmother how to sew these, and the recipe for pomegranate cordial came from her too. It's her signature fruit! You'll see why.' Valini pulled the ruby-red thread and began to stitch.

'Each telling is as delicate as tying threads. It needs time and care.' Valini smiled, straightened her back and seemed to grow in stature as she prepared herself. She began quietly, and slowly at first, staring at the candle as if speaking to the flickering flame.

'When I was a small child, an Indian woman named Lakshmi came to live with us. This is how the story has been passed down in the old tongue.

'One night, my mother was carrying me in her arms, rocking me to sleep. It is told that she was so tired herself that at first she thought she was dreaming when she looked down into the water to find an angel with white wings floating there. When she saw Lakshmi's face emerging, she screamed for my grandfather, who leant over the barge and hauled her out, wrapping her in blankets. He blew his warm breath into her, pressing on her chest for the water to leave and her life-stream to return. That angel was Lakshmi, though she hardly knew who or what she was for her mind had flown in pain and grief. But in her delirium she spoke in a tongue not so strange to us. For five days, my mother and grandmother sat by her side and nursed her, placing hot bread poultices over her to draw the heat from her body. She was skin and bone but in time she began to eat and the water seemed to heal her as we travelled up and down the ways. She spoke little at first, but my mother told of how whenever she sang her lullabies all us children would calm.

'Lakshmi grew happy on the slow tide of barge time and

began to sew, embroider and paint. She even shed her white sari and made her own bright skirts, blouses and shawls. But when I was older she taught me how to wear a sari. I remember how happy she was when I finally got it right!' Valini smoothed her fingers over the silk and gestured around the barge. 'Little by little she began to talk of her ordeal – how the matron in Wilmington Manor tried to lock her away, forbade her to paint or pray.' Valini sighed deeply, turning towards Lucky. Imtiaz noticed her shoulders relax to find her sleeping.

Lowering her voice to a whisper Valini tied off the last threads of her embroidery and placed it on the table. 'You know, a pomegranate's a symbol of love and all of us loved Lakshmi. She had a special way with children and we thought she might have a grown-up family of her own in India, but she confided in my mother that she'd never had children and the husband she had been married off to at age twelve—'

'Our age!' Imtiaz gasped.

Valini inclined her head. 'Lucky's husband had died before her thirteenth birthday and she was taken in as a housemaid by Lata's family in a village on the outskirts of Kolkata, where she lived in a bungalow beside a pomegranate grove.'

'In that newspaper clipping of your grandparents' marriage it said that they both came from Kolkata too, remember?' Imtiaz fingers tapped the table.

Usha nodded. 'I would love to find that place one day.'

'Me too,' Imtiaz said and they smiled at each other. Maybe they would.

Valini stopped to sip the sweet cordial that had stained everyone's lips ruby-red and as she did, Usha picked up the three sari squares.

'I think when she stitched these, she must have been thinking of home and the promise she made to Lata,' Valini said, running her fingers over the corners of one. 'Just before Lata died, weeks after Saraswati was born, Lakshmi gave Lata her word that she would look after her daughter till her eighteenth birthday. Lakshmi was heartbroken that she could not fulfil that promise because the matron of the school threw her out. In return for her promise, Lata gave Lakshmi this conch shell to travel with, so it's little wonder that all those secrets and promises and bargains' – Valini looked at both girls pointedly – 'are whispering through its ear, her music playing on the ebb and flow of time and carried across oceans.'

Usha and Imtiaz reached for each other's hands.

'When Lata died, her husband, Louis Wilmington's heart was broken, but he scattered her ashes in the sacred Ganges and decided to return to England to be with his family. As his own father had been killed in the First World War the plan was that his mother and sister would help to care for the baby.

'So he made the long journey to England, bringing Lakshmi with him, but he always missed India and his beloved Lata. He was fond of Lakshmi because she had loved Lata, and their child too. He enjoyed speaking Bengali to her and encouraged her to teach it to Saraswati.

'On the three-week-long crossing from India, Lakshmi made friends with other ayahs on the ship.'

Imtiaz and Usha nodded at each other, Gladys's story about Mina and the ayahs, who at this moment were looking after Kali Ma on the top deck, filling both their minds.

'It was such a long journey and the women kept each other company with songs, dancing and storytelling and passing around the conch. It is said that when Lakshmi sounded the conch, whales and dolphins surfaced, blew fountains of water and danced on the waves, making baby Saraswati laugh.'

Usha and Imtiaz shook their heads in amazement and, smiling knowingly, Imtiaz tapped the space between her eyes.

'Louis's mother and sister were happy to see him home but they did not take to Lakshmi, saying she had the eyes of a witch.'

'What about the baby?' Imtiaz interrupted Valini's telling.

'It was a cautious welcome. They were at least happy that Saraswati, who they called Sara, was pale-skinned and could pass for an English child.'

'Racists!' Imtiaz blurted out.

'That's what Cosmo says! This is an old, old story.' Valini nodded. 'Mother and sister decided that it would be better for Sara if Lakshmi, who they renamed "Lucky", didn't stay for long.'

Imtiaz had wrapped her arms around herself tightly as she listened. Usha squeezed Imtiaz's hand as she folded the stories of baby Imtiaz and the baby who was her great-grandmother together in her heart.

'Then the Second World War came and Louis had to go and fight. Once he was gone the household grew heavy with resentment. Now times were hard, even for the wealthy, and Louis's mother and sister turned their home into a school for girls that Sara attended, while they went to live with a relative nearby. Lakshmi continued to live there in separate quarters, in a castle tower hidden away at the top of the house.'

Usha traced her fingers over the paintings on the prayer box. 'The tower where we found this,' she whispered.

Valini nodded. 'It was decided that Sara and Lucky should become Christians and on Sara's confirmation day she was officially renamed "Sara". There was an attempt to get Lakshmi to convert too, but she refused. Even though forbidden, Lakshmi continued to pray to her Hindu "idols" – as the matron called them.

'As she grew up, Saraswati's grandmother and aunt visited her rarely and she came to understand that she was tolerated by them rather than loved.'

'What were they called?' Usha asked.

Valini shook her head. 'Lakshmi never spoke their names. But she told of their coldness and how they forbade her to speak in her own tongue.' Valini shook her head in disgust. 'More than once they advised her that she might make more friends if she didn't have Lakshmi in tow. But, despite their efforts to break their bond, Sara and Lakshmi were as close as any mother and daughter.

'One happy day Louis wrote to Lucky to say that, much to his own amazement, while serving in France he had met, fallen in love with and was going to remarry a woman called Alice. Louis and his bride-to-be planned that when the war was over they would find their own home together, away from the school, and have Saraswati and Lakshmi come and live with them. It was not to be. Louis Wilmington was killed only weeks before this marriage.'

Usha picked up one of the sari pieces and handed another to Imtiaz. Valini held the third, sighing. 'We'll need these for our rivers of tears!' she said, pausing to wipe her own eyes. 'Saraswati's grandmother and aunt were heartbroken when Louis died and left the running of the school to the matron, who was overburdened. Lucky was happy to help her with cleaning and washing at first but Matron began to treat her like her servant and also came to resent Sara, who was turning out to be a clever and studious girl with dreams of becoming a doctor.

'Sara's education was paid for and instructions were given for Lucky's passage home to be financed so she could make the return journey to India whenever she was ready. But this money was intercepted by Matron.

'One day, when Sara was having her lessons, Matron found Lucky praying and, in a fit of rage, ripped up her travel documents, giving her an ultimatum that unless she stopped praying to her "idols" she would have to leave the house with no payment or documents.'

Usha picked up the school photo of Matron standing at Saraswati's shoulder.

'See!' Valini said. 'Eyes and heart of ice.

'When Lucky refused once again to convert to Christianity, Matron had little sympathy. "Your promise to an Indian native woman is no business of ours," she told Lucky.

'It broke Lucky's heart that she could not fulfil her promise to Lata. She painted Saraswati a little postcard, tore a small square from her sari, embroidered her beloved pomegranate on to it and hid it in the brickwork next to Sara's bed, hoping she would find it. That day, Matron marched Lakshmi to the gates of Wilmington Manor without a penny in her pocket, refusing to let her take her prayer box containing the torn pieces of her identification. Heading into the woodland clutching her conch to her heart, wearing only sandals, a white sari and a cardigan, not even a coat, she discovered the canal in deepest winter. Ice coated her hair, her lips were dry and chapped. The way she described it, her mind became a fog of white and mist swirled around her ankles. Catching sight of a beautiful swan, she called to the goddess Saraswati. Following the great bird, she sailed on dream clouds until the freezing water bit at her skin.' Valini dabbed the tears from her cheek.

'This is the story that has been passed down from when I was just a babe in arms myself. As I told, my family took

Lakshmi from the water and nursed her back to health and when she was ready, took her to a place she had heard of where she might find help to travel back to her home in India.'

'Our house. The Ayahs' Home!' Usha and Imtiaz whispered together and Usha glanced over to Valini's bed, feeling within touching distance of being able to see Lucky.

'Is she listening?' Usha asked.

Imtiaz shook her head. 'Sleeping.'

'That house,' Valini continued, 'was where the missionaries looked after ayahs abandoned on the streets.'

'We know about the house!' Imtiaz interrupted. Valini nodded.

'She didn't stay there for long because she could not stand to have her faith taken from her twice. On the eve of Indian Independence in 1947 she decided that she would return to us. She called us her long-lost family and lived here for the next twelve years.' Valini smiled over to Lucky.

'I was the first of seven children and she taught me so much.' Valini paused and adjusted her sari train over her shoulder. 'One day, she was ill with her sore chest and none of our remedies worked to draw out the infection. My mother heard of a free clinic at the Elizabeth Garrett Anderson Hospital so we took her there. Lakshmi was so tiny and thin, it felt like carrying a child. We're not used to receiving such a rapturous reception as we did that day. There was a young doctor called Sara, just qualified, who bawled like a baby when she saw Lakshmi, kissing and hugging her, and that was it. Though she was so weak it was obvious that Lakshmi too was overjoyed to be reunited with her Saraswati once again.

'The young doctor learnt that Matron had lied to the Wilmington family, telling them that she had secured a passage home for Lakshmi accompanying a child at the school who needed to leave immediately. So there had been no time to say goodbye.'

'Poor Saraswati. No wonder she was messed-up!' Imtiaz whispered, wiping her eyes.

'Painful though it was for us to lose our Lakshmi, Dr Sara made us a promise that she would carry out Lakshmi's wishes. To return to Wilmington Manor and retrieve Lakshmi's prayer box and to bring Lucky's ashes to us on the *Sara Kali* barge when her time came, because we Roma, she said, had become her "floating family". I think this last honour, to bestow her ashes, was her way of thanking us.

'Life is epic, if you open your eyes!' Valini smiled, taking Imtiaz's slender wrist and turning over her hand. 'We discovered later that a few days after Sara and Lakshmi were reunited, Lakshmi died of pneumonia, but no one informed us and the ashes were never returned. We were angry and so my family traced Saraswati to her doctor's surgery, the very same house as the Ayahs' Home' – Valini paused – 'your home. We made an appointment as if we were patients. Saraswati was shocked to see us and said she had been to Wilmington Manor but not found the prayer box and that she was sorry to have broken her promise about the ashes but wanted us to understand. Saraswati laid her hand on the wall beside her desk and said, "I lost her for so long, I need her right here with me, in everything I do. I need to keep her ashes."

'We pitied her, clinging on to Lakshmi like that. Saraswati kept her conch, too. The only possession she had that belonged to her own mother. We argued with her, saying that our way is also to bury our dead, but she must respect that Lucky was a Hindu, that she believed she should be released into sacred waters to set her spirit free. But Saraswati told that she might one day take Lakshmi's ashes to India and release them into the Ganges herself. What could we do? But I'll never forget what my mother said that day as she left. "You can't lock a story away, Valini, no matter how painful, no matter how close you keep it – one day the truth will be released. Lakshmi doesn't belong to Saraswati, she can't keep her like one of her possessions. We will keep Lakshmi's memory alive by telling her story. So she'll never be forgotten and she'll always be there, whispering in that family's ear to be released."

'On the way out of the surgery, we bumped into Saraswati's doctor husband but she didn't introduce us. He saw she was upset and went hurrying into the room. As we passed the surgery window I heard her say, "They were just passing and popped in to have a little reminisce about Lucky.""

'You don't think my great-grandad knew about the promise to return her ashes to you, then?' asked Usha.

Valini shook her head. 'But my mother was hopeful that Saraswati would one day release Lakshmi's ashes into sacred waters. Poor Lakshmi, having to wait so long.' Valini stood up and walked over to the bed, helping Lakshmi up and gesturing for her to be seated next to Imtiaz at the table. Imtiaz turned to her side and nodded gravely as Valini spoke. 'This is the story that Lakshmi and her ayah friends have waited for you to bear witness to. Now it is time for you young ones to take up the conch!'

Valini handed Usha and Imtiaz Lucky's shell and raised her own conch to her ear. Lucky's lullaby and the soothing words flowed over them as, with bated breath, Imtiaz and Usha leant in to listen for new words.

To right a wrong
Sail a new passage
And write me in
I'm locked behind the surgery wall
Knock down the bricks
Open the safe for me
And finally let the dust fly free

With these words, the barge bashed into the bank. Imtiaz and Usha both sprang up.

'Surgery wall? Her ashes have been in The Hearth all the time?' Usha gasped.

'So it seems. In the heart and in The Hearth.' Valini

nodded. 'It must have been a heavy burden for Saraswati to keep that secret all to herself. You had better go and see what's hidden there. But remember your bargain. We're still waiting for that promise to be fulfilled! For Lucky's ashes to be returned to us.'

'We won't forget,' Imtiaz assured her.

'We're here!' Cosmo shouted, standing at the top of the steps, peering down at Usha and Imtiaz. 'Your eyes are bloodshot. Cuts me up too that one. You going to change her ending or what?'

'We're going to try.' Usha sighed.

'And from now on, Lakshmi, we'll call you by your proper name,' Imtiaz said as they pushed her back along the towpath on the front seat of the tandem, past the sleeping homeless girl where a white butterfly had settled on a purple flower in her hair. 'May it bring you butterfly freedom and good luck!' Imtiaz whispered the girl's wishes back to her and her words made Lakshmi smile.

When they reached London Fields, Usha and Imtiaz pedalled in perfect balance as they passed back and forth the revelations of Valini's truth-telling.

Last Will and Testament

Leaning the tandem against the hallway wall, they strode into The Hearth.

'All the ayahs are here!' Imtiaz whispered.

'Kali Ma, too. They're waiting for us,' Usha replied, hurrying through to her mum's meeting room, pointing up at the plaque of 'Dr Sara Gopal' over the door.

'Where were you two? We didn't see you go out. Lem and Tanvi are worried! Tanvi's not in there!' Nilam attempted to stop them, but Imtiaz and Usha had only one focus.

'This room's so small. It can't be that hard to find.' Imtiaz's fingers traced over the wall to the right of Tanvi's desk. 'Here, look, where the plaster ridges.' Eyes darting frantically over Tanvi's things, Imtiaz picked up a paperweight and began bashing the wall with all her force.

'What on earth's going on in here?' Lem shouted, rushing in from his room, shaking his head. 'Where have you two been? We were about to call the police . . .'

But Lem's voice drifted far away as Imtiaz continued to smash away at the plaster. Together they now clawed at the wall to reveal the familiar wallpaper from the black and white photo, the remains of which still clung on in the 'hell-hole'. Imtiaz felt the eyes of Lakshmi and the ayahs at her back, encouraging her, helping her to peel away the hidden layers of house history, travelling back in time. Lem yelled again for Imtiaz to stop and attempted to catch hold of her flailing arms, but was stunned into silence when a large section of the wall crashed down, turning to rubble on Tanvi's desk. 'You take it out, Usha.' Imtiaz stood aside and Usha reached in, grabbing the copper wheel of a small safe.

Tanvi appeared in the doorway, eyes wide with shock, words blurted in an endless stream as she demanded answers. 'What are you doing, wrecking the place? You two have got so much explaining to do, where have you been? The fire escape's falling off the side of the house – I know you went down it! You could have died! As if we haven't got enough problems without Councillor Puttock calling round, accusing us of not being fit to look after our own children. Says he's going to report us for letting you rampage around the streets at dawn, and I can't say I blame him!'

'Shhhh, Mum . . . Just wait!'

Imtiaz began whispering Lakshmi's words over and over like a mantra and Usha and Kali Ma joined her. 'Esimorp niagrab ykcul sterces.'

'What language are you speaking? What's happening?'

Drowning out Tanvi's questions, their voices rose, lending them power as they tugged hard at the safe, edging it closer towards them and striking Tanvi speechless. Behind them, Lakshmi and her ayah friends looked on.

The room had never felt so crowded as on that day, when generations, some seen, some unseen, some who flowed in bloodlines and some who flowed in love and friendship lines, stood together and watched the wall of secrets, broken bargains and promises crumble.

Usha and Imtiaz placed their hands together on the safe's copper wheel and twisted the stiff handle with all their might. Inside, they found a tied white bundle. Imtiaz backed away. Usha placed a comforting hand on Imtiaz's arm and gently lifted the sari bundle free.

'Lakshmi's ashes,' she whispered, as Imtiaz reached for an envelope under the bundle addressed to . . . she read the name aloud, 'Saraswati Wilmington'.

'My grandma?' The lines on Tanvi's forehead furrowed deep in confusion as she took it from Imtiaz's hands.

They huddled close, Lakshmi at Imtiaz's shoulder, Kali Ma at Usha's, as Tanvi opened the thick parchment envelope and read the letter aloud.

Dear Saraswati,

I am Alice, a stranger to you, I know, but I was almost your stepmother. I was engaged to be married to your late father, Louis Wilmington. He was the love of my life and I am sure we all live with the sadness of his death. He died in service before our wedding could take place. It has been a lifelong struggle to come to terms with that turn of events in my life, as I am sure it has in yours.

I am deeply sorry and regretful that we never met, but Louis told me so much about your mother, Lata, whom he loved very much, and about you and Lakshmi. Your father and I shared a love of India as I was born in Calcutta. I, too, made that long journey home by ship, but not as a baby, as you did.

Louis confided in me that you were not welcomed with open arms by his family and that they rather covered up your Indian heritage. I was deeply saddened to learn of that.

On one occasion I attempted to make contact with you and Lakshmi. I had an idea to invite you both to stay with me but my approach was not welcomed and I was told that your ayah had returned to India.

I have made myself useful in the intervening years. One great pleasure in my life has been to work with my dear friend Aneurin Bevan to set up the glorious National Health Service. How wonderful to see that all people will be cared for from now on, no matter their circumstances.

Suffering frequent bouts of malaria myself, I have been bed-bound for some time. I never married and therefore am in the curious position of looking for someone to bequeath this house to. It is special, because it used to be where ayahs stayed before going home. Feeling a personal link to this story, I was lucky enough to buy it with some family money.

Imagine my amazement and delight to open the paper and find news of you qualifying as a doctor. Congratulations, your father would have been so proud of you. And I also saw in the newspaper that you are marrying another Indian doctor and making your working lives together too. I was interested to read that you hope to find a doctor's practice here in the East End of London where, as you know, there is much need. Not being of a religious bent I'm not one to believe in souls or fate or any such notions, but recently I have felt very strongly that your father's spirit may be at work here, that he is intent on me helping you as my last deed on this earth. I have no dependents at all and so it is with great pleasure that I now bequeath the Ayahs' Home to you and perhaps your future family, to build your surgery and life here. I hope that you will be very happy in it.

Attached is the legal documentation from me to you; I leave this in the hands of the lawyers. I hope you will approve of my caveat – by way of ensuring the community good is continued through the generations.

I wish to make a change in the grand scheme of stories told and stepmothers do tend to get a rough write-up, so I hope you will think of me as your kind almost-stepmother.

Alice Durand

Tanvi collapsed in the chair that had once been Saraswati's, her chest heaving with emotion as she steadied her breath and wiped her eyes to read in a fragile, shaken voice. 'Alice Durand bequeaths this house to Saraswati Wilmington. This legally binding document ensures that Saraswati Wilmington and the benefactors of her will thereafter will own the freehold of this property in perpetuity. With the proviso that the ground floor be given over to the benefit of the community, in keeping with the spirit of this house.'

Tanvi's hands trembled as she let the documents drop on to the desk. She turned to the wall and stared from the ashes into the void, unable to speak.

'Tanv! This is it! This is just what we need!' Lem grabbed her shoulders and planted a mammoth kiss on her forehead. 'Can you believe these two have found it?'

'Not only us,' Imtiaz and Usha said at the same time as the tiny consulting room crowded with their ghosts.

'Come on, Tanv, we've got to take this to the council, now!' Lem shouted, jubilant. 'Question time's later. For now, we've got to save this Hearth.'

Usha shoved the envelope into her mum's hands and as she did Tanvi grabbed hold of both Usha and Imtiaz and enfolded them in her arms. 'Thank you, my girls, I love you,' she whispered. Smiling through their tear-stained eyes Imtiaz and Usha felt the weight of Lakshmi's ashes as they carried them upstairs together, closely watched and followed by a procession of ayahs.

Opening the Globe Window, they took the ashes outside, and without speaking began to unwrap the bundle, discovering that they were double-bound. The outer layer was a sari with three missing pieces. They laid it out over the length of the deck. It reached all the way from among the swaying bamboo, across the rope bridge to the Helm wall where the ship's wheel slowly turned. When fully spread out, Lucky sat at one end of it, fingers sealed to her third eye and Kali Ma stood at the other. A gentle breeze rippled the delicate material and it threatened to fly away but Usha and Imtiaz stepped barefoot across it to fit Lakshmi's embroidered squares into the empty spaces.

Afterwards, when they had stowed the pieces safely away inside, Usha and Imtiaz were directed on how to fold the sari by Kali Ma and Lakshmi. They began at opposite ends of their room folding and fanning the material backwards and forwards till Imtiaz and Usha met at the anchor with a length of beautifully folded cloth.

'Neat!' Imtiaz laughed as they caught sight of each other reflected through the Globe Window.

That night, despite the blustery weather, Lem, Tanvi, Usha and Imtiaz all crammed into the roof garden tent, along with Lakshmi and her ayah friends and a fast-fading Kali Ma, to hear how promises, secrets and bargains made so long ago had now fallen to their generation to be fulfilled.

Sacred River

Cosmo appeared at their door the very next day with Valini's detailed instructions regarding Lakshmi's ashes. She had done her research and discovered happily that some decades ago the Thames had been blessed and was deemed now a sacred river for Hindu people. First, she instructed that the sari and its embroidered pomegranate pieces should be brought to her to sew back in. This she did with large, even stitches, making no attempt to cover up the tears.

But there were gifts of thanks from Kali Ma to Valini too. She insisted that Valini be given her jade skull necklace because she said, 'Myush, I don't think you'll get much wear out of it!' And her bunting because, Kali Ma reasoned, 'That woman appreciates beautiful textiles and I like the idea of it dancing in the breeze up and down the waterways!'

It was a still grey day when Usha, Imtiaz, Valini and Cosmo walked down to the Thames.

Standing barefoot on a mudflat, Valini produced from her basket three hollowed-out pomegranates, into which she had carefully distributed Lakshmi's ashes, and handed the fruit to Usha, Imtiaz and Cosmo.

In her own palms she held the sparkling, scooped-out ruby seeds. Usha lit the candles that had been placed inside the pithy hollows. To the communal gentle hum of Lakshmi's lullaby they set her ashes adrift on the sacred Thames.

'For those who paved the way,' Valini said, as she scattered thousands of seeds that shone like a flotilla of sparkling jewels lighting up a sullen grey sky.

Valini sounded the conch and in the time it took to reach the end of her breath, a shaft of sunlight illuminated the dull water and, before all their awe-struck eyes, right there rising from the river, Lakshmi and Kali Ma materialised.

'I see your Kali Ma,' Imtiaz whispered, staring at the shimmering water.

Usha reached for Imtiaz's hand. 'And I can see your Lakshmi.'

Cosmo nodded. 'And see who else has come to wave them off!'

Imtiaz and Usha gazed up to find the bridge lined with ayahs.

As the ghosts' flickering light slowly faded into the choppy surface of the Thames, so too the ayahs took their leave.

'It is time,' Valini announced as she raised her arms to

release Lakshmi's sari to the tides. They watched, mesmerised, as it swirled out over the river and within seconds, drifted out of their reach.

Above them, the clouds parted into a portal of delicate blue.

Both girls felt heavy-hearted and hugged each other close as Lakshmi's sari sank beneath the water.

'Let's go home, Immy,' Usha whispered as her sister's tear-stained eyes followed the dance of a single white butterfly skyward.

That Summer . . .

On long, lazy days travelling the waterways, Kali Ma's bunting wafting around the *Sara Kali*, Valini taught Imtiaz, Usha and Cosmo how to sound the conch. Most days the three of them swam at the lido. It took every scrap of Imtiaz's patience to teach Usha and Cosmo how to dive to the bottom of the pool to catch blue diamonds, but they managed it on the day before they started secondary school.

Imtiaz kept her bargain with Dr Devi and took the Promise Book to show her. They also invited her to see how they'd adapted Charles's idea and made their own 'Passport to History Booth' to tell their story of Lakshmi and the ayahs. 'A fitting legacy!' Dr Devi declared, and requested that the pod-sized exhibition be installed along with a family portrait from Wilmington Manor, in her old office.

The guests of honour at the grand opening of the miniature but perfectly formed 'Conch Gallery' were Delyse and Merve, who not only brought Imtiaz's story book, but themselves back home.

Visitors to The Hearth were often welcomed by Imtiaz or Usha sounding the morning conch. Spirit, although often looked for on starry nights camping out among the whispering grasses, never returned. On those last summer evenings before school started Imtiaz and Usha found themselves drawn, time and again, to the driftwood bench, where, surrounded by the sweet scent of roses, the sisters took the conch to their ears to listen to the ebb, flow and breaking of the waves.

Author's Note –
Inspirations for the Ayahs' Story

This novel is the culmination of many patchwork pieces of my life working in community and the arts. It is written in a time of great upheaval and I hope that some of this story will inspire you to explore the local history where you live and the threads that reach from there across the globe.

There are many inspirations for this ayahs' story that began to grow sixteen years ago when I was commissioned by the Royal Shakespeare Company to create an oral history installation called 'Maps at Midnight'. One element of the installation consisted of talking to South Asian elders in Residential Care Homes about their memories of arriving in Britain and America and the many struggles and joys they had experienced throughout their lives.

In one of the recordings a woman spoke about her memories of the treatment of ayahs. I was not a children's author then, but thought how many stories about the contribution of migrant people in history around the world are untold.

For several years I worked with Director Kristine Landon-Smith to co-create and script a theatre production (Tamasha Theatre Company) inspired by Shaun Tan's graphic novel *The Arrival* . . . and in this story I have continued to look through 'memory's porthole' at the timeless story of migration, inspired by Tan to place the magical and epic side by side with the real world story.

Since then I have seen my friend and wonderful playwright Tanika Gupta's celebrated play *The Empress* at the RSC that featured the stories of ayahs and I thought once again how important it would be for young readers to hear their story. I worked with my friend Tania Rodrigues (the talented actor who is the audio voice of this and almost all of my stories) to help develop her play *Invisible* about the hidden voices of Asian women in history and once again heard the ayahs' story call to me.

My own father, the late Dr A.K. Brahmachari and nurse mother, Freda Brahmachari worked in the NHS since the late 1950s. My father's evocative stories of the long passage to Britain were an early inspiration as was accompanying him on visits to ships when he was 'The Dock's Doc', in Hull.

The 'Hearth' is a homage to the community spirit of The Islington Centre for Refugees and Migrants where I am Writer in Residence alongside artist in residence, author, illustrator and dear friend Jane Ray.

In the character of social worker Delyse many of my friends will see themselves. In Delyse I pay homage to all those British citizens of the Windrush generation who answered the call of 'The Motherland'.

This book could not have been written without the incredible research of Rozina Visram into the history of ayahs and lascars and of South Asian people in Britain. A little of her truth-questing spirit resides in Dr Devi.

Through my work at Amnesty UK and in Sheffield Libraries I have discovered the appalling disparity in life expectancy of Roma children as well as the still rare representation of Roma children in stories. Without Cosmo and Valini this truth-quest could not have been completed.

As I presented *When Secrets Set Sail* to my publishers I discovered an event at Hackney Libraries at which Rozina Visram was speaking about her research, celebrating the fact that the Ayahs' Home has been nominated for a blue plaque to commemorate the history of the women who lived there. I was heartened to hear that this campaign has been led by researcher and activist, Farhanah Mamoojee, who lives nearby. On discovering the story of the ayahs she has campaigned to have the house recognised and the ayahs' history better known just as my characters Imtiaz and Usha living in the house do. You can find Farhanah's amazing discoveries @ayahshome on Instagram.

Sometimes truth and fiction sail closely together, driven by urgent winds of change or the spirit of impatient ghosts demanding that their untold stories arise from the shadow places in history.

Thank you to all whose energy, empathy and integrity, past and present have helped me untie the knots, find a voice and sail this story home.

Sita X

Imtiaz and Usha had to research a lot to discover Lakshmi's story, as I did to write this book! Here are a list of books that inspired me, that you might like to discover too.

Homecoming: Voices of the Windrush Generation by Colin Grant

The Stopping Places: A Journey Through Gypsy Britain by Damian Le Bas

Asians in Britain: 400 Years of History by Rozina Visram

Ayahs, Lascars, and Princes: Indians in Britain 1700–1947 by Rozina Visram

We Mark Your Memory: writings from the descendants of indenture edited by David Dabydeen, Maria del Pilar Kaladeen and Tina K. Ramnarine

Farhanah Mammoojee @ayahshome

Acknowledgements

First thanks go to my loving family, husband Leo and grown children Maya, Keshin and Esha, who understand more than most what goes into these stories. Thanks to my wonderful sisters and brother, aunts and uncles and family. This story, with its wide diaspora tides across time, could never have been written without your journeys. I love you all.

I wish to thank my agent Sophie Gorell Barnes who is such a supportive force in my writing and for sending me healing joysticks just when they were needed!

Thanks to the wonderful creative team at Orion: Sarah Lambert, Ruth Alltimes, Tig Wallace, Dominic Kingston, Emily Finn, Samuel Perrett, Ruth Girmatsion, Felicity Highet, Hannah Cawse, Helen Hughes, Rachel Boden, Tracy Phillips, Annabel El-Kerim, Eshara Wijetunge.

With special thanks to Tig Wallace (Senior Commissioning Editor) for being such a skilled, sensitive, insightful and empathetic guide whose passion for all things nautical has hugely enriched this book. Thank you for helping me steer my course through the many threads and strands of this story and for keeping me focused on the quest.

Sincere thanks to Ruth Girmatsion (Senior Desk Editor) who has worked so patiently with me on the last stages of this journey to steer *When Secrets Set Sail* safely into harbour during the unpredictable choppy waters of this period.

Huge thanks go to Dominic Kingston (Head of Publicity) who has shared in the vision, potential and scope of my intergenerational novels from the start.

Samuel Perrett (Senior Designer) and Evan Hollingdale (Illustrator) for the beautiful blue sky, London brick cover and artwork that so captures the spirit of this story.

Samantha Swinnerton (Freelance Editor) for sharing in early discussions and especially for her encouragement for me to explore a love of magic realism in storytelling.

Felicity Highet (Marketing Manager) for seeing the scope of these stories to inspire projects in education and curriculum. I hope this novel will inspire many to explore their diaspora histories and help to ignite a passion in new writers and for untold and uncharted stories.

To humanitarian Angela Neustatter for the total inspiration of a home with a top deck as well as a family hearth.

To ace Librarian Gill Ward – you will spot our oral history project when we were Patron of Reading partners and a homage to your creative approaches to Reading for Pleasure.

Thank you to great friends Tanika Gupta (Playwright) for

Bengali references, inspiration and advice and to wonderful friend and artist Natalie Sirett for her embroidered handkerchiefs and the gift of a conch.

It's an honour to have the Arundhati Roy quote from *The God of Small Things* at the opening of this story.

Finally, thanks to Nicky Parker (Publisher) and all the dedicated people I've met at Amnesty UK as part of my work as an Ambassador there. Your communal spirit has kept me lighting candles and writing stories through these times.

SITA BRAHMACHARI

won the Waterstones Children's Book Prize with her debut *Artichoke Hearts* and is one of the most interesting and important voices in children's books today. *Tender Earth* was awarded an honour by the International Board of Books for Young People, and her most recent novel, *Where The River Runs Gold*, published to great acclaim in July 2019. Sita's books have been shortlisted for the UKLA Book Award, nominated for the CILIP Carnegie Medal, and have been translated into many languages around the world.

She was the 2015 Booktrust's Writer in Residence and is the current Writer in Residence at Islington Centre for Refugees and Migrants. Sita is also an Amnesty International ambassador. She lives in London with her family.

@SitaBrahmachari
facebook.com/sita.brahmachari
sitabrahmachari.com

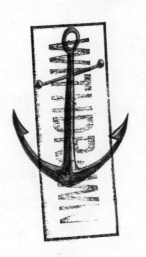